THE DARING NIGHT

In the company of murder

ROBERT McCRACKEN

Published by The Book Folks

London, 2021

© Robert McCracken

ISBN 978-1-913516-09-3

www.thebookfolks.com

THE DARING NIGHT is the second standalone title in the DI Tara Grogan mystery series.

Prologue

Daily Mail. Monday, 29 April 1968.

POP HEART-THROB RODDY CRAIG
DEAD AT 22

*Birkenhead singing star, Roddy Craig has died in
what is believed to be a drowning accident in the
Mersey. His body was recovered from the river on
Sunday morning close to Canada Dock. The city is
reeling from the shock of the passing of its newest
musical star and lead singer of The Moondreams.*

*The band's manager, Tony Walker, said that
everyone in the band was devastated by the news.
They were due to begin a UK tour to promote their
debut album, The Food of Love, released last month.
The death of the lead singer, one half of songwriting
partnership with guitarist Paul Gibson, has now
thrown the tour in doubt. Indeed, speculation is rife
that Craig's death could mean the end for The
Moondreams. None of the band members were
available for comment.*

*The family of Roddy Craig are deeply upset by the
loss of a cherished son and brother. A spokesman for
the family said that no words can express the shock
and distress they are suffering at the news of Roddy's
death. He was described as a fun-loving young man
with the whole world at his feet. An announcement
regarding funeral arrangements will be made later in
the week.*

CHAPTER 1

Liverpool was under high alert. Police cordons had been set up in three areas within the city centre. Traffic was in chaos. Workers had been ordered to go home and stay indoors. Pubs and restaurants were closing. A football match, scheduled for the early evening at Goodison Park, had been postponed. Public transport was still operating, but services were likely to be suspended before nightfall. John Lennon Airport had already closed, and the evening sailing of the ferry to Belfast had been cancelled.

The reason behind these emergency measures had yet to be established. The authorities were aware that two people had died, but the exact cause was unknown. Rumours abounded. Novichok – Salisbury – nerve gas – terrorists – hostages – Russian agents – explosives – radiation – Islamists: were the words circulating, as some people chose to stay and watch proceedings rather than follow police instructions and make for home.

DI Tara Grogan felt useless. She was uncomfortable, too. The stab vest she wore was tight over her tailored jacket. She felt constrained. And she was freezing. A biting October wind funnelled through the city streets and whipped across the open spaces. She'd been standing now for nearly two hours on the corner where Tarleton Street joins Williamson Square. The entire area had been sealed off. From where she stood, she could see the body lying in the open air, undisturbed, unattended. A team of forensic specialists, immersed in full-body protective suits and breathing apparatus, worked steadily around the male figure on the ground. The man was dead — at least that much had been established. But no one was taking any chances, not in this day and age.

She wasn't entirely at ease standing this close, but where did you draw the line? One street away? Two streets away? The only way to be a hundred per cent certain was to evacuate the entire city, and that was just not practical. It may not be what everyone feared: a terrorist attack with a chemical weapon. But two people were dead so far and another seriously ill from incidents in three separate areas of the city.

Tara and DS Alan Murray remained on standby. If some kind of dangerous contaminant had been released, then they were powerless to assist. Police detective work would come later. Right now, the immediate threat must be neutralised. Once security had been restored, then they could go after the perpetrator.

The two detectives had at least managed to interview eyewitnesses who had seen the man collapsing in the square. One married couple in their forties had been coming out of a shop when the man walked by.

'I thought he was drunk,' said the woman. Her attractive face was flushed from shock and she blinked nervously. 'We'd just come out of TK Maxx. He staggered past us. Then he fell over, right where he is now. It's terrible.'

'Did he say anything to you?' Tara asked.

Both husband and wife shook their heads.

'Did he touch you in any way?'

'No, he didn't come that close, but I saw his face,' said the husband who looked towards the stricken body. 'His mouth was twisted, and his tongue was hanging out. He looked really scared.'

'Thank you for your help,' Tara said. 'Please give your name and address to the constable, in case we need to contact you. And if you feel unwell in the next few days, contact your GP immediately.'

Tara spoke with two more witnesses, both of them telling similar stories. They described a man, in his fifties, wearing a blue anorak and dark trousers, staggering into Williamson Square. He appeared drunk and his face was contorted, but within seconds he had collapsed. By the time the emergency services arrived, he was dead.

Now, Tara felt sorry for those passers-by who had rushed to the man's aid. They may be at risk from whatever had claimed his life. At least six people had gathered around the victim. They became victims, too, each one having been rushed to a hospital to be examined as a precaution. The fear could be seen on their faces. Would they still be alive by this evening?

DS Alan Murray, Tara's colleague for the past two years, paced up and down next to a length of incident tape stretched across Tarleton Street. He was a sturdy man, mid-thirties, gaining weight by the day and losing patience by the minute.

'I can't see us getting anywhere near the victim today, Tara.'

She glared at him, and Murray knew well the reason. Tara was a stunning woman. Too beautiful to be a cop, many thought, but she had a put-down look for her sergeant that could reduce the strongest of men to puddles on the floor. It seemed at times that Murray would never lose the habit of calling his superior by her first name, instead of ma'am. Today, he was lucky. As Tara was about to reprimand him, she heard the sound of a disturbance from behind them. There was a mêlée of hurried footsteps and shouted warnings.

'Armed police! Stay where you are, armed police!'

'Don't move!'

'Keep your hands out!'

Tara and Murray were bystanders. A group of uniformed and armed police officers had surrounded a figure in the centre of the street. People scattered amid the screams. Tara saw a youth, his arms raised in the air, one

4

hand holding something. It might have been a weapon, or possibly just a bottle or can.

'Down on your knees, now!'

The youth dropped to his knees, and Tara, from forty yards away, saw the look of terror on the young man's face.

CHAPTER 2

Tara lay on her sofa, a late-night film on TV but she'd lost interest in it. Her gaze fell upon the chipped varnish on her nails. She hadn't tended them in weeks. The length of time was significant only to her. If she had explained to a friend, or even to that shrink at the Police Treatment Centre, they would appreciate her reasoning. They could offer sympathy and show understanding. But she didn't want any of it. She had lost her baby. None of their carefully chosen words, their advice or their sympathetic smiles would ever bring him back. She, Tara, had to deal with it. Suck it up. Get on with things, she told herself. No point in mulling it over all the live-long day.

Sleep had never been easy since becoming a detective in Harold Tweedy's squad. In just a few brief years, she'd chalked up several tragedies and was expected to take it all in her stride. Now there was a serious incident in the city. The whole of Liverpool was at risk. And what was she doing about it? She'd found herself hoping that the lad caught by armed police was the end of the issue. That the aerosol can he'd held in his hand as he was ordered to his knees, contained the poison: the stuff that had already killed two people and thrown an entire city into fright. Then and there, she'd hoped that the lad was the culprit and that the uniforms would just open fire and put an end to it all. It was bloody bizarre, and she seldom swore. But Saturday afternoon in the city centre, with one man lying dead in the square and a youth causing panic with a can of deodorant, spraying it on his girlfriend for a lark – it was simply bizarre.

Her mobile sounded. Mechanically, she stretched her arm out to the coffee table and grappled for the phone. Her eyes were fixed on the TV.

'Ma'am? Sorry to wake you at this hour.'

It was DC John Wilson, his Scouse accent cutting through her head like a serrated knife.

'What is it?'

'Ma'am, we have an incident.'

'Not another one. Where?'

Her tone was abrupt and impatient, demanding details before Wilson could even string the words together. A year ago, she would never have spoken to anyone in such a manner, never mind a young man she valued as a colleague and a friend.

'Can't say if it's connected to Saturday afternoon, ma'am, but some guy has jumped off the Liver Building.'

'Can somebody pick me up?' She had no desire to reveal that she had been drinking.

'Yes, ma'am. Murray is on his way.'

CHAPTER 3

Except perhaps in advance of a royal visit, Tara had never seen such intensive police activity at five o'clock on a Monday morning. On the short drive, with Murray at the wheel, from her apartment at Wapping Dock to the entrance of the Liver Building, she counted six patrol cars and a minibus carrying a Matrix team. Two patrol cars and an unmarked vehicle were parked at the front entrance of the building. Murray jerked to a halt, and Tara, having shed her seatbelt in anticipation of stopping, shot forward, her hands landing on the dash to prevent her head from doing so.

'Sorry, ma'am,' said Murray.

She couldn't be arsed replying. Everything she thought lately, began and ended with a profanity. It was her newly adopted default state of mind.

They both climbed from the car and strode through the lobby of the city's iconic building. DC John Wilson, the detective who had telephoned her, who believed he had disturbed her from a night's sleep, greeted them in the foyer.

'Morning, folks,' he said, trying to sound jovial, despite the hour and the circumstances.

'Morning, John,' Tara managed. 'What have we got?'

Wilson, a strapping bloke in his thirties, Scouser to the core, always looked out of place in a suit and tie. He more resembled a nightclub bouncer or a rugby player wearing his ill-fitting club suit, but Tara would never swap her DC, or DS Murray, for anything. She cherished them as colleagues and as friends.

'A Mr Richard Andrews was found dead on the terrace above the entrance porch.' Wilson nodded to the place from where Tara and Murray had just entered. 'Looks like he jumped off from one of the upper floors of the building. We're getting security staff to run through CCTV.'

'Let's have a look at the body,' said Tara. She gazed around the foyer for an indication of how she might reach the victim.

Wilson walked from the reception desk toward the lift lobby at the opposite side of the foyer. Tara and Murray followed.

'It's not pleasant, ma'am,' said Wilson.

Tara glared at him. A year ago she would have appreciated the head's up and the concern shown by Wilson. She was a big girl now; she'd learned the hard way; she didn't need to be cosseted anymore.

Tara and Murray stepped onto the roof terrace on the first floor of the building, above the semi-circular entrance porch. Dr Brian Witney, forensic pathologist, a thickset man in his fifties, to whom Merseyside Police were frequently indebted, had just stepped away from the body. Tara saw the grey suit, blood-stained, but from her position, she couldn't yet see the state of the dead man. Witney, by his explanation, would spare her some of the trauma.

'Good morning, Tara,' he said with his habitual warm smile that he seemed to hold in store exclusively for her. Quite often, Tara thought, it was the only warm thing at a crime scene.

'Good morning, Brian. What do we have?'

Murray slid past her to have a close look for himself. A police photographer was taking as many shots of the body as he considered necessary.

'Male. Late-thirties to early forties. I imagine his death came instantly as a result of a fall.' Witney looked upwards. 'Must have fallen from a fairly high point, I would say, judging by the state of the body. Poor bugger didn't have a clean fall either.'

Tara followed Witney's gaze to one of the flagpoles that pointed skywards from the terrace. There was no flag flying, but she saw a streak of red down the white pole.

'Looks like he hit the pole, headfirst. It prevented him from making it all the way to ground level. Instead, he flipped sideways and smashed onto this terrace. I'm sure CCTV will establish the time of the jump or fall, can't say which, I'm afraid. The post-mortem might show something more. You can have a look if you wish. Not a pretty sight, though.'

Tara joined Murray beside the body and soon wished she'd stayed where she was. The victim's head was nothing but a pulp of bloodied red flesh and white bone, ruptured brain tissue having oozed to the floor. Death from a traumatic brain injury is how they would describe it. The legs of the victim sat askew but one arm had been cruelly trapped under the body and was probably dislocated from the shoulder. Strangely, the body had come to rest in what could be regarded in first-aid terms as the recovery position. For Richard Andrews, the term was meaningless. An inquest would probably conclude suicide unless the CCTV showed otherwise.

CHAPTER 4

Murray examined the wallet that had been found on the man's body. It contained credit and bank cards, a gym membership card, some cash, amounting to seventy pounds, and a driving licence.

'He lived in Caldy.'

'What's the address?'

Tara snatched the wallet from Murray and examined the licence. Her parents still lived in Caldy, on The Wirral. She had grown up there. The street name was not familiar. She imagined it was one of the modern developments close to Caldy Golf Club.

'Get someone out there to break the news,' she said to Murray. 'We'll call at the house later on.'

Murray re-entered the building, passing Wilson on his way out. Tara did not care to linger within sight of the stricken body of Richard Andrews. She stared at the photograph on the driving licence. Andrews was handsome; had been handsome: a bright face, strong-looking with a confident expression. She noted his date of birth which made him thirty-seven years old. A few years older than her. She couldn't help wondering if he was married, a father, perhaps. If so, a family was about to receive some devastating news.

'Ma'am,' said Wilson, 'we can view CCTV footage now when you're ready.'

'Yes, good. Let's get out of here.'

Her final glance at the appalling scene of the broken man sent a shiver through her body. With all that had happened to her in recent months, she should have been hardened to these scenes by now. Instead, this most recent vision blurred and merged with horrific images of crime scenes past. Closing her eyes for a second helped to dispel the pictures, but it did not erase the memories.

Inside the security lodge of the Liver Building, the head of security Mr Daniel Browne, a tall upright man in his early sixties with silver hair, large nose, and sporting the odour of a delicious after-shave, guided Tara and Wilson through the overnight recordings of the CCTV in the building. Browne had a forthright manner, suggesting perhaps that he was ex-military. He spoke in a direct factual tone.

'Cameras one and two are mounted on the outside below the entrance…'

'Please, Mr Browne, just show us the place from where the victim fell.'

Wilson raised an eye at Tara's abrupt command. Her clipped tone had unnerved the security officer, too. Quickly, he navigated to the relevant footage.

'The time was 11.46 p.m.,' said Browne. 'Camera number eleven.'

They watched as Richard Andrews, wearing a suit and tie, emerged from the building onto the roof terrace on the twelfth floor. The camera view did not cover the exact spot where Andrews had fallen to his death.

'Is that it?' snapped Tara.

'I'm afraid so, Inspector,' Browne replied, rising from his stooped position at the desk.

'So, at 11.46 Mr Andrews steps onto the roof terrace. At 11.47, a minute later, he's dead. There's no one else in the vicinity? No one entered the area before or just after Andrews?'

Browne shook his head.

'Unlikely then that he was pushed,' said Wilson.

'Cameras one to six are mounted for perimeter and entrance security,' Browne explained. 'Only camera number five shows anything of the incident.' He adjusted the mouse beside the monitor, clicked once and there appeared on screen the briefest glimpse of Richard Andrews. Browne reset the footage to view again. 'It's very quick. The time recorded was 11.47 p.m. yesterday.'

Tara watched the monitor. For two seconds there was nothing to see but a view of the terrace on the roof of the entrance porch and a partial view of the esplanade beyond the building. Suddenly, an object slammed to the floor.

'I can zoom in,' said Browne.

'No! We don't need to see it in detail, thank you,' said Tara, alarmed by the idea of watching the smashing of a skull once again.

'A definite suicide,' said Wilson.

'Seems that way,' said Tara.

They met up with Murray in the atrium on the ground floor. He held aloft a security pass, dangling on a red lanyard.

'Dr Witney managed to get this off the body before they took it away. Richard Andrews worked here for a company called Harbinson Fine Foods. The head office is here in this building, but they have several factories on Merseyside and several others around the country.'

Tara grasped the security pass and saw another photo of Andrews. It only added to her view that he had once looked a handsome and perhaps a happy man. Her pondering was interrupted by Murray who was reading a text message on his phone.

'We have to get to the station, ma'am,' he said. 'There's been a development in the poisoning case. Tweedy wants to speak with us.'

Tara frowned. *Please*, one thing at a time, she thought. She could tell that Murray was waiting for instruction, but all she could manage was to puff air through her lips. Already, it felt like a day's work had been done and yet it hadn't gone six-thirty in the morning.

'Right,' she said at last. 'Leave this for now. We can speak with the family and Andrews' employer later. You can drive me to St Anne Street. Let's hope there hasn't been another incident.'

CHAPTER 5

Tara had always admired Detective Superintendent Harold Tweedy. His demeanour was calm, controlled and polite but he was very effective in getting results. Tweedy was seated in his office, organised, tidy, in his neat grey suit and smart golf club tie, his hands closing the leather-bound Bible that he always kept on the top-left corner of his desk. Tweedy had a strong faith that Tara not only admired but envied. That was how the man, tall and lean, looking all of his fifty-seven years, coped with the rigours of police detective work. His faith was his strength, his conscience and the basis probably for every decision he'd ever made on how to deal with villains.

But how could his faith explain the past few days? That's what she would like to know. Innocent people dropping dead in the street, a young man throwing himself from the twelfth floor of the Liver Building, and then there was all the crap she was still dealing with in her head. The previous cases. They wouldn't leave her alone. And the loss of her baby sat to the fore of it all.

When Tara, Murray and Wilson entered the office, Tara noted the expression on Tweedy's face. It was one of obvious concern for the well-being of his prized officer, DI Tara Grogan. Embarrassed, she failed to hold eye contact with her boss as he began their meeting.

'Good morning, folks,' Tweedy began in his grandfatherly tone. 'As you are all aware, shocking events have occurred over the weekend. A further fatality has just been reported in the Speke area. No details yet, but it is thought to be connected with the other deaths.'

Tara shifted uncomfortably in her chair. She had difficulty processing the news when the vision of a smashed skull was uppermost in her mind. She barely listened to the rest of Tweedy's announcement.

'A special task force has already been assembled with staff from Admiral Street and from here at St Anne Street. This team is liaising with national security from London and with specialist forensic investigators from Porton Down.'

'Any information yet on what material was used?' Murray asked.

Tweedy shook his head.

'Nothing, I'm afraid. For now, though, we can stand aside and allow these specialists to do their jobs. Until we know exactly what toxic substance we're dealing with, we can't carry out a normal homicide inquiry. It would be too dangerous for us to go stumbling through an investigation until we ascertain whether it is terrorist-related. Could be connected to Russian spies or even an individual acting alone. Lessons have been learned from the events in Salisbury.'

The incidents in Salisbury in 2018, where two Russian nationals had been poisoned with the nerve agent, Novichok, was still fresh in the memory of UK security and police authorities. The evidence had pointed to an assassination attempt by Russian agents and although the intended targets survived, an innocent British woman had died as a result of coming into contact with the source of the toxin.

'Who is going to put together the connections, if any, between the victims?' Tara asked.

'I can appreciate your frustration over this, Tara. I'm sure it will not be long before we're called back into the investigation. Once this substance has been identified, it will surely become clear what type of operation will be involved. We might be dealing with a terrorist organisation, an individual or, strange as it may seem this morning, these deaths might be accidental.'

'Do you mean like an outbreak of *E. coli*?' Wilson asked.

'Food poisoning!' Tara was alarmed. She was struck by the image of the young lad, nearly shot dead because he was fooling around with his girlfriend in the street.

Before the meeting descended into loose chit-chat, Tweedy called a halt.

'Right, folks, for the time being, please turn your attention to the other cases you have been working on. Tara, I understand you're dealing with a fatality at the Liver Building?'

'Yes, sir, an employee of one of the tenant companies in the building.'

'Suicide?'

'It seems that way.'

'Carry on then, folks. I'll keep you informed of any news regarding the emergency.'

Tara, Murray and Wilson filed from Tweedy's office and resumed conversations in the operations room. Murray and Wilson were soon embroiled in football banter – Murray was the red of Liverpool and Wilson, most devotedly, Everton blue.

'Calling off the game on Saturday, did your lot a favour,' Murray jibed, 'saved another defeat.'

'An away draw to Newcastle is hardly worth getting excited about,' Wilson replied.

Usually, Tara could blank out the banter while she scrolled through emails and the Merseyside Police bulletins, but not this morning.

'Give it a rest, you two,' she barked. 'There's more to life than bloody football.'

Wilson went back to his desk in silence, but Murray was brave enough to approach his DI.

'Is everything all right, ma'am?'

'No worse than usual, why?' Tara replied without looking up.

Murray sat at the edge of her desk while she feigned her continued reading of the BBC News.

'If you're going through a hard time, you can talk to me. I know things have been difficult since…'

'And? You think I should press on, put it all behind me – leave it at home?'

'No, I think you should remember, ma'am, that there are plenty of people around here who care for you. But if you can't talk to us maybe you should speak to a professional.'

'So you think I'm losing it?'

Her voice was raised, and Murray could only stare back at the young woman he was so used to seeing cheerful and upbeat despite the woes of their job. Her large blue eyes seemed full of venom, ready for a fight. A sudden chasm of silence had been opened between them. Finally, Tara broke the stares and the silence. She jumped from her chair and grabbed her handbag.

'Right. Enough said. Let's get out to Caldy.'

She marched off, and Murray, with a pained shrug, had little option but to follow her.

CHAPTER 6

She had been right about the address. Murray stopped the car on the road opposite a set of electric metal gates through which Tara could see an impressive modern house built of red brick and a lot of glass. The windows of the entrance hall stretched from the ground to the roof above the first floor; it resembled a modern church building. At the rear, beyond the house, Tara could see one of the fairways on Caldy golf course. She pictured the view from a room at the rear of the house. Her parents' bungalow, though extensive, did not come close to the opulence before her. Murray whistled.

'How the other half lives and all that,' he said.

Tara inwardly agreed, and yet they were about to meet with someone going through a most unenviable experience. What did the future hold for the lady of the house, the widow Andrews?

'I want you to wait here,' said Tara. 'There's no need for the poor woman to be inundated with police officers.'

'Fair enough.'

'I won't be long. While I'm gone, why don't you set up an appointment with the company Andrews worked for?'

She stepped from the car and straightened her clothes and hair. She was far from presentable, wearing stretch jeans, a long-sleeve T-shirt, black hooded anorak and white trainers, but there had been no time to get home to shower and change.

By this stage, Tara was aware that Richard Andrews' wife, Nicole, had been informed of the tragic news. An older brother of the deceased had already gone to the morgue to formally identify the broken body. Nothing

16

peculiar was found on the roof terrace of the Liver Building, and everyone interviewed within the building so far had not seen or heard anything suspicious. Andrews' car, a silver BMW 5 Series, had been discovered in a multi-storey car park close to the Liver Building.

All indications were that Andrews had simply taken the lift to the twelfth floor and stepped outside to keep his appointment with death. The latest Tara had heard, before leaving St Anne Street, was that Andrews' wife that morning had opened a letter left for her in her kitchen to find all explained.

Very sad – a jumper – more so than any other way, Tara believed. Not only was a jumper ending his life, but it seemed he was reaching out for something, for another world, a place of refuge perhaps, a place where all his troubles would be over. There was forlorn hope in a jumper, that's how she viewed it. Still, she had work to do. It was up to her to tie it all together. She would speak to the widow and make her report when she was satisfied that Richard Andrews had taken his own life.

The double gates were closed but, to her right, Tara found an intercom next to a letterbox mounted on the stone gatepost. She pressed the button but heard nothing for almost a minute. Then a female voice answered.

'Hello?'

'Hello, Mrs Andrews?'

'No. I'm her friend from next door. What do you want? Mrs Andrews is resting at the moment.'

'I'm Detective Inspector Grogan, Merseyside Police. I would like to speak to Mrs Andrews, if possible.'

There was a pause before the intercom sprang to life again.

'Just a minute, I'll open the gates.'

Tara heard a buzzer sound and, without another word from the woman, the gates began to swing open. On her approach to the house, she couldn't help a glance at the property next door, presumably where this neighbour lived. The architecture was equally impressive. Clearly, people around here were not short of a pound or two.

There was little sign of life about the place until a tall, strong-looking woman in her thirties, wearing navy-blue gym leggings and vest opened the front door. Her face looked strained, probably worse for the absence of make-up. She swept a long mane of straight dark hair behind her shoulders.

'Mrs Andrews?'

'No. You'd better come in,' she said, stepping back. 'I'll just call Nicole. She was lying down for a while. I'm Marjorie, her friend from next door. I've been looking after the kids.'

Tara merely nodded her understanding of the situation as Marjorie continued to reverse nervously down the wide entrance hall.

'Have a seat in there, Inspector.'

She pointed through a set of glazed double doors to a bright and extensive lounge, the light enhanced by a huge picture window affording a magnificent view of a professionally landscaped garden, with fishpond, decking, a modern stone folly, and of the golf course beyond. Briefly, Tara scanned the room. She was looking around for a picture of Richard Andrews, a family portrait perhaps, when a petite woman in blue jeans and ballet pumps appeared at the door. She could easily pass for a teenager and, for a brief moment, Tara wondered if she might be a daughter of the late Richard Andrews. Her features were fine, although pale, bordering on deathly white, and she wore a large degree of exhaustion, her dark eyes heavy, her short brown hair ruffled from a fitful sleep. Tara knew what it was like to be taken for someone much younger than her age. She had never looked her true age and had never seemed old enough to be a police detective. She smiled at the woman.

'Hello, Mrs Andrews. I'm Detective Inspector Tara Grogan. I'm very sorry about your husband.'

The woman ventured into the room and sat down on a deep sofa, indicating that Tara should do likewise.

'I've already spoken to the police, this morning,' she said in a shaky voice. It was faint, and she sounded more like a bashful schoolgirl than a grown woman.

'I understand that, Mrs Andrews. It's been a horrendous experience for you, but I need to ask you a couple of questions. A few minutes of your time and I'll try my best not to bother you again.'

Nicole Andrews produced a tissue from the sleeve of her black jumper and used it to wipe the tears rising in her bloodshot eyes.

'I'm sorry, this may sound very callous, but we need to be satisfied that your husband took his own life.' Tara knew instantly that it didn't sound right. 'What I mean is, we have to be sure that a murder has not been committed.'

The harsh idea of murder seemed to startle Andrews and she looked gravely at Tara.

'I believe that you found a letter from Mr Andrews?'

Nicole pulled a crumpled envelope from the pocket of her jeans and handed it to Tara, remaining silent as she read. The first couple of lines were full of apology to Nicole and the children for causing so much pain. Andrews' reasoning for taking his life was contained in the last line:

I'm sorry, but I can't live without her.

Tara inspected the page on which the brief message had been roughly scribbled. It was headed paper, the logo of Harbinson Fine Foods in red and blue at the top left, an abstract though obvious image of a liver bird surrounded by the company name. She noticed at the bottom of the page, where the company directors were listed, that the name Richard Andrews had been scored out.

Nicole Andrews was staring into space as Tara attempted to return the letter.

'Do you think you could elaborate a little bit, Mrs Andrews?'

For a second, the woman glared at Tara, cold, indignant, nearing anger. Then she rose from the settee and went to the window.

'We were separated, Inspector. Richard left us eight weeks ago. He moved in with her. He claimed that he still loved us, but he couldn't bear not being with her. So, off he went.'

Tara was waiting for the name. Purely academic now, but she felt obliged to listen. It was tragedy piled upon tragedy for Nicole Andrews. Tara knew all about that – been there, got the T-shirt.

'Is there any reason why he should then take his own life?' Tara asked.

'She threw him out – four days ago. He couldn't handle that. I would have taken him back, you know, but all he could say was how much he loved her and that he needed to be with her. He cried down the phone to me, can you believe that? His wife, the mother of his children?'

Her voice began to fail, and she wiped her face with the already tear-soaked tissue. Tara gave her a few moments, but she felt so powerless to help the woman.

'So, Inspector,' Nicole said tearfully, 'it's her you should be talking to, not me. I didn't feature in his life. Go ask her.'

'Does she have a name?'

'She has, but I'll never speak it. She is my father's secretary. Richard worked for my father's company. At least, he did until yesterday.'

Tara assumed that she meant until the moment when her husband jumped to his death, but Nicole Andrews had not finished.

'Richard was asked to resign from the board yesterday morning. I imagine that was the final straw. He lost everything within three days: his lover, his career and his family.'

Nicole's eyes were set to infinity once more. Tara reckoned she had heard enough. It certainly wasn't the sort of story to set you up for a relaxing evening in front of the telly.

'Thank you for your patience, Mrs Andrews. Once again, I'm so sorry for your trouble. I'll see myself out.'

The woman was unable to acknowledge Tara's leaving.

Outside in the driveway, she sighed with relief, taking a deep breath of chilled morning air. That should be that, she decided. A definite suicide, tragic for the family concerned but as far as police business went there was no further need for the Serious Crime Squad. Why then did she feel the sudden inclination to have a word with this other biddy?

CHAPTER 7

As Murray drove them back to St Anne Street, Tara stared at the blank screen of her mobile.

'You all right, ma'am?' said Murray. 'You're very quiet.'

'Fine,' she said, trying her best to blink away the tears.

They arrived back at the office to hear the news of another death in the city and linked apparently to the ongoing emergency.

'Are we needed down there?' Tara asked.

Wilson shook his head.

'The *special ones* have everything under control,' he said sarcastically, while reading the latest developments on his screen.

'What the hell is going on?' Murray blurted. 'That's four deaths and we still know fuck-all squared!'

Lime Street station had been closed, and all trains cancelled. The body of a young woman had yet to be removed from a carriage that had been due to travel to Manchester at ten-thirty. Tara read the latest bulletin over Wilson's shoulder. It wasn't hard to picture the scene at the city train station: traffic chaos, police cordons, men in full-body protection suits and breathing apparatus. And what of the other passengers? How many had been in contact with this young woman? How many more would fall ill or die?

Tara was irritated by her lack of involvement. She felt useless. Three days into an emergency and they still had no idea what they were dealing with. Questions raised at Westminster, Government statements, press conferences by the Chief Constable of Merseyside and still no one had any clue. The media were having the proverbial field day. Pages filled with back-story on Salisbury and references to earlier incidents: Alexander Litvinenko and even as far back as Georgi Markov in 1978.

Tara just wanted to speak with the families of victims. Maybe then they could find connections, circumstances that linked each death. Had they all been in contact with the same perpetrator? Had they all at some point visited the same place contaminated with goodness knows what? Drank from the same glass, eaten the same meal at the same restaurant? Were all of the victims complete innocents? Or was someone amongst their number an intended target? But as yet they had nothing, and here she was spending her time dealing with a case of suicide.

* * *

Wilson set a piece of paper on her desk.

'Ma'am, this note was found in Andrews' car. It doesn't say much.'

Tara lifted the A5-sized paper, torn from a notebook, and read the handwritten line.

'Toby, I've been such a…'

'Fool, maybe,' Wilson suggested.

'Seems likely. Or perhaps, failure or complete bastard.'

Wilson looked at her, bewildered.

Following a brief lunch, where she ate only strawberry yoghurt and drank some coffee, she decided that there was little point in moaning about her lack of involvement in the poisoning cases while she had still to close her inquiry into the death of Richard Andrews. On her way from the office, she called out to Murray.

'I'm off to speak with the company that Andrews worked for.'

'You want me to come with you?'

'No need. It shouldn't take long.'

Tara strolled from the station building, savouring the fresh air and the feeling of solitude. She made a call to check that the appointment that Murray had set up was with the chairman of Harbinson Fine Foods. She learned also that Edward Harbinson's secretary, a Miss Riordan, had gone home early; due to illness, it was said.

She had forgotten when refusing Murray's offer to accompany her to the Liver Building that she didn't have her car. It was Murray who had picked her up from her flat at Wapping Dock in the early morning. She could hardly believe she was still living through the same day – so many different issues had flowed through her mind. It was no more than a mile and a half on foot to the Liver Building and she decided to walk.

Despite the early twentieth-century exterior of the Liver Building, the head office of Harbinson Fine Foods on the fifth floor was ultra-modern in concept: plate glass and polished granite with desks and counters trimmed in chrome. It felt cold and clinical, almost intimidating, and yet Tara was greeted at reception by a polite and attractive girl dressed in a royal blue skirt and cream blouse. The receptionist already had a note of Tara's appointment and led her through a smoked-glass doorway into a short corridor that housed several rooms. The girl opened the second door on the right and showed Tara inside. She was met by an empty desk in an anteroom, but the receptionist told her to go straight through to the chairman's office.

Edward Harbinson was putting down his telephone as Tara came in.

'Hello, Inspector Grogan?' he said, glancing at a notepad where, Tara assumed, her name was written. 'Merseyside Police are turning them out young and pretty these days.'

She didn't care much for his sexist retort and cared even less to comment upon it. Instead, she got straight to the point.

'I am here to ask some questions regarding your son-in-law.'

'Please, sit down. A terrible business this morning. My daughter, Nicole, is devastated. You'll appreciate that I don't have much time. I'm on my way to see her. How can I help you?'

Harbinson had recently entered his seventies, but he appeared to be a fit man in good shape. If it wasn't for his silver-grey hair, combed back on his head, he could pass himself as ten years younger. He knew also how to dress well, in a tailored suit, white shirt and striped tie, and he spoke politely.

'Just routine, Mr Harbinson, very awkward I know, but we have to convince ourselves of the cause of death.'

'Yes, of course. I appreciate that.'

Tara was intrigued because, since taking her seat opposite him, Harbinson had yet to look her in the eye. His head was down, staring at his open diary as he flicked through the pages. He lifted his head at intervals but did not engage his visitor.

'If you could confirm for me that Mr Andrews was your son-in-law and that he worked for your company?'

'That's correct, yes.' He shifted in his leather swivel chair. His face reddened slightly.

'Your daughter, Nicole?'

Harbinson nodded.

'She told me that Mr Andrews was dismissed from the company yesterday?'

He cleared his throat as his face became more flushed.

'That's not strictly true,' he replied, defensively. 'The board felt that his position in our company had become untenable. We suggested that he should resign.'

Bloody hair splitter, Tara thought. She waited for the chairman to elaborate but silence ensued. Eventually, after a deep sigh, Harbinson again spoke.

'I know what you're thinking, Inspector. That his departure from the company caused him to do what he did?'

Tara would leave that for the man to ponder for himself.

'I gather from your daughter that Mr Andrews was no longer living at the family home?'

Harbinson nodded.

'I believe also that he was in a relationship with your secretary, a Miss Riordan?'

For the first time, Harbinson stared Tara in the face. His eyes looked weary behind gold-rimmed glasses, but he removed them to glare at her.

'And I believe, Inspector, that the relationship had ended,' he said curtly and with increased volume.

'It's just that I will need to speak to her,' said Tara impishly. 'For the sake of completeness.'

She had a poor first impression of this callous man. In truth, there was probably little to be gained in speaking to Andrews' former lover, but something told her that in doing so, she would piss off Edward Harbinson. And that was something she was happy to do.

'She's not here.'

'A home address will do fine. Oh, and one more thing. At what time did you last see your son-in-law?'

'The board meeting was at four. It was an extraordinary meeting, an emergency if you like. Richard left after a few minutes.' Harbinson's voice became choked. Tara was not convinced that it was genuine sadness. 'We never spoke again.'

Harbinson provided the home address of his secretary, and Tara left.

Everything appeared quite straightforward. Andrews had left his wife for another woman who happened to be his boss's secretary, except that his boss was also his father-in-law. The love affair breaks down and his boss gives him the heave-ho. Just as his wife had explained, he lost everything in a few days, it seemed. There wasn't any need for Tara to visit this *other* woman except to satisfy a little of her curiosity. Andrews had abandoned a beautiful wife and young family; it would be interesting to see the woman he had left them for.

CHAPTER 8

When she reached her apartment building close to the Albert Dock, rather than calling it a day, she collected her car and drove to the address that Harbinson had given to her.

Before arriving at the home of the woman, Tara had realised it was an exclusive address in the city. She parked on a tree-lined road in Woolton, outside a large rambling house secreted behind a stone wall and double wooden gates. The short avenue was enclosed on three sides by several schools; the area was well sought after and commanded some of the highest property values in the city. Quiet and attractive, she thought, gazing at the house. She tried to conjure an image of the woman who lived here, a woman who had played a part in the destruction of a marriage and possibly a man's life. An impressive-looking house for someone who worked as a secretary, it was only natural to wonder how this woman might afford such a property.

The house exuded character. It gave a feeling of tradition. The style was, Tara supposed, mock-Tudor with black and white exterior detail and leaded windows. The blinds were drawn at one of the front windows, and she couldn't tell if there was anyone inside. She pushed the doorbell twice. A few moments later, a light came on. Tara could see the figure of a woman through the small side panes to either side of the solid wooden door. The door opened on a chain and the woman's face appeared at the crack. Even at this limiting view, Tara could see the face of a stunning woman.

'Miss Riordan?'

'Yes?'

'I'm Detective Inspector Grogan, Merseyside Police. I wonder if I may have a quick word.'

Tara presented her warrant card for inspection. She could see the doubt and alarm on the woman's face as she peered at it. Another moment passed, while she studied Tara's face before the door was closed, the chain was released and the door re-opened. Tara's eyes did a double-take. She was everything Tara imagined that she had to be. For Andrews to abandon a beautiful wife and then top himself when his affair ended, she had to be special. She was barefoot and yet towered over the slight figure of the detective. A long white bathrobe was pulled closed across her waist with one hand. Long tussled black hair sat on the thick collar of the robe. Her eyes were a vivid blue and rather piercing as if to inspect the very mind of her visitor. Riordan's mouth sat in a seductive pout before she spoke, although her voice sounded weak and tired.

'You'd better come in.'

She stepped back holding the door, allowing Tara to pass through into a dimly lit hallway. Both women observed each other nervously. Riordan slipped past Tara and padded to the rear of the house and into a spacious lounge. Tara felt obliged to follow. The walls of the room were adorned in colourful paintings. One wall housed an extensive collection of books, CDs and DVDs within a dark-wood bookcase. Out of character with the rest of the room, Tara thought.

'Apologies for my appearance,' said Riordan, 'but I wasn't expecting company. It's been one hell of a day.'

'I'm so sorry for your trouble, Miss Riordan, but I'm afraid I have to ask these questions.'

Tara had yet to decide on the woman's age, but for some peculiar reason, she wasn't interested in such trivia. Riordan nodded her understanding of the situation and motioned for Tara to sit down. The living room was square, although a second door, a few feet from the other one and wide open, revealed a spacious modern kitchen. Tara sat down in a soft brown leather sofa and found herself facing an attractive raised fireplace where a gas fire was flickering away.

'Firstly,' she began, 'just to confirm that you work at Harbinson Fine Foods, is that correct?'

'Yes,' Riordan replied, resigning herself to an armchair that matched the sofa.

'Am I right in thinking that you knew Mr Andrews well?'

A bemused smile broke on the woman's face.

'Come on, Inspector, I'm sure that someone has told you by now? Richard and I were lovers.' She left it at that as if to tease Tara, inviting her into prying further. It worked, too.

Tara wasn't usually so easily embarrassed but she was feeling rather in awe of this confident woman. Now that she had opened the can she would have to deal with the worms.

'When did you last see him?'

'Yesterday.'

'At what time?' She felt the room growing warmer, or was it just her?

'Not long after four o'clock. He walked out of a board meeting and kept on going.' Her eyes filled with tears. 'That was the last time I saw him. He left, Inspector, without a word.'

'I need to get an idea of his state of mind…'

'The chairman had just shown him the door. I think it's fair to say that he wasn't terribly happy.'

'Am I right in thinking that your relationship had also ended?'

Riordan raised an eyebrow then dabbed a tear with a tissue she'd pulled from the pocket of her bathrobe.

'Do the police usually send a Detective Inspector to investigate suicide?'

'We have to be sure it is suicide. Some are more obvious than others, Miss Riordan. We have to be sure that there was no foul play.'

'Oh,' she said, seemingly regretting having raised the issue.

'And your relationship with Mr Andrews?' If she had been trying to avoid answering the question it hadn't worked.

'Was over.'

'Right, thank you, Miss Riordan.'

'I know what you must be thinking, Inspector?'

Two bloody mind-readers in one day, thought Tara. First Harbinson and now Riordan. She got to her feet.

'That our breaking up was too much for him to bear? That he wouldn't be dead if we'd stayed together?'

'I'm sorry, but it's not my place to pass judgement. If someone has it in them to take their own life then they will eventually find a reason for doing so. That's what I think, for what it's worth.'

'You must think me very selfish, Inspector?'

'No, not at all. It's very difficult for all concerned, so I won't take up any more of your time.' Tara was already at the lounge door before Riordan rose from her chair. 'Is there anyone close, to keep you company?'

'I'll be fine, thank you.'

'I see that you have an interest in art,' said Tara, her clumsy attempt to lighten the tone on her way out.

'They're all mine, I'm afraid.'

Tara took the opportunity to glance around the room once again. Her experience of painting was confined to looking and a little reading of art history in some of her more studious moments when at Oxford. But she knew what she liked. There were several landscapes, fairly large canvases, vivid greens and blues of rare summer days. She liked open spaces, hills and sky. Wasn't it Constable who was the master of sky? she mused. It never seemed a difficult thing for someone to paint until you tried it for yourself. So many shades of sky. But here was a definite, bold, overwhelming blue. This had been no trouble at all. Riordan watched patiently as Tara inspected her work.

'I have a studio upstairs,' she said. 'Call in some time. I'll show you around.'

'Thank you,' said Tara, without conviction as if the last minute had just been wiped from her memory. 'I'll be on my way. Good night, Miss Riordan.'

'Good night, Inspector.'

Case closed, Tara thought, as the front door was shut behind her. Now she could turn her attention to the current emergency. She was not a part of the investigation team but she hoped that would soon change.

CHAPTER 9

Tara ate less than half of a lasagne she'd bought from Marks and Spencer. The remainder, still within the foil tray, lay abandoned on the coffee table. The bottle of chardonnay, bought at the same time on her journey home from Woolton, was more welcome than the food. She poured a third glass and sat back on her sofa, cradling her mobile in her right hand and texting with her thumb. She had managed only one night out in six months. It had not exactly been a wild evening. Dinner at a restaurant in the city, a couple of drinks and then home early.

She couldn't help smiling, though, at the picture her friend Kate had sent of Adele, Tara's god-daughter, in her Christening gown.

'She's a sweetie,' Tara replied. It made her feel cosy inside. It made her feel human. Kate responded with a lol emoji and there ended the exchange.

She flicked on the television to catch up on the latest news. On the ITN bulletin, there was a recap of events to date on the unexplained deaths of four people in Liverpool. Beside her on the sofa, she opened up her laptop. Soon, within a variety of newsfeeds, she read all manner of commentaries on the 'Merseyside Mystery' as it had been titled by the media.

The names of the four victims and also the number of those who had taken ill had just been released. One article on Sky News stated that there were no apparent connections between any of the dead. Tara read the names.

David Leigh, aged fifty-two years and from Bootle, died in Williamson Square on Saturday afternoon.

Emma Whitehouse, thirty-one, married with two young children, from Speke, died at Broadgreen Hospital early on Saturday morning.

Norman Forbes, eighty-three, a widower, and also from Speke, was found dead in his home by his daughter on Sunday night.

Marsha Ross, twenty-two, died on board a Liverpool to Manchester train at Lime Street station. She was single and came from the Orrell Park area.

Twelve-year-old Kaley Watson from Everton remained seriously ill at Alder Hey Children's Hospital where she was admitted late on Friday evening suffering severe nausea, headache and difficulty in breathing.

Three other people, two men and a woman, were critically ill in the Royal Liverpool Hospital, their cases also being linked to similar incidents.

Finding the connections: that's exactly what she and Murray should be doing, instead of her writing up a report of an obvious suicide.

She lifted her mobile and composed a text to her DS. He responded immediately and in complete agreement with her stance. Questions were piling up before her, and for now, she had no power or authority to do anything about it. What if there were more fatalities? Why Liverpool? If it were a terrorist plot, then it could happen anywhere. If it was a case of accidental food poisoning, then why weren't they going into all the supermarkets and food outlets in the city? Maybe they were; maybe they already knew the source of the poison; maybe it was a matter of national security. Maybe, maybe, maybe: she could scream with frustration.

She typed a few words into Google. She had already studied the story several times in recent weeks, never believing that such an attack could happen in her home city. She read:

> *On 4 March 2018, former Russian spy Sergei Skripal, 66, and his 33-year-old daughter, Yulia were found seriously ill on a bench in the centre of Salisbury. They had been poisoned by a nerve agent, in an attack likely to have been sanctioned by the Russian state.*
>
> *A bitter exchange of accusations and denials from the highest levels of governments came in the months that followed, culminating in diplomatic expulsions and international sanctions.*
>
> *The attack on Sergei Skripal and Yulia left them hospitalised for weeks.*

In June, Wiltshire Police linked the attack to another
poisoning in which Dawn Sturgess and her partner
Charlie Rowley were exposed to Novichok in nearby
Amesbury, after handling a contaminated perfume
dispenser. This dispenser was believed to be the
container used by the Russian agents in their attempt
to kill Skripal. Ms Sturgess died in hospital in July.

An hour later, and well into a second bottle of wine, Tara had covered the stories of Alexander Litvinenko and Georgi Markov.

On 1 November 2006, Litvinenko suddenly fell ill
and was hospitalised in what was established as a
case of poisoning by radioactive polonium-210. He
died from the poisoning on 23 November. He became
the first known victim of lethal polonium-210-
induced acute radiation syndrome. The blame for the
attack was firmly set at the door of Russia.
Litvinenko was a British naturalised Russian
defector and former officer of the Russian FSB secret
service.
On 7 September 1978, Georgi Markov walked
across Waterloo Bridge in London and waited at a
bus stop to take a bus to his job at the BBC. He felt
a slight sharp pain, like a bug bite or sting, on the
back of his right thigh. He looked behind him and
saw a man lifting an umbrella off the ground. The
man hurriedly crossed to the other side of the street
and got into a taxi which then drove away. The event
was reported as the 'Umbrella Murder' with the
assassin identified as Francesco Gullino, codenamed
'Piccadilly'.
When he arrived at work at the BBC World Service
offices, Markov noticed a small red pimple had
formed at the site of the sting he had felt earlier, and
the pain had not lessened or stopped. He told at least

one of his colleagues at the BBC about the incident.
That evening he developed a fever and was admitted to
St James' Hospital in Balham, where he died four
days later, on 11 September 1978, at the age of 49.
The cause of death was poisoning from a ricin-filled
pellet.

It felt more like fiction when it happened far away,
thought Tara. Once it enters your hometown, however,
fear quickly surpasses surprise. What the hell could she do
if Russian agents were involved? How many of the victims
had been targets? It was no wonder that the mystery had
taken on national significance.

Reluctantly, and now quite drunk, she abandoned her
laptop, left the television blaring with some futile celebrity
game show and traipsed to her bedroom. If she was to
take on the world in the morning, she must get some
damn sleep.

* * *

They arrived at St Anne Street at the same time and,
following a brief greeting, they quickly decided they were
of the same mind. Tara and Murray would approach
Tweedy and request that they were assigned to the special
investigation team dealing with the present crisis. Neither
officer had envisaged what was to happen when they
walked into their operations room. DC John Wilson leapt
from his chair to greet them. His face was beaming and
much too cheerful for the news he was about to impart.

'Morning, ma'am,' he said. 'I might have something for
you.'

She turned to Murray.

'Go and see if Tweedy is here yet. I'll catch up with
you.' She slipped an arm through John Wilson's left and
walked him towards her desk. 'OK, John,' she said,
playfully, 'tell me your story.'

'Housebreaking, ma'am. The super wants us to look at some recent burglary activity.'

Tara flopped into her chair and looked at Wilson with the sad eyes of a bored pubescent teenager.

'Burglaries? But we're a serious crime unit. What the hell is going on, John? The entire city is under siege and Tweedy assigns us to a case of burglary?'

CHAPTER 10

Wilson could do little but shrug his large rounded shoulders. He was so used to seeing his boss full of vigour, motivated and determined to see things through. He paused, but eventually felt inclined to deliver the details of the case they were to investigate. He felt some relief when Murray joined them, although his expression, matching Tara's, was scorched with frustration.

'I reckon Big Beryl's been at it again,' said Wilson.

'Why, what's up?' Murray asked.

'Three houses yesterday, all done the same way. Nothing touched except for mobile phones, plasma screens and jewellery. All three houses were entered from the rear, and the doors were smashed in with a sledgehammer. Two of the properties had alarms fitted, both were activated but it didn't seem to bother the perpetrators.'

'And why Big Beryl?' Tara asked, more from idle curiosity than genuine interest.

'Usual routine, which is no routine, just barge straight in, to hell with anybody who happens to be in the house. Beryl's the main operator in the Kirkdale area.'

'Is that it?' Tara snapped.

'And…'

'What?'

'We got a positive ID on the bugger.'

'You're joking me?' said Murray, who at least was showing some interest.

Tara, aside from scoffing, was already doing other things. She logged into her computer, checked her mobile phone for messages and listened to the discussion between Wilson and Murray.

'A Mrs Henshaw,' Wilson explained, 'was coming down her stairs just as Big Beryl was struggling in the hall with her telly. She recognised him straight away. He washed her car the day before.'

'At that Speedy-Klean place down by the docks?' said Murray.

'Yes, Great Howard Street.'

'Brilliant, bloody brilliant. Time we paid Big Beryl a visit.'

'I thought you might want to do that,' said Wilson with a satisfied grin.

Tara went along – reluctantly. Murray and Wilson were brimming, particularly Wilson who seemed to relish a reunion with an old adversary. Tara sat next to Murray in the marked car, thinking of how best to approach Superintendent Tweedy over what she now firmly believed was her sidelining.

Wilson had come along to supply physical support. Murray drove a marked BMW 3 Series just over a mile from the station to the Speedy-Klean attended car wash in Great Howard Street, a former heavy industrial area now, in patches, within the throes of re-development. Murray thought it wise also to have a couple of uniforms in a second car, for the same reason he had brought Wilson.

'Want your motor cleaned, love?' said a husky and rather high-pitched voice. Big Beryl stood in navy blue waterproof gear with a power-hose in his burly hands. Tall, heavily built, no one would ever deny him the first word of his nickname. The second, however, as the story went was acquired during a stay at Her Majesty's pleasure in a youth detention centre when Beryl was thirteen. His fellow inmates were rather taken with his female-sounding voice and man boobs. Billy, his real name, was lost forever. In those days, his expertise lay in stealing car stereos. Although he sounded cheerful, his face was scrunched to a permanent scowl such that his eyes were little more than slits in a chubby face.

'You're a funny man, Beryl,' said Tara, flanked by Murray. Wilson had remained by the entrance to the car wash compound. 'And it's Detective Inspector Grogan to you.'

Beryl gave a few token squirts of water across the bonnet of a red Astra as Tara and Murray drew closer. Close enough, for him to suddenly aim the jet in their direction. Their recoil gave him just enough time to leg it past them towards the open street. He had not bargained on running into Wilson, his equal in height if not in weight. Wilson thrust him sideways into the wire mesh fencing, but Beryl merely bounced off and hurried on his way. The two uniformed constables were quickly out of their car and formed another obstruction across the pavement. Beryl barged through with ease, knocking one officer flat on his back. Several passing cars were the first thing to slow him down. He couldn't get across the road. He wasn't a fast runner, either. Forty yards along the pavement, Murray and Wilson finally ran him to the side, colliding with a heavy metal railing. Big Beryl wasn't hurt, but even after such a short run was gasping for breath.

'Now that wasn't very nice, Beryl,' said an out-of-breath Tara, catching them up. The front of her blouse and trousers were soaked. 'I only wanted a word. Now we'll have to do it down at the station.'

Still panting, Beryl smirked at Tara.

'Did you ever think of entering one of those Miss Wet T-shirt competitions, love?'

Instantly, Tara drew her arms across her chest. She glanced at her colleagues and caught their smirks.

'Get him out of here,' she snapped.

Wilson held Big Beryl in an elbow lock, gladly applying pressure each time he tried to move. Once he was handcuffed, the two uniforms marched him to their car. Three people in the car wash, two men in a Nissan and a young woman, in the Astra, were gazing through the fence looking stunned and mystified by the activity before them and no doubt wondering who was now going to wash their cars.

'I'm sayin' nothin'. I want my brief, *now*,' Beryl shouted as he was squeezed into the patrol car.

CHAPTER 11

It was evening before they had the opportunity to interview Big Beryl. Tara left Wilson to do the honours.

'Beryl, have you no sense?' said Wilson. 'It's a simple question. What did you do with the gear?'

'What gear?' Beryl, resting on his arms, was slumped over the table, his bald pate beading with sweat.

'There you go again. I thought you knew how to play this game. You tell us what we want to know and then I can go home for my tea, simple.'

But the big man wasn't having any of it. He continually smirked at Wilson who was at a loss for what to do or say next. His inexperience at working an interview was driving him along dead-end streets. Beryl was a seasoned campaigner of police interviews. Exasperated, Wilson rose from his chair opposite Beryl and made for the door.

'You can bloody stew here for all I care. I'm away for my dinner.'

'Get that cute detective or Murray. I'll talk to him. At least his balls have dropped.'

It was a swipe at Wilson, who didn't like it.

'With a voice like that, Beryl, yours must be in your throat.'

Tara and Murray were chatting in the operations room sifting through a pile of papers, neither one looking at all happy.

'Will you look at this pigging mess!' said Murray as Wilson approached. 'Tweedy wants me to go through all of this before Thursday.'

'What is it?' Wilson ventured to ask. It was as if Murray had been willing him to do just that so that he could rant for another ten minutes.

'Case notes. Dot every I, cross all the bloody Ts, he says. We can't afford to slip up on this one, Alan, he says.'

Wilson listened in silence feeling it wiser to say nothing.

'It's the Hurley case, booze smuggler extraordinaire,' said Tara with a sigh. It comes up to court next month, you know how Tweedy likes to have everything neat and tidy, well before the time.'

'What's going on, ma'am?' Wilson asked. 'I thought we were supposed to be a serious crime squad?'

'I wish I knew, John. I'm beginning to think I've done something wrong.'

Wilson acknowledged her comment with a nod of his head. 'If you want a break, Big Beryl says he'll only talk to one of you.'

'Playing hard to get is he, John?'

Murray enjoyed the odd poke at his junior colleague. Wilson and Murray were good lads. They had been in Tweedy's section longer than Tara. They more or less clicked right from day one. She was fortunate, two good cops; they understood her, and she was happy to allow them some scope. Wilson was relatively quiet, never said too much but Tara knew he had a wild streak in him. He liked a few drinks and a hand of cards. Murray, however, was making another attempt at settling down. Lately, he was not always available when Wilson fancied a late night at cards or a game of squash after work.

'He's acting as if he's just snatched the bloody crown jewels and won't tell us where he has them stashed,' said Wilson.

Tara tossed a bundle of paper onto her desk, sat back in her chair and stretched.

'What time is it?' she asked.

'It's after seven, nearly half past,' said Murray.

'Sod it. I think I'll take this lot home and look over it in front of the telly.'

'What about Big Beryl?' said Wilson, as Tara stood, gathering her bag and coat.

'Give him his tea and put him to bed. I'll speak to him in the morning. He might be more forthcoming after a night in the cells.'

'Fair enough,' Wilson replied. 'That means I can be on my way too. I'll see you in the morning.'

Tara gathered up the files that Tweedy had given to her, walked from the office and took to the stairs. She contemplated the remainder of her evening. Once she got home, there was little chance she would even open the files. This day, as if she could get much lower, had dragged her down.

But she did not go straight home.

CHAPTER 12

Tara needed activity and had a yearning for company. There weren't many options open for her. Maybe she could drive around for a while, or go to the pictures, but then she wouldn't get any work done. She could turn around and go back to the office, or she could go for a long run.

Somewhere between driving to Kate's or the local Cineplex, she still hadn't decided, another idea popped into her head. Scarcely realising she had done it, and instantly feeling nervous, she stopped her car outside the house. The double gates lay open, but she felt better leaving her car in the street and walking up the drive to the front door. The blinds were closed at the lounge window, and she was unable to tell if there was a light on inside. She rang the doorbell and waited for a light to come on in the front porch. Her tummy gave a little flutter — nerves or hunger — she couldn't decide which. Within a few moments, Jez Riordan appeared by her door. On this occasion, she drew it open wide and recognised Tara instantly.

'Hello, Inspector,' she said with a smile, her wide-eyed expression suggesting that she was intrigued by Tara's presence.

'Miss Riordan.' She attempted to sound informal, failed miserably then lied. 'I was just passing. Thought I might take you up on your offer.'

'Offer?'

'I'm sorry, perhaps I got it wrong...'

'No, no, no,' she said. 'My studio! Of course, please come in, Inspector.'

Two and a half feet was about the measure of Tara as she stepped inside. What a stupid idea. What was she doing here?

'Would you like a drink?' Jez asked. 'I was just about to open a bottle of wine.'

She walked to her kitchen, while Tara stood in the middle of her lounge, the little girl lost, in a quandary over whether to stand or sit. She watched as her host uncorked the bottle.

Tara thought Jez looked better than last time. It was the clothes and make-up, she supposed. She wore a dark grey skirt with a white blouse, black stockings and expensive-looking shoes.

'I'm sorry about turning up like this. I hope I'm not interfering with your plans for the evening.'

'Turning up like what?'

'Out of the blue, unannounced.'

'You don't need an appointment, Inspector. Not for a social call anyway. I had no plans for tonight other than this bottle of wine and the television.'

'Please, call me Tara. I suppose I also wanted to check that you are all right.'

'That's really thoughtful of you, Tara. And you can call me Jez.'

She handed Tara a hefty wine glass, one-third full of a fruity red. 'Please, make yourself comfortable,' she said.

Tara was glad for the drink; it moistened her dry mouth and throat and settled her uncharacteristic nerves. She stole the chance to examine Jez as she sat in an armchair to her right, while she was plonked sheepishly in the middle of the sofa. Tonight, Tara thought, Jez looked younger, at least by five years, her hair brushed into waves which dropped to her shoulders. Her eyes seemed bigger and brighter. She appeared less strained and more confident than when they'd first met.

'I had the evening free, unexpectedly,' Tara felt compelled to explain, 'and the idea of looking around your studio came into my head.' Did that sound all right? Or did she sound like Inspector No-mates?

'I'm glad it did. I don't often get the chance to show anyone around. I wonder sometimes if people feel that I'm being pretentious when I start talking about my painting. Lately, though, it's got me through some rather dark times.'

'And how are things at the moment?'

'Fine, I suppose. It's never easy getting over the loss of someone you cared for.'

'You're still working at Harbinson's?'

'Yes, of course.' She sounded a little put out by the question. It sparked an alarm in Tara that told her to quit

43

work for the evening and to stop asking such pertinent questions.

'Come on,' said Jez, rising from the chair. 'I'll show you around, after all, that's what you came for.'

She led the way up the thickly carpeted stairs, pushed open a door on the landing and switched on the light.

'It's supposed to be the master bedroom, but I thought that I could put all the space and light to better use. I sleep in one of the rooms at the back of the house; it's perfectly adequate when you're living alone.'

The room was indeed spacious and would appear more so in daylight with the French windows open onto the balcony.

'It must be a lovely room when the sun is shining,' Tara commented.

'Mmm. In summer I can easily lose track of time up here. I do all my real living in this space.'

Tara began to relax and to wander around, inspecting the half-dozen pictures on the walls. There were several canvasses stacked on the floor, paper sketches too, paint boxes and two easels. The smell of fresh air mingled with the odour of oil paints and new paper. Jez remained by the doorway, her arms folded, allowing her visitor to browse in silence.

Being honest, Tara wouldn't know if Jez's work was any good in the commercial sense, but she didn't have to be told what to like and what to dislike. She stood for a moment, lingering over a painting that sat on the floor and against the wall, of a place familiar to her.

'I used to love going there when I was a kid. You've captured it very well.'

'Funny you should say that. I painted it from a photograph when I was living in London. I've never been there. Don't even know where it is.'

'You're joking? You've never been to Llanberis?'

'I'm afraid not. I didn't get the chance when I was a child and I moved to London when I left school. I did the painting while I was at university.'

'Let me know when you have a day free, and I'll take you for a drive. Then you can see how you've done the place justice.'

'Thank you, you're very kind, Tara.'

They smiled at each other and at last Tara felt at ease in this woman's presence.

They spent nearly an hour going through Jez's collection, discussing each one that interested Tara. Jez explained a little of how she chose a subject and what she tried to convey in the work. Mostly, Jez's paintings were traditional landscapes, but Tara uncovered several canvasses which seemed a tad bizarre. She held one before her in both hands.

'Oh, that was part of an exhibition theme I did a few years ago,' Jez explained. 'I chose some beautiful landscapes and then blighted them with something horrible. A big environmental statement, I suppose, but they sold well.'

Tara was holding a picture, shaking with laughter, as she gazed at a beautiful rural scene of cows in a meadow. In the background, however, the cows had formed an orderly queue which led to the front door of a McDonald's restaurant.

'For that one, I had no takers,' Jez said.

* * *

'So tell me, how do you like being a police officer?' Jez asked, having insisted upon making supper after Tara had let it slip that she had not eaten.

'It has its moments, I suppose. It certainly gives me plenty to think about.'

'You mean that you bring your work home?'

'Sometimes it's hard to switch off. It's probably the type of job that a woman like me should have. Not married, no kids, not much else to worry about.'

Jez set a bowl of spaghetti with smoked salmon in a cream sauce and a basket of garlic bread in front of Tara. She was ravenous and tucked straight in.

'How come you're in Liverpool and working as a secretary? I'd have thought you'd have done pretty well with your painting in London?'

'I suppose I did do well, but I needed a break. I wanted to be somewhere else, and I decided to do something ordinary for a change. Being a secretary pays the bills. The money I make from painting allows me to enjoy myself from time to time.'

'You don't feel awkward working at Harbinson's, after what happened?'

Jez's expression told her that she was pained by the question. Prying off-duty was an anti-social habit she would have to stop.

'Why should I? Richard and I hadn't done anything wrong, except fall in love.'

'I'm sorry, Jez. I shouldn't poke my nose in. I didn't come to interview you.'

'It doesn't matter. Already in the past, I suppose, and I'm on my own, again.'

Jez took a drink of her wine as if to wash the thought away. Tara caught the look in her sad blue eyes and offered a sympathetic smile. Jez smiled, too.

'Do you have family in Liverpool?' Tara reckoned the question was less intrusive than her previous faux pas. But she was wrong again.

'No, not really,' Jez replied, her eyes watering. 'My mother died when I was three and my father when I was seventeen. There's no one here really, no one I'm particularly close to.'

She seemed to wander off with her thoughts for a while as Tara continued with her supper. When the meal was

46

finished, an awkward silence ensued and Tara began to think she had overstayed her welcome.

'That certainly hit the spot,' she said, wiping her mouth. 'But I think I've taken enough of your time.' She glanced at her watch. 'God, it's after eleven. I'm sorry for spoiling your evening, having to entertain the likes of me. I'd better be on my way.'

'Finish your wine first,' said Jez, topping up her glass.

Tara found this woman hard to refuse.

CHAPTER 13

It was the first board meeting since Richard's death, and Maggie Hull was frightened. She set a tray of glasses and jug of water in the centre of the table and looked around the room. There would be an empty chair this morning unless Edward had already found someone to replace his son-in-law.

She had worked for the company for more than thirty years. Edward had been in charge for longer, but she remembered the day that Toby had joined in the shadow of his father Jimmy. Then Richard came along and he and Toby soon became a double act, bosom pals and tricksters of the highest order.

Soon, though, Richard had begun a relationship with Nicole, Edward's daughter. She had worked there during the summer months while she was a student, but when she and Richard married, and the children came along, she was happy to stay at home. Everything had turned sour when Jez showed up. Maggie could see trouble brewing once Richard and Toby both began paying Jez too much attention. At first, it seemed merely a light-hearted competition between the two lads to see who could impress Jez the most. But the harmless flirtations developed to something more serious. She could see that Richard and Toby were fighting each other for the affections of the stunning woman. Jez had been her friend for a time also but she could never approve of such behaviour. She never thought that Richard would go as far as he had done. To leave his family for Jez was only asking for trouble. He hurt so many people.

But Maggie knew the secrets of this place, far more than she was supposed to know. She had seen how Jez had eased her way into working for Edward, a job that she, Maggie, had done for years. There was a hostile atmosphere about the office. And now she was afraid. She knew things about Jez, and she knew the secrets of each of the directors. Such knowledge, she feared, might one day get her into terrible trouble. How was it all going to end?

* * *

'Good morning, Maggie,' Skip McIntyre called to announce his presence in the room. He enjoyed making an entrance.

She could barely summon a reply. 'Morning,' she mumbled, but the man's ego didn't stretch to him being concerned by the lack of warmth in her greeting. He was thick-skinned and had never cared a damn for his employees, including Maggie. At times she wondered how a man like McIntyre gained any satisfaction from working at the firm. Then again, she knew how he had come to be here.

Toby came in next and sat down at the table where she had already laid out his files for him. He had a report to present to the board this morning and she knew he was ill-prepared. As always, she did her best to cover for him. He looked his usual nervous self, well-dressed, well-groomed but there was little of substance between his ears.

A few minutes later, his father Jimmy hobbled in on his walking stick, puffing heavily from having struggled from his car to the lift and then to the boardroom. Nowadays, effectively retired, he maintained a presence on the board, more to ensure that he was not getting ripped off by the rest of them than to contribute anything worthwhile to the company. Years ago he had enjoyed groping her each day when she came into his office. Now he was incapable of anything, and she could make him feel inadequate merely by brushing her body against him.

Last to arrive was the chairman, Edward Harbinson, son of the company's founder and the man responsible for making Harbinson Fine Foods a profitable company and national success. She thought that he looked drained and was sure it had everything to do with what had happened to his son-in-law. He might also be aware of the trouble that surely was soon coming his way.

When Jez strode in elegantly to record the minutes of the meeting, Maggie quickly made her escape. It was her nature, though, to express her distaste of the woman by staring coldly into her eyes as Jez took her seat. Once, they had been friends but now Maggie Hull knew better. This woman had destroyed Richard's marriage and now he was dead, and yet she still had the nerve to continue working there. Any decent woman would make herself scarce.

Maggie missed her regular bus home because, after the board meeting, Toby had a ton of things needing to be done. He had disappeared off to the factory in Speke, or so he said, while she was left to sort his problems. On her way out of the office, she shared the lift with Skip McIntyre who was full of his usual monotonous chat about holidays drawing near and questions on her plans for the weekend. He knew damn well she had few plans; she lived alone, never married, no family in Liverpool, no real interests outside of work, while he could boast of a rich social life, his country cottage in the Lakes and his bloody villa in Marbella.

Maybe it was time for her to think of a new job, or perhaps retirement. But where could she go, or what else could she do? Harbinson's was all she had ever known. This company was her life.

On the walk from the bus stop, rain coming down heavily with the sudden drop in temperature, she deliberated over what to have for her dinner. She could fetch some fish and chips on the way home, or else pop a steak pie in the oven and settle down for the night with *Eastenders* and *Coronation Street*.

Having opted for the steak pie, she slid her key into the lock and pushed open her front door. She shook the water from her raincoat as she pulled it off, hung it on the post of the bannister and went down the hall to the kitchen to switch on the oven. Her doorbell sounded. She froze. She didn't even dare to look behind her. So often these days she had a reluctance to open her front door. The last time they had called at least she had the money to pay them. But not tonight. She'd promised herself that she would not rack up any more debts. She had decided it was so unnecessary. Most of the things she bought were useless to her anyway. Pretty to admire, but that was all. And before she knew it her spending was out of control again. She'd maxed out her credit cards weeks ago. She was behind on payments. As she'd done several times before, she turned to the local guys who were quick to lend her cash but at a huge rate of interest. Now she had no money to pay them back and no friend this time to step in to help her.

She tried to make out the figure beyond the frosted glass. It might be someone else, about something entirely innocent. Mormons, Jehovah's Witnesses, charity collectors or even a neighbour. Maybe it was Toby, or someone from the office, calling to drop off files for her to work on before the morning. But the outline of the figure in the dying light didn't look as though it could be Toby.

The caller was persistent, ringing the bell and hammering with a fist on the glass of the door. She heard the muffled voice calling to her. She switched the oven off again and eased slowly down the hall. Her hands trembled as finally, she opened the door. Immediately, she drew back, sighing with relief as her visitor, dripping wet, stepped into the hall. Maggie turned and walked towards her living room as her caller closed the front door. But it was a disastrous mistake to assume she was safe.

The first blow to the back of her head knocked her cold and she fell across the doorway into the lounge. The frenzy that followed quickly sucked the life from her.

CHAPTER 14

Despite feeling less motivated even than the day before, Tara dealt swiftly with Big Beryl.

'I suggest that you tell DC Wilson of your involvement in these burglaries,' she said.

Beryl scoffed as if her words meant nothing.

'We have a witness, Beryl. Someone who can identify you as the man who was making out of her front door with her television.'

Beryl rubbed his chubby hand across a day's growth of beard. Suddenly, he didn't look so confident.

'I'll leave you with DC Wilson, and you can make your statement.'

She sighed as she walked from the interview room back to her desk. Only twenty to eleven and she was praying for the day to be over. She glanced across the room at Murray who was engrossed in paperwork. The remainder of her day promised the same, and yet her mind was busy with the information she had digested on the poisoning emergency. She had composed a mental list of the people she would like to interview. Whoever was running the investigation may have already done so, but why had no progress been reported? It seemed that with the involvement of national security services everything was being kept under wraps. The public was not to be told. And she was not allowed to get involved.

Scrolling through the Merseyside Police bulletins, she was trying to conjure some interest in her work when her desk telephone rang.

'May I speak with Detective Inspector Grogan, please,' said a woman's sedate voice.

'Speaking,' Tara replied.

'Inspector, this is Jez Riordan, how are things?'

Tara was startled by the call. She was certainly not expecting it, and yet somehow she felt elated to hear the friendly voice.

'Up to my eyes in tedious paperwork,' she replied. 'Not the most interesting of days.'

'Oh dear,' Jez said. 'Maybe I can change that. Are you free this evening? I have two tickets for the Philharmonic tonight. I wondered if you would care much for an Elgar Cello Concerto?'

'Classical music? Can't say that I've tried that before. I'm more a Foo Fighters fan.'

'A what?' Jez said incredulously.

'Rock music.'

'Oh, I see. I thought about asking you last night, but I'm afraid I chickened out. I didn't want to appear forward.'

'No, not at all.'

'It's fairly light – lowbrow, you might say.'

'Why not? You've talked me into it. I'm happy to drive.'

'Great. You can pick me up at seven if you like?'

'See you then.'

'Bye.'

Tara could have talked more. She could have chatted to such a friendly soul all day. With a wistful smile, she wondered about her new friend. Was Jez, like her, in desperate need of companionship?

* * *

Her afternoon's work paled away. It was a battle with her mind to concentrate on the Hurley case. The paperwork was four months old, the case having first come to light almost a year ago. After a tip-off and then several weeks of surveillance, police had managed to seize two tanker lorries. Five men were caught at the scene and three others, including Jack Hurley, the overlord of the smuggling operation, were arrested within the day. The lorries had been especially converted to carry alcohol in tanks hidden behind the refrigerated compartments used for transporting dairy products. Thousands of gallons of booze had been smuggled from Poland ready to be bottled and sold as a major brand of vodka.

The police had managed, not only to catch the smugglers but also to smash the distribution network for the booze once it reached Liverpool. The case being prepared for the courts was built upon the surveillance evidence. The objective had been to disrupt a major alcohol smuggling operation. Jack Hurley was the number one target; his previous convictions ran to two pages, mainly related to drug activities. The rumour was that his old associates were upset to learn about Jack's smuggling operation because they had been excluded from the scheme. Hurley was probably thankful that the police got to him before his old comrades did. Chief Superintendent Tweedy was pleased with the work and hopeful of a positive result when the CPS took it to court.

As Tara read through the various reports she could see the flaws, mostly the minutiae of police procedure but a half-alert barrister could still decide to muddy the water sufficiently for a judge to order a dismissal. She had seen it happen many times before. That's what worried Tweedy. Unfortunately, events and occurrences could not be changed. Having got to this stage they would simply have to make do.

* * *

By six o'clock Tara could take no more, her head buzzing, the cocky face of Jack Hurley flashing like a Belisha in her head. She felt elated at the prospect of a night out with new and friendly company. A quick shower and change at home and, twenty minutes late, she dashed to the house in Woolton to pick up her new friend.

'Did you think I wasn't coming?' Tara asked.

'I was beginning to wonder if you had some kind of allergy to Elgar.'

They were standing in the foyer of the Philharmonic Hall before Tara dared to comment on Jez's appearance. Until then she'd been covered in a black, full-length overcoat, protection against the cold October rain.

'You look...'

'What?'

'Very different from last time,' said Tara. 'If I'd knocked on your door instead of you running out to the car I might not have recognised you.'

'Oh thanks very much,' Jez said.

'Sorry, I mean you look fantastic – just different.'

Jez looked rather striking. Her eyes were heavy with liner and mascara, her face deliberately pale, milky white, in contrast to her black hair. She wore a mid-length, slim-fitting black dress, cut away in front to reveal the edges of a black lace bra and cleavage. Around her waist was a broad leather belt with two shiny silver buckles, and she stood tall on five-inch-heeled, black ankle boots. The thought occurred to Tara that if you passed this woman in a crowded street you would still remember every detail of her four weeks later. Tara had made some effort to look presentable. She wore a maroon off-the-shoulder dress and matching high heels. She noticed that Jez seemed to inspect her in a similar manner.

The auditorium was full, a great venue for music, Tara realised, although she had only been there once before with her mother to see Cliff Richard. She also had to admit that the cello concerto was at least relaxing. She wasn't as struck on the other composer, she'd forgotten his name, but the time passed gently and as they drove back to Jez's house, she felt that the evening had been enjoyable.

'Thank you, Tara,' Jez said softly. 'I really enjoyed your company. It's the first time I've been out since Richard, you know.' A trace of a tear sparkled in her eyes, and Jez again looked vulnerable in the same manner Tara had noticed when they'd first met. 'I've had the tickets for ages; it would have been a pity to waste them.'

'Thank you for thinking of me. A night out was just what I needed,' Tara said with a smile.

Suddenly, Jez leaned across and kissed her on the lips. She lingered for a second, enough time to flash her blue eyes at Tara. Then she opened the car door before Tara could react. It was bold and mischievous, but Tara had no clue whether she should read anything more into the kiss.

'Next time we can do the Foo Fighters,' said Jez.

'Definitely.'

'Goodnight, Tara. Sleep well.'

Jez closed the car door and strode confidently toward her house. Tara was suddenly trembling. As she drove away, her confusion over what had just occurred suppressed her enjoyment of an evening spent with a new friend.

She was on her way home to Wapping Dock when she got a call on her mobile. It was a duty officer from St Anne Street. Another fatality.

CHAPTER 15

The death was suspicious, but she had no idea at this point if it was linked to the spate of poisonings in the city. If it was another such incident, then she was surprised to have been called to the scene. After all, she had been sidelined. That case was in the hands of a specialist team. She turned the car at the next junction and headed to Wavertree.

The rain was coming down in bucketloads. Now close to midnight, it was cold, and she was standing with Murray outside a small terraced house in Bartlett Street. Her jacket and dress were soon soaking wet despite the shelter from Murray's umbrella, and her heels were impractical for wearing at a crime scene. Two police vans were parked either side of the house and arc lighting had been erected above the front door, from where forensic personnel were coming and going. There was no sign of a team of special investigators in protective suits, so she assumed that it had already been confirmed that this scene was not linked to the poisoning emergency. She was curious to know how such a conclusion had been reached so quickly.

A cordon of fluorescent incident tape sealed off the lower end of the long street, while at the opposite end, and closer to the house, a crowd of more than fifty people standing in the road were held at bay in a similar manner. Tara noticed the looks of shock on the faces of some, horror on others and pure inquisitiveness on the remainder, all sheltering under umbrellas, baseball hats or hooded anoraks. Someone in their quiet little street was dead; the police were involved, so it must be murder.

Wilson ducked beneath the crime scene tape and joined Tara and Murray.

'Well, John, what's the story?' Tara asked him.

'I've just been speaking to the woman who lives two doors down, a Mrs Bailey.' He paused for a moment and drew a breath. He'd been the first detective on the scene and looked pale and cold for it. 'She found the body.'

'I assume it's not another poisoning incident?'

Wilson shook his head.

'Not this one, ma'am.'

'What time did she find the body?'

'About two hours ago. She knocked on the door, got no answer then took a peek through the living room window. The light was off, but she saw the body lying on the floor. According to her, it is the body of Maggie Hull. She lived alone.'

'Do we know what happened?' Murray asked, visibly shivering.

'I got a quick peek before forensics moved in. Looks like she was battered over the head, what's left of it. She's lying on the floor between the living room and hallway. I didn't get to see much else.'

'We'll have a good look around when forensics have finished,' said Tara. 'Have a word with some of the other neighbours. Ask if they saw or heard anything. Tweedy will be here soon; he'll want to know all the biz. Alan, you and I can have a chat with Mrs Bailey.'

An elderly man, Mr Bailey, Tara presumed, was standing by his door, beneath a small porch affording him shelter from the rain. Tara introduced herself and asked to speak with Mrs Bailey.

'She's very upset,' said the man in a flustered tone, his face pinched and his mouth drawing tightly on a cigarette. Despite wearing only a white cotton shirt and dark trousers, with braces despatched from each shoulder, he didn't seem troubled by the damp and cold. His hair was black, thinning, and greased to his bony head. His eyes seemed to bulge outwards as he spoke.

'She got a hell of a shock; we all did. I can hardly take it in – that it's Maggie.' He shook his head and exhaled a barrage of smoke.

'I take it that you knew her well?' Tara asked.

'Maggie? Of course, we did. We've lived here forty-four years. She was only a nipper running about the street when we moved in. Wouldn't hurt a fly; a kind girl, if ever there was one.'

'Does anyone else live in the house?'

'With Maggie?' He drew back as if astounded by the question. 'No, no,' he said, shaking his head each time with increased fervour, dismissing the very notion that his neighbour shared her home. 'Not Maggie. She never married, you see. Didn't bother at all with men, as far as I know. You can ask our Betty; she'll tell you. No not Maggie.'

Tara was about to speak again, but the man hadn't finished.

'Now, she did have her mother until about five years ago. She died. Only seventy-two; it was sudden like, you know. A stroke.'

'Tell them about her brother,' said a voice from within the dimly lit hallway.

Mrs Bailey, a handkerchief at her nose, wobbled to the door. Her chubby face was flushed from expended tears. She was slow, her ankles and feet were swollen with fluid.

'Maggie has a brother,' she said in a croaky voice. 'He lives in Canada. Kenneth's his name. He'll take this badly. He was home last year on holiday, and he told me himself that he wanted Maggie to come and live with him in Toronto. I don't know how anybody is going to break the news to that lad.' The woman turned away and disappeared again in floods of tears.

Tara glanced at Murray who had been writing every word said into his notebook. She wouldn't be surprised if he had gone to the bother of recording every action, including the old woman crying her way back into her living room.

'Is there anyone you know of who would want to do Miss Hull any harm?'

'Maggie?' This habit of repeating the victim's name as a question was beginning to wear on Tara, but she understood that the man was elderly and upset by the evening's events. 'I wouldn't know a soul with anything bad to say about Maggie. Not a soul.' He seemed to drift away on his thoughts and memories. Tara thought it best to leave things until morning.

* * *

Superintendent Tweedy's arrival coincided with an opportunity for the group of detectives to have a limited viewing of the crime scene.

'What's happening, Tara?'

Tara ran through what information she had so far gathered as Tweedy made it clear that he was eager to see inside. They continued their discussion as they put on the requisite white protective, hooded overalls and blue overshoes. Wilson consulted with an officer from SOCO in charge of guarding the front door and thereby the precious crime scene and vital evidence. He nodded to Tara that it was all right to proceed. He needn't have bothered because Tweedy was not about to be kept waiting. All three detectives filed inside: Tara, then Tweedy and finally Murray.

The entrance hall, with a staircase to the right, was long and narrow and led to a galley kitchen. Off to the left, was the living room although at that moment none of them could get that far. The body of Maggie Hull lay straddled over the doorway. From where the three officers stood, only her legs were visible. The victim wore dark shoes with a medium heel, black or navy, plain tights on fairly trim legs and what appeared to be a knee-length dress or skirt, also in black or navy blue. The rose-coloured light shade in the hall, although bright and enhanced by the arcs from outside, betrayed the natural colours.

Blood, copious amounts of it, was the sight that hit them when they stepped closer to the threshold. Tara hung back, but she knew that she must look. This evening, she felt as though she could never stand over another corpse. Tweedy sighed, tutted and shook his head. The body lay face down, the back of the head was nothing but a mass of deep-red pulp fused with hair, the colour of which was indiscernible. The beige shag pile carpet of the living room was soaked red around the head and shoulders of the body. There were splatters of blood for several feet beyond. One side of a mink-coloured sofa was darkened red, and a cushion had been pulled from its place and lay close to the victim's left hand.

They didn't enter the living room. It would have involved them stepping over the body, and it was clear from the activity around them that the SOCO team still had work to do. Tweedy scanned the scene, absorbing as much information as he could. Tara, reluctantly, did the same. She studied the body, and gazed about the living room, saying nothing. It was a tiny place, filled with furniture and ornaments and a woman's touch. Little seemed out of place to her, meaning that she didn't think a long, protracted struggle had occurred. Murray stole a glance at the stricken body as Tara moved away. When they had seen enough, they stepped back into the heavy rain, the droplets a refreshing tonic for Tara's clammy face.

'Right,' said Tweedy, 'try to put everything together, as much as we can tonight. I'll see you all in the morning, at nine sharp.'

'Sir, does this mean we have this case?' Tara asked. 'Only, I was getting the feeling that I was being sidelined.'

Tweedy looked sympathetically at his young DI. It was not a conversation to hold in the pouring rain, but Tara was eager for a response.

'No, Tara, you have not been sidelined. It's just that I felt that this poisoning emergency would be just too much for you right now. You're not long back on duty; you've had a torrid experience. It can't have been easy for you. But now, needs must, you have a murder to investigate.'

'Yes, sir.'

Tweedy strode away, scraping off the white suit before retreating to his car.

'Right, I'll see you two at nine sharp,' said Tara to both Murray and Wilson with a satisfied smirk on her face.

Murray looked peeved, knowing he was here for some time yet.

'Have a word with some of these onlookers,' she said, 'they don't seem too keen on going to their beds.'

CHAPTER 16

At nine o'clock in the morning in Tweedy's office at St Anne Street station, Tara watched with Murray and Wilson as the Superintendent worked with his notorious flipcharts. By the time they were finished most of the paper would have something written on it, a word or phrase, a roughly sketched diagram, lists of evidence, lists of people, witnesses or suspects. Every thought from every person involved with the case would find its way onto Tweedy's charts. That was his way. He had been using them since Babbage was a lad, in other words, long before anyone ever saw the benefit in using a computer. He was not dismissive of new technology, but he did not believe that it necessarily had to replace his tried and trusted methods.

No one in the room looked particularly fresh. Murray and Wilson had no more than three hours' sleep, a quick shower and down to the station. Despite getting home earlier than her colleagues, Tara was not feeling the better for it, her head throbbing and her stomach crying out for nourishment. Tweedy always looked drained nowadays, although his voice somehow portrayed a brisk and jovial manner. He flicked over the cover of his chart.

'Right,' he began like an auctioneer, 'who'll start me off?'

'The latest,' said Wilson, who'd spent the night in liaison with SOCO, the police doctor and the pathologist in charge of post-mortem, 'is that the estimated time of death was between six and seven yesterday evening. The post-mortem is to begin at eleven-thirty this morning after formal ID. There were no signs of forced entry to the house.' Wilson paused while he flicked from one page to another in his notebook.

Tweedy scribbled fervently on his chart with a felt pen. The information was not coming in the manner he would prefer, that is, in a logical order. It meant him having to write the time of death on one page and then turning over several pages before noting facts from the crime scene. He wrote the time for the post-mortem in the bottom-left corner of the first page.

'Thank you, John. Who's next?'

Tara looked at Murray who merely returned her gaze. Tara couldn't help grinning at their playful indecision. Tweedy was oblivious to the silent remonstrating, but finally, Murray felt compelled to jump in.

'The victim has been unofficially identified as Maggie Hull, aged forty-nine, un-married and lived alone at the house in Bartlett Street.' He paused, giving Tweedy time to construct his lists. 'The victim was found by her next-door neighbour at approximately ten-fifteen. The front door had been closed normally; there were no signs of forced entry. So far, there are no witnesses to any disturbance in the area.'

'Thank you, Alan,' said Tweedy, always keen on using first names at the office.

'The victim appears to have been beaten to death,' said Wilson reading again from his notes. 'No evidence as yet of motive. No signs of sexual assault. It seems as though the victim had just returned home from work when the attack took place. Her overcoat was found hanging on the bannister, and a handbag was discovered close to the body. Some cash was found inside the bag. Bank and credit cards also, so it doesn't appear that robbery was a motive.'

Tara was busy making her notes, jotting down reminders to herself to check certain details. At times she was not fully aware of what was being said.

'No weapon found as yet,' Wilson continued.

Tweedy quickly devised another table relating to weapons.

'The victim was found lying face down between her living room and hall, little sign of a struggle except for a displaced cushion from the sofa. From what neighbours say, Miss Hull had no known enemies, no boyfriends and no family, except for a brother in Canada. The victim worked as a secretary in the city centre at the head office of Harbinson Fine Foods in the Liver Building. She seemed to live a solitary existence.'

The mention of Harbinson Fine Foods suddenly pinched at Tara's sides, disturbing her thought patterns. The company where Richard Andrews had been a director. The office also where Jez Riordan still worked. Tara's mind raced.

'Tara?' said Tweedy.

'Sorry?'

'Anything to add?' Tweedy remained at the ready with his marker.

'Just to remind you, sir,' said Tara, her attention to proceedings now restored. 'It seems that Maggie Hull worked for Harbinson Fine Foods. That's the same company as that jumper at the Liver Building, Richard Andrews. A possible connection?'

'Or tragic coincidence?' replied Tweedy. 'Have a look anyway. It's a start.'

Tweedy stepped back and examined his handiwork.

'Right,' he said, a little perplexed. 'What we need this morning is a plan of attack and a list of priorities.'

Within a few minutes, a sizeable list of tasks had been committed to paper. Tweedy shared them out among the officers assembled and then called for any further thoughts or suggestions regarding a lead to quickly solving the case.

Tara wanted a second, more detailed inspection of the murder scene before she set about doing anything else.

* * *

A squad of uniformed officers had begun a series of house-to-house inquiries in Bartlett Street and several roads on either side. The home of Maggie Hull remained cordoned off, while forensic examination continued. Another team of uniforms were busy searching the back alleys and gardens of nearby houses for a murder weapon or indeed anything that might shed some light on this dismal case.

Murray accompanied Tara into the house as he had done in the early hours of the morning. On this occasion, with the body removed from the crime scene, they were able to stand inside the living room.

'There doesn't seem to be a thing out of place,' Murray commented.

Tara agreed.

'And yet there's hardly room to move,' she said. 'Look at all this stuff.'

The pair of them examined the contents of the compact yet overfilled room. A plump three-seater sofa sat against a wall directly opposite a grey-stone fireplace. An armchair, matching the sofa, sat in the bay of the window and another one by the door. A heavy, dark-wood cabinet with glass doors and shelves was squeezed between the wall and chimney breast and housed an extensive collection of glass crystal: Waterford, Edinburgh and Swarovski. Between the fireplace and the window sat the latest in home entertainment: 3D Smart TV, Sky Box, DVD and an iPod docking station. Behind the TV, a bookcase housed a multitude of CDs and DVDs.

'Will you look at the size of that TV,' said Murray. 'Maybe this is where Big Beryl keeps his loot?'

'Miss Hull certainly had the best of gear,' Tara agreed. 'I'm sure that carpet and suite cost a bit, never mind all that crystal. It's a hell of a CD and DVD collection, too. She must have spent a fortune.'

The room, despite being filled to the brim with all sorts of personal luxuries, was also quite tastefully decorated. The walls were painted an inconspicuous mild cream, allowing several expensive-looking paintings to catch the eye. One, in particular, had Murray looking baffled.

'Take a look at this,' he said, his head cocked to the side. Above the sofa, a picture, three feet by two and a half, showing a waterfall, had posed him with a problem. 'Do you see what I see?' he said, bewildered.

Tara studied the scene. At first glance, it appeared simply as an oil painting of a vibrant waterfall in a leafy glen. It was brightly coloured: fast-flowing water over dark-grey rocks amid emerald ferns and silver birch. On closer inspection and indeed, once noticed, it was difficult to believe that it could have been missed in the first place, stood two young boys above the falls and among the mosses and ferns, their hands by their crotches. Suddenly, it became apparent that their behaviour, both of them having a pee, was entirely responsible for the torrents of water cascading over the rocks.

'Who the hell would paint a picture like that?' Murray asked.

It immediately occurred to Tara who might have devised such a scene.

They continued their inspection of the ground floor of the house. In the kitchen, they were once again amazed to find such an expensive range of utilities. Murray whistled.

'Wow! These kitchen units must be top of the range, never mind that oven and hob.' He opened one of the cupboard doors to find a well-stocked refrigerator. 'Jeez, look at the stuff in here.' Champagne, smoked salmon and several expensive, pre-cooked meals from luxury ranges of Waitrose, and Marks and Spencer were stacked on the shelves. 'She certainly didn't make do with beans on toast. She knew how to treat herself.'

'The joys of living alone, Alan,' said Tara, closing another cupboard door upon expensive-looking crockery. 'Let's take a look upstairs.'

It was the same story – compact rooms made to look even smaller by extensive bedroom furniture, fitted slide robes and a king-size bed in the master bedroom.

'Did she own part of that company she worked for?' said Murray. 'Makes you wonder where she got all her money from. She lived well for a secretary.'

Tara slid open one of the wardrobe doors. By this stage, she was no longer surprised to find a vast array of expensive clothing hanging inside. Behind the next door and, woman-typical she thought, was the accompanying collection of shoes and boots. Murray handed her a photograph in a heavy brass frame.

'This our Maggie then?'

In the colour picture was a woman of about thirty-five sitting on a bench beside an older woman who looked around sixty. The scene behind them was of a riverboat, the type you would see cruising on the Rhine.

'Maggie and her mum?' said Tara. She looked closely at the photo, the first she had seen of the victim if indeed it was Maggie Hull. She seemed a happy sort but then she appeared to have been on holiday and well relaxed. Tara couldn't tell much else. She was not that pretty, a step above plain maybe; her hair was long and curly, her smile a little fixed. Again, Tara concluded it was a holiday snap, nothing more.

'Well, Maggie love,' she said to the photo. 'For whatever reason, some bastard took a strong disliking to you.' She handed the frame back to Murray who replaced it on the bedside table. 'Right, Alan, let's go see the people she worked with.'

CHAPTER 17

On this occasion, Tara didn't bother to make an appointment. She was certainly intending to speak with the company chairman once again, but she wished also to speak with the ordinary staff, the people who had worked day in, day out with Maggie Hull, those who knew her best and those who may even have been her friends. It might well be that she worked at one of the company's factories of which there were two on Merseyside, one in Speke another in Birkenhead.

From the moment she and Murray walked through the door of the head office in the Liver Building, however, it was obvious that the news of Maggie Hull's murder had reached them. Officially, her name had not yet been released to the media because the formal identification had not yet taken place. Her address, however, and the scene outside her home had already featured on the breakfast-time news and social media.

'Good morning, can I help you?' asked a girl on the desk.

She wore slim black trousers and high heels, but Tara couldn't recall if it was the same girl she'd met on her previous visit. She shrugged off the notion as unimportant.

'I'm Detective Inspector Tara Grogan, Merseyside Police and this is my colleague, Detective Sergeant Murray.' The girl's face reddened but she managed to nod acknowledgement. 'Can I assume that you have already heard the tragic news this morning regarding Miss Maggie Hull?'

'Yes, we have,' she replied, tearfully.

'Can you confirm that Miss Hull worked for this company?'

'Em, yes, she worked for Mr Ewing; she's his secretary. Would you like to speak to him?'

'I'll certainly do that, but first, can you tell me if Maggie had any close friends in the office? Anyone who might have known her better than most?'

'Maggie's been here a long time,' she said. Her voice faltered as she realised that she'd been talking of Maggie in the present tense. 'I'm sorry, we're all very shocked. I'll get someone to speak with you.' She returned to the group of people who by now had ceased their conversation and were listening to the exchange with the police.

'Poor Maggie, we can't believe it,' said a woman who had volunteered her services, leaving the other girl behind to settle herself with a cup of coffee. 'What happened to her? I hope you get them, lock them up and throw away the key. She never did anybody a button of harm.'

The small and stout woman with greying hair and well-powdered face was saying all the things that would spring naturally to anyone who'd just learned of a murder and especially that of a friend. She dabbed her eyes with a crumpled tissue as Tara repeated her introductions.

'I would like to speak to anyone who knew her well,' she said.

'All of us knew her well,' the woman replied. 'Maggie was a very private person, though. She mixed well in the office; we went out to lunch, did some shopping. Beyond that, I don't think anyone in here was close to her. As far as I know, outside of working hours she never really socialised.'

'Thank you, Mrs…?'

'Hodges, Muriel Hodges.'

'OK, Mrs Hodges, I'll speak with Mr Harbinson now if he's available.'

'Certainly, I'll just check.' She walked to a desk, picked up a telephone and punched in a number. A few seconds later, she was back with Tara. 'That's fine, Inspector, Mr Harbinson can see you now. I'll take you there myself.' She led them along the corridor that Tara remembered from her previous visit. 'Go on through,' she said when they had reached the door to the chairman's office. 'Oh, Inspector, just one thing.'

'Yes, Mrs Hodges?'

'I should have mentioned it earlier, but Maggie was quite close for a while with one member of staff. At least, I believe they used to spend some time together outside working hours. She'll probably explain to you herself.'

'And who is this person?'

'Oh sorry, I nearly forgot to tell you that part. Her name is Jez Riordan. She and Maggie are both secretaries to the directors. I expect that's how they became friends.'

'Thanks very much, Mrs Hodges. You've been very helpful.'

The woman smiled with closed lips, turned on her heels and hurried away, no doubt relieved to be finished with the police and their questions.

Edward Harbinson must have overheard the conversation because he opened his door to greet them. There was no sign of Jez at what Tara presumed to be the secretary's desk in the outer office.

'Come in, Inspector,' he said, holding the door open.

'Mr Harbinson, I'm sorry to bother you again on the back of more tragic news.'

'I understand. You'll have to excuse me, but I'm devastated about Maggie. My phone hasn't stopped this morning with colleagues and friends, even clients who knew her well. Everyone is very shocked.'

Harbinson was certainly more animated than when Tara had first met him. On that occasion, he'd sat with head bowed and seemed rather indifferent to the passing of Richard Andrews, his son-in-law.

He had sat down as Tara and Murray had taken their seats, but in seconds he was on his feet again, pacing, fidgeting with his tie then tidying around his desk. He was a man on edge; his hands shook when he lifted some papers and his voice teetered and threatened to fail.

'We were wondering if you could fill us in a little on Maggie Hull's background. I gather that she's worked here for a long time?'

Harbinson sighed but his breath seemed to pass nervously. He fighting to remain composed.

'All her working life, Inspector,' he replied. 'She walked into our office in Birkenhead the day after she left school. Her mother had to bring her in, she was so shy. My father was chairman at the time. I was still learning the ropes. A long time ago.'

Tara didn't want him drifting off on some nostalgic trip, she needed hard facts regarding Maggie Hull because so far she had precious few.

'Can you think of any reason why anyone should want to do her harm?'

'I was about to ask you the same question. If you had known Maggie then you, too, would be confounded at the thought that anyone would have reason to kill her. She worked hard in the office; there's nothing she didn't know about this company; everyone trusted her; everyone liked her. What more can I say?'

'What about her personal life?'

'Of that, I'm afraid, I know very little. She kept her personal life to herself. She never brought her problems into the office. She never appeared as anything less than happy. I know she never married, and I don't believe there was anyone in particular. Her mother died a few years ago. I was unable to attend the funeral but Maggie understood. That's the sort of person she was – very understanding.'

'OK, Mr Harbinson, I think we've heard enough. If you don't mind, we'd like to chat with other members of your staff.'

'Yes, of course, please feel free.' He rose from his desk visibly relieved as if he'd just been given the all-clear by a cancer specialist. He walked his visitors to the door. 'May I ask you a question, Inspector?' he said shakily.

'Go ahead.'

'How did she die?'

'Someone battered her to death, Mr Harbinson.' Tara studied the man's reactions and could have elaborated but the vision she'd planted was more than sufficient. Harbinson's face drained of colour. 'One last thing, Mr Harbinson. Can you think of any connection between Maggie Hull and Mr Andrews?'

He had to swallow hard before attempting to speak. The idea had given him something of a jolt, and Tara had noticed.

'Not beyond the office, no,' he answered as if he were running the idea through his mind for the first time.

CHAPTER 18

They were shown into the office of Toby Ewing by a young lad who didn't look old enough to be a school kid on work experience let alone a full-time employee. Thin, scrawny, with spots, his white shirt and bright red tie did little to enhance his maturity. The office was at the far end of a bare corridor, in a functional red-brick building within the Harbinson Fine Foods factory at Speke.

Toby Ewing had his back to them as they entered, and he was speaking on the telephone. When eventually he turned around and noticed that he had company, he nervously called an abrupt halt to his conversation.

'I'll have to go,' he said, sounding flustered. 'I have people waiting to see me. I'll see you tonight.' He put down the receiver. 'Sorry about that,' he said, although he didn't yet know who he was addressing.

'Mr Ewing?' Tara asked then continued with her introductions and explanations as to why she was there.

Ewing stood and listened but couldn't hide his being distracted. He was pale, fine-featured and wore designer spectacles, oblong lenses in dark blue frames. His suit, also, well in vogue, complemented a neat white shirt and a sensible tie. His body was thin, almost wimpish. It occurred to Tara that he seemed quite young to be a director in such a large company, but then again Richard Andrews, also, was only thirty-seven when he died.

'I'm sorry, Inspector,' said Ewing. 'As you can imagine things are a bit hectic here today. The phone hasn't stopped, and Maggie isn't here to field my calls.' His mention of her name suddenly halted him in his tracks. It allowed Tara to begin her enquiries.

'Miss Hull was your secretary, I believe?'

'That's correct.' He'd, at last, dropped into his leather chair and sat with his arms resting on the desk. 'Maggie was a lot more than a secretary, though.' His voice cracked and he wiped tears from behind his glasses. 'I'm sorry,' he sobbed. 'I meant to say that Maggie had been here a long time – long before me. And Richard. We were just kids; she taught us everything about this place. She was like a big sister to us, keeping us in check and covering up for us when we stepped out of line. The products, the accounts, dealing with clients, how to handle Edward: there's nothing she didn't know.'

'You mentioned Richard, would that be Richard Andrews?'

'Yes, poor Richard. I can't believe all this is happening. First Richard and now Maggie.'

Tweedy had referred to it as a tragic coincidence, but Tara wasn't entirely sure that she believed in such things. In her experience of crime investigation, a coincidence was merely something that lacked a credible factual explanation. It did not necessarily mean that two happenings could not be linked.

The telephone rang.

'Hello, Toby Ewing speaking?' He paused to listen. 'I'm sorry, John, I'll have to get back to you on that one. I don't have the file to hand … Tomorrow morning. Bye, John.' He replaced the receiver. 'Sorry for the interruption, Inspector.'

'No problem,' Tara replied. 'Can you tell me, Mr Ewing, when you last saw Miss Hull?'

'Yesterday. She was at work as usual. At head office, I mean. She didn't spend much time down here. I'm the director in charge of primary production here at our Speke factory. My time is divided between here and head office in the Liver Building.'

'Primary production?' Murray asked.

'Yes, we process our meat products here, mainly poultry, and some pork and lamb, then pass them on to Birkenhead where they prepare our "Fine" ready meals. We also supply fresh chicken directly to retail outlets.'

'And at what time did she leave work?' Tara asked.

'Quarter past five, I assume.'

'You assume?'

'That's her usual finishing time. I was here in the afternoon. I didn't make it back to head office.' The phone rang again. 'Sorry,' he said before answering. 'Toby Ewing speaking … e-mail? No, I'm sorry, Mr Soames. I haven't got to it yet. Things are a bit upside down at the moment…'

Tara looked at Murray who rolled his eyes. This man had spent his entire morning fielding a barrage of client phone calls. When he was finished, he apologised once again. Tara remained largely indifferent, wishing only to get the interview over and done with.

'Do you know of anyone who might have wished to harm Miss Hull?' she asked.

'No one could ever have reason to hurt Maggie. She was a saint.'

'Do you know of any problems that she may have been having? Did she seem troubled about anything? Perhaps, not her usual self?'

Ewing rolled his head, dismissing all of the suggestions. His eyes watered heavily as he struggled to answer.

'No, Inspector. I can't help you.'

'In that case, Mr Ewing, we'll let you get on with your work. I can see that you're very busy.'

The phone was ringing again as they left his office.

* * *

At the Harbinson factory in Birkenhead, they were introduced by a secretary to Skip McIntyre, another of the company directors. Put bluntly, McIntyre was of a non-impressive yet memorable appearance: slim, tanned and wrinkled face, and balding but with long strings of dark and grey hair hanging to the back and sides of his head. Tara tried to guess at his age but found it impossible. McIntyre wore an open, collarless shirt, brown tweed waistcoat and jeans. His face was pinched, and he sported a grey goatee beard. He looked like a geriatric hippie.

His office was quite lavish and certainly better furnished than that of the company chairman. A glass and chrome desk occupied the middle of the floor, a computer monitor and keyboard the only things sitting upon it. There was an expensive-looking black leather sofa, a heavy, smoked-glass coffee table and, set against a wall, a well-stocked, glass and chrome drinks cabinet. Judging by the number of bottles, some full and several nearly empty, it was put to regular use.

'So, how can I be of service to the Merseyside Police?' he asked, quite chirpily and sporting a churlish grin.

Tara returned the grin in equal measure. She didn't expect every colleague of Maggie Hull to be in floods of tears at the news of her death, but where had this guy been this morning? On the happy pills?

Tara quickly ran through her line of questions regarding Maggie Hull. It soon transpired that McIntyre also thought highly of her concerning her work and her long service at Harbinson Fine Foods. Tara, however, was conscious of a pattern emerging. Everyone they had interviewed so far was in wholehearted agreement that Maggie Hull had been a cherished employee, one which any company would be privileged to have on their payroll. Strangely, though, not one of them seemed to know or even care very much about her personal life – her life beyond the office door. She had worked at the company for a very long time, but it seemed that she was part of the furniture to leave behind at the end of the working day.

'She left about ten to six,' said McIntyre in reply to Tara's question. 'I shared the lift with her.'

'That was a bit late for her,' said Murray. 'Mr Ewing reckoned that she usually finished shortly after five?'

'Yes, he would,' said McIntyre, frowning. 'Since Maggie became his secretary, about a year ago, she never left the office before five-thirty. Most days it was closer to six. Toby wouldn't notice that sort of thing. He's a bit of an idiot. That's why she became his secretary in the first place. Edward believes that Toby needs to be taken by the hand.'

'And what do you think?' inquired Tara.

'Me? As I said, Inspector, he's a complete disaster. If it were up to me, he wouldn't be here. But daddy keeps an eye out for him. Toby and Richard were supposed to be the future of this company. The rest of us are a bit long in the tooth. Now that Richard is gone, I can't see Toby taking control by himself.'

'Daddy?'

'Yes, Jimmy Ewing is a retired partner of the firm or a sleeping partner you might say. Young Toby is the apple of his eye.'

Tara quickly realised that she wasn't going to get much more information on Maggie Hull from this particular company director. The man seemed to have a rather hefty chip on his shoulder regarding his business partners. Perhaps within such an attitude there lurked a motive for murder. But why kill Maggie Hull, a much-loved servant of the company? They left McIntyre to get on with his work, although of all the executives they had met this morning, he appeared the least busy.

'They're a strange bunch,' said Murray on the drive back to St Anne Street.

'What do you mean?'

'To be directors in a big company – they don't strike you as high-powered businessmen.'

'Harbinson seems business-like.'

'But the other two: Ewing is only there because of daddy, and McIntyre looks as though he'd rather be at Glastonbury.'

CHAPTER 19

Tara could not recall ever feeling such relief to have made it to the weekend. Having made it, she wondered why she had been looking forward to it in the first place. She had no plans. Continuing to regard herself as having been sidelined at work concerning the ongoing poisoning scandal, she did not expect to have anything to do with policing until Monday. At the counter in the kitchen area of her flat, she sat over a chicken korma ready meal and wondered if it had originated from Harbinson Fine Foods.

Most of the company's product was not sold under the Harbinson name but rather appeared as home brands by all the major food supermarkets in the country.

As she ate and tried to get into a paperback novel about lost love in the eighteenth century that she thought she should be reading, she pondered her options for the weekend. A visit to her parents was long overdue, but she decided that if it was going to happen she would leave it until Sunday afternoon. It was more likely that on Saturday her mother would be lunching with friends and her father playing golf. Sunday was the best time to find them both at home, and also she could invite herself for lunch. Only a few months ago, she would have been under pressure to free up her time to be out on a Friday and Saturday night. It had been even longer since she'd been on a date with a man, and she could scarcely remember the last time she had sex.

The prospect for this Friday evening was to sit in front of the telly and wonder about the terrifying events taking place in the city. The belief now was that the incidents of poisoning were not as they had been in Salisbury. The victims seemed random and no specific target had been identified. The use of chemical nerve agents like Novichok had been ruled out, although the toxin responsible for the deaths had still not been identified. None of these developments could rule out the actions of terrorists or of an individual acting alone. No motive had been established for the deaths of four innocent and unconnected members of the public.

Her appetite remained poor and she gave up on the korma with rice and scraped what was left on her plate into the bin. Automatically, it seemed, she reached into the fridge and removed a bottle of white wine, twisting off the cap and filling a stemmed glass. She retired to her sofa and scrolled through her mobile. There were no texts, there were no WhatsApp messages from Kate in reply to her cinema suggestion and there were no missed calls. At the end of the news on TV, the weather forecast for the weekend sounded promising – late autumn sunshine and no rain. A rare opportunity to be out and about.

A sudden notion came into her head, and she went immediately to fetch her notebook from her handbag. On a fresh page, she had jotted down a telephone number. When she had made the call, she sat back in the sofa and contentedly sipped her wine and selected a movie from Netflix. Her weekend was looking up.

* * *

'Right, you can open your eyes now,' said Tara.

'Oh my word, it's beautiful,' said Jez. 'But I certainly didn't do it justice. Look at the colours of the trees.'

'It's autumn. You painted a scene of early summer.'

Tara had parked her car by the side of the road and led her companion along a narrow path before climbing on to a rocky outcrop that stood above Llyn Padarn. Jez struggled with the climb, unprepared for walking on rough ground, wearing heeled boots. Tara had less trouble in flat shoes, and her excitement to be at this place where her father had often brought her as a child, quickened her step. Soon though, they stood on the rock known as Craig yr Undeb, or the Union Rock, and gazed over the lake towards Llanberis. It was the vista that Tara had seen among Jez's paintings.

'I thought you might like to see the place,' said Tara.

'Wonderful, thank you.'

The pair sat down on the rock with their legs outstretched. The air was cool but there was little wind and the clouds were absent, leaving a milky-blue sky. For a time they sat in silence admiring the view. Tara, when she had left home that morning, had no motive in her mind other than to bring Jez to this spot. Now, however, she couldn't help her thoughts drifting towards the investigation of Maggie Hull's murder. She realised she still had to quiz Jez over what she knew about her late colleague. Worse still, she was well aware that if Jez was considered a person of interest in the murder case then she was breaking every rule in the book by socialising with the woman. If Tweedy were to find out he would bounce her out of his squad in a flash. But Tara's mindset lately was to care little for protocol and even less for her well-being.

'I take it you've heard the news about Maggie Hull?'

Jez flashed a look of irritation. She was not expecting to be questioned at this time. She continued to gaze into the distance.

Tara had the chance to study her face more closely. She saw that Jez's eyes were puffy as if she'd been crying but she'd made some effort to perk herself up again, perhaps in anticipation of their outing.

'Maggie and I were very close, very close indeed. She took me under her wing when I started working at Harbinson's. I learned most things about the company from her.' Jez did not look at Tara as she explained but continued to absorb the scenery. 'We got on well together; we became great friends. She was Edward's secretary when I arrived, but after a few months, with her excellent teaching, I took over and she moved along the corridor to look after Toby.'

'Was she happy with that arrangement?' Tara asked.

'I think so. We didn't discuss it in those terms, but Maggie, as I'm sure you've already heard, was not one for complaining. She just put her head down and got on with the job.'

'Did you see each other outside of working hours?'

'Oh yes, we spent a lot of time together. I had just moved back to Liverpool and I'd lost contact with all my old chums. Maggie and I became soulmates, I suppose.'

'Can you think of any reason for her being murdered?'

For a moment, the question went unanswered. The frankness of it seemed to induce some tears. Jez wiped her eyes and then blew her nose.

'I'm sorry,' she cried. 'It's just so terrible. I can't believe that anyone would want to hurt Maggie.'

'Do you know anything about her personal affairs?' Tara asked.

'No, not really. The only problem she ever seemed to have was money. She was always in debt. She didn't seem to care how much something cost. If she wanted it, she bought it.'

Tara's mind glanced over the scene in Maggie Hull's home: the expensive furniture, the huge collection of CDs, crystal glassware and the vast wardrobe of clothing.

'When I first met her,' Jez continued, 'she was spending a lot more than she was earning. She showed me some of the things she was buying: not just clothes and jewellery but silly things, too, like joining wine clubs and ordering special edition porcelain – things that she didn't need. I tried telling her to be more careful, but she told me that it made her happy. "What good is money if you don't spend it?" she used to say. I tried to steer her towards things that would at least give her some lasting enjoyment, a social life even. We went to the theatre and the cinema together and several concerts. I enjoy painting, so I suggested that she attempted a hobby.'

'And how did that turn out?' asked Tara who, although listening intently to Jez's softly spoken tones, was irked by the fact that Jez had taken over Maggie's role in the company.

'Oh, she attempted to paint and went to a few evening classes. I gave her a few tips as well. Last year we went on an artists' weekend to the Lake District. She did all the things I suggested and more, but she remained as carefree as ever with her money.'

'And her debts were mounting?' said Tara.

'Absolutely dreadful. I found out that over a year ago she'd been refused a debit card by her bank. I advised her to throw away her credit cards. She had at least fifteen that I knew of: Visa, MasterCard, American Express, store cards like Marks and Spencer. She did it too, I watched her cut them up one day during lunch. I offered her some money to help pay off some of the bills until she got back on her feet but she wouldn't accept it, not at first anyway.'

'She changed her mind?'

'I changed it for her. I found her one morning, about four months ago, crying in the ladies. She refused to tell me anything at first until I noticed the bruises. She'd taken a beating from someone who had lent her money. She hadn't been able to pay them back, so they'd turned nasty. She'd been kicked in the ribs. I told her to go to the police, but she wouldn't hear of it. I gave her the money to pay them off – nine hundred pounds – she'd only borrowed three hundred! Can you believe those people? That was the last time she involved me in her problems. I asked on several occasions how things were, but she always shrugged it off and said that she had learned her lesson. It's strange because after that incident we were never really close again. I think it must have embarrassed her deeply.'

'How did she seem when you last saw her?' Tara asked.

Jez thought for a moment, her face losing some of its colour.

'It was one day last week, I suppose, before a board meeting, but as I said we were no longer very close. Apart from discussing work, we hadn't spoken for months.'

She gazed directly at Tara as if searching for an ounce of comfort.

* * *

Jez insisted on paying for lunch when they stopped at a pub in Llanberis.

'It's my treat,' she said. 'You were kind enough to bring me here. It was really sweet.'

Tara smiled coyly. She had enjoyed the time spent in this woman's company, a world of difference from the empty times at home brooding.

'Better than Elgar?' said Tara.

Jez laughed. 'If you like.'

After lunch, they started immediately on the drive back to Liverpool. They didn't chat much. Tara played the radio, and at one point Jez dozed off. When she awoke, she was suddenly all biz about what they could do together: another concert, a visit to the theatre, dinner in mid-week and a proposed trip to London for early Christmas shopping. As she pulled up outside the house, Tara felt strange. Her tummy tightened and she was suddenly tingling with nerves.

'Would you like to come in?' Jez asked her. 'We could order Chinese and watch TV?'

'Oh thanks, Jez, it sounds great but I really must be getting back.' Her reaction was instinctive and defensive. She couldn't think why; it was an innocent proposal, but already she'd gone too far in her association with a woman who might well be considered a suspect in a murder. She felt uncomfortable suddenly with Jez staring at her.

'Well maybe some other time,' said Jez with a smile.

'Definitely.'

'Thank you for a lovely day, Tara.'

In a flash, she moved closer and kissed her as she had done on the previous occasion. It was intended to be a long and passionate kiss, but Tara snapped her head back. She knew it was too much, too much for her to understand and yet it did not feel unpleasant. Certainly, it was a step further than the last time. Jez smiled devilishly and searched Tara's eyes. Tara knew she had to leave.

'I'd better go, Jez.'

'I'm sorry, I went too far...'

'It's fine. I just have to go.'

Jez climbed from the car, and Tara roared away from the curb. She fought to see the road beyond her floods of tears. The only mechanism she had to deal with her confused emotions was to think of murder and death and the case of Maggie Hull. Had Jez and Maggie been lovers? Is that the reason they had stopped being friends? The idea fought the logic. Jez had been in a relationship with Richard Andrews – she wasn't gay. Why was she reading so much into a kiss? Maybe Jez was simply an over-affectionate woman. But there was mischief in the look she had after the kiss. Tara had no idea what to think.

At least Jez had provided a possible lead in the case.

CHAPTER 20

Murray was sitting alone at a table in the canteen as Tara entered. He was feasting on a full English accompanied by a mug of strong and sweet tea. Tara didn't know how he managed it. She had left her flat with nothing more than a cereal bar in her hand, and by the time she'd reached the station two-thirds of it remained. After ordering a filter coffee, she joined him at the table.

'I don't know where you put it.'

'Hollow legs.'

'So, how was your weekend?' she asked him.

'Great,' he managed between mouthfuls of sausage and fried bread. 'How about you?'

'Fine, I suppose.' She couldn't erase the image of Jez kissing her, and worse still could not work out exactly how she felt about it. 'I went out for a drive on Saturday with that secretary from Harbinson Fine Foods.'

Murray looked puzzled. Tara suddenly remembered that Murray was not with her that first time she had met Jez. He hadn't a clue what she was talking about.

'Jez Riordan – she had an affair with Richard Andrews – the suicide?'

'OK.'

'We have a few things in common, and she *is* a friendly type.'

'You do realise since she works for Harbinson's that she could be considered a suspect for killing Maggie Hull,' said Murray.

'I know.'

'Tweedy would go nuts if he found out, Tara.'

'He's not going to find out, is he, Alan?' Tara gazed sternly at her colleague. On this occasion, she excused him calling her Tara.

Murray looked exasperated.

'I hope you know what you're doing, that's all.'

'Yes, I can manage perfectly well, thank you. Besides, she gave me a possible lead concerning Maggie Hull. It seems that the woman was prone to running up large debts. How much do you know about loan sharks in Liverpool?'

'Not much, but I know of someone who does. Joe Melling.'

'Is he a loan shark?'

'A loan shark? Definitely. Heavy-handed with bad debtors? Might be. A murderer? Not likely.'

When they entered the operations room, Murray went directly to a filing cabinet. Unsuccessful in locating the file he wanted, he sat down at his computer and ran a search through the police database until he came across several cases relating to recent incidents of theft in the Bootle, Walton and Aintree districts. Somewhere, within the files, was an address for Joe Melling. He was the *go-to* for information on petty criminal activity in those areas of the city.

* * *

To look at the house from the outside, anyone would find it difficult to believe that a man capable of lending money, hefty sums at that, could wish to live there. It was a three-storey, mid-terrace house, but well overdue its demolition order in a street not far from Anfield Stadium.

Several of the houses in the same row were already bricked up, a sign that the rest would not be too far behind.

The curtains on the upstairs windows were open. Hopefully, the people inside were up and about. It was only eight-fifteen in the morning. Children hurried past Murray's car on their way to school. A miserable bloody day to be going to school, Tara thought. The clear skies of the weekend had succumbed to a thick, billowing grey mass, unleashing its store of rain that pelted against the windscreen.

Scurrying to the solid, brown door with its peeling paint, she gave the knocker four definite clouts, stood back and waited. Murray, from his time spent in CID, knew Joe Melling by reputation only. Included on Joe's record were three convictions for theft, the reason being that when he struggled to collect debts from clients he tended to collect in kind by carrying away the family television, the mother's wedding and engagement rings, the baby's pram and, on one occasion it was rumoured, the family Labrador. Joe Melling was the local moneylender and, assisted by a couple of young louts, the district bailiff rolled into one.

'Good morning, Mr Melling, how are you?' said Tara.

A rotund, squat man of sixty-five, wearing a dark-grey suit, in places shiny with age, peered out from a dim hall at his early-morning caller. The ruddy face was not the friendliest, more a face of suspicion and concern.

'What can I do for you, love?' he asked, the words fired at considerable Scouser speed.

Tara introduced herself and Murray, stating their business and was rewarded by a modicum of recognition and an invitation to step inside. The house was awash with the smell of food frying as they followed the man through a gloomy hall to a room at the back. Melling intimated for them to sit at a table, laid out for a cooked breakfast for two; salt, pepper, HP sauce, Yorkshire Relish, a carton of milk and a bag of sugar. Through a crack in the doorway to the kitchen, Tara spied a plump woman in a heavy maroon dressing gown busily tending to her frying pan on the cooker.

'I've more or less retired, you know,' Melling said. Tara recognised the defensive tone of his statement. 'I don't lend much these days,' he continued. 'To tell you the truth, Inspector, I don't have it.' He laughed at his quip.

'C'mon, Joe, a man like you?' said Murray. 'I hear you're rolling in it.'

'Where'd you get your hearing aid, son? I don't even give the wife the housekeeping these days.'

'The old shares portfolio giving you gyp then?'

'Now you're getting the idea.'

'Fair enough, Joe,' said Tara, bringing a halt to the banter. 'What I'm looking for is a list of names.'

'Names?' Melling's watery eyes widened at the suggestion. 'What sort of names? You're not after my books, are you?'

'Sharks, I need to know who else is operating at the moment, especially around Wavertree.'

Melling sat back to consider the question, his rickety chair creaking under the strain.

'Somebody overstepping the mark?' he asked. He gazed from Tara to Murray as if he was unsure who was the most senior of the two detectives. It didn't enlighten him when Murray answered.

'Could be, Joe, but for the moment we just need to know what sort of people are conducting business and are likely to turn nasty with customers who can't make their repayments.'

It was obvious to Tara that naming names to the police went against Melling's life philosophy. Either that or he feared the consequences if the wrong people got to hear about it.

'I'm not sure if I'm the man to ask, Inspector, know what I mean?'

'Ah c'mon, Joe, where's the harm?' said Murray, his impatience kicking in. 'Strictly between us, we may not even be talking to these guys. We just need to run a few checks, that's all.'

Melling's wife emerged from the kitchen with two plates of fried food; bacon, eggs, sausages, mushrooms, beans and fried bread – very healthy. For the benefit of her visitors, she also carried a scowl, not at all amused at her breakfast being disrupted by her husband's business. After setting the plates on the table, she traipsed back to the kitchen only to return moments later with a stainless-steel teapot. They were not offered tea, not that Tara cared, although she reckoned that Murray could still manage some despite his earlier feast.

'Ray Dempsey,' said Melling, breaking free of his deliberations, 'still operates around Wavertree.'

'Anybody else?'

'You might do better asking around a few of the clubs if you know what I mean?'

'Snooker clubs?'

'Snooker clubs, supporters' clubs, working men's clubs, take your pick.'

'Tommy Gracey is another one, but he's a bad lot. You'd have to stand your granny as collateral before he'd give you a penny.'

'Any idea where I might find him?' Tara asked.

Melling looked incredulous.

'Sorry, Inspector, I'm not that daft. Now if there's nothin' else, me and the wife would like to eat our breakfast in peace.'

* * *

From the car, Tara called Wilson at the station and asked him to check out the names that Melling had given to her. What she feared most was that Maggie Hull had borrowed heavily from a highly organised gang. It would be hell getting any information out of an organised crime group.

When she arrived at St Anne Street she found a copy of the post-mortem report for Maggie Hull lying on her desk. She fetched a coffee from the machine and sat down to peruse. There were no surprises, nothing much to supplement what she'd already heard from Tweedy. Drugs and alcohol were not a factor in the death, and no sexual assault had occurred. Judging by her inspection of Maggie's house, there had been no robbery either. A motiveless killing? If so, they would have to consider the possibility of a psycho on the loose. She shuddered at the thought.

CHAPTER 21

Rebecca Thomas was late for her lecture only because she couldn't bear to see the kitchen left in such a mess. The others were happy to leave it. Eventually, somebody would get around to clearing up. And they were right, somebody did. It was always her and never the others. Even the girls took advantage of the fact that she couldn't abide seeing the house left in a state. First thing this morning, as some of them hurried out to lectures and one or two slept off last night's binge, she raced around the downstairs of the house, gathering empties, bottles and cans, crisp bags, pizza boxes, trays of chicken curry and chilli con carne, taking all of it out to the bins. Then she washed the glasses and plates, dried them and put them away. All the work surfaces and the big table in the kitchen were cleaned down with disinfectant wipes. At least the place would be habitable before anyone cooked dinner this evening. All of her efforts left her fifteen minutes behind schedule. She grabbed her bag and folder, pulled on her jacket and rushed outside.

The air was cool and damp, the pavements wet from the early rain. It was a ten-minute walk to the lecture theatre. She would miss the start to 'The relevance of the nineteenth-century novel to modern society.'

As she hurried along, she sent a text to her friend Laura, saying that she was on her way and asking her to save her a seat. With all of her clearing up, she hadn't had time for breakfast, although she thought it best to give her tummy a rest. She felt a bit delicate this morning. She hadn't drunk a lot the night before, a few bottles of Budweiser, but maybe it was something she had eaten. Her throat felt tight also. But she had been singing and laughing so much last night. The guys in their house: Josh, Gary and Mark were very funny when they got a few drinks in them. And she quite fancied Josh, although so far nothing had happened. Early days, she thought as she tried to pick up her pace. She felt herself sweating beneath her long-sleeved T-shirt and corduroy jacket. She knew she wasn't fit. Never had been into sports that much, except for dancing and it wasn't really a sport. She reached Abercromby Square, not far to go now, she thought. Her head was throbbing, and now she had difficulty swallowing. She must have eaten something bad. Veering to the railings by the side of her building, her stomach suddenly heaved and she bent double. But this was more than simply throwing up. Her throat was pulsing in a spasm, she was boiling hot and suddenly she felt sharp pains across her chest. She cried out for help. A lady who was standing at the bus stop across the road hurried towards her. Rebecca dropped to her knees; she could no longer see clearly; she couldn't breathe and finally dropped face down on the damp pavement.

In a laboratory within the Chemistry department of the university, Rebecca's housemate, Mark, suddenly let go of the conical flask he was holding. It smashed on the floor, and he collapsed over the pool of dilute sodium hydroxide solution it had contained.

The lecture Rebecca had missed was halted ten minutes before the end when one of the students was taken ill. Laura had become nauseous then found herself gasping for breath as she was gripped by a terrible pain in her chest.

At the student house where Rebecca had so diligently cleaned up, two students, Catherine and Philip, sharing a bed and feeling wretched, would not rise in time for their lectures.

CHAPTER 22

Wilson handed over a single sheet of A4. Upon it were printed the names and addresses of both men. Under Dempsey's name was his National Insurance number and date of birth. The same details were stated for Gracey, along with a list of criminal convictions that included, assault, theft, ABH, membership of a proscribed organisation and, to cap it all, attempted murder. Murray whistled his amazement.

'Well, well, Tommy Gracey, *this is your life!* John, can you dig up a file on this guy please?'

Tommy Gracey was forty-eight years old and was enjoying his years of freedom under the early release scheme, a consequence of the Good Friday Agreement in Northern Ireland. Before 1998 he had been detained at Her Majesty's Prison Maze, serving fourteen years for the attempted murder of a Catholic taxi driver, illegal possession of a firearm and a list of other offences, minor in comparison, linked to the same incident. In short, he was the archetypal loyalist paramilitary who'd been fortunate enough to have served only three years of his sentence before the political situation swayed in his favour.

Before, during and following that period, he had participated in several other ventures associated with paramilitary groups. A quarrel with his fellow gangsters in Belfast had resulted in his resettlement in Liverpool. Moneylending was his strike for independence from the organisation. His activities, however, had already come under scrutiny from Merseyside Police. At least four vicious attacks in Liverpool were suspected by the police to be retribution by Gracey for unpaid debts. In light of this, Tommy Gracey seemed a plausible suspect for the murder of Maggie Hull.

Tara and Murray called firstly to Gracey's ground floor flat off Priory Road in Anfield. There was no one at home but a mousey-looking teenage girl, his next-door neighbour, told them that Gracey could usually be found around lunchtime at his local bar, The Hallowed Turf.

The pub stood at a busy road junction, its outer walls curving around the street corner. It was the type of place that was packed on match days and Friday and Saturday nights. The rest of the week, the pub had a dedicated but limited clientele.

Tara and Murray entered the bar and looked around the dingy room which was in dire need of renovation, quite obviously searching for a particular individual. A pair of old men, both with a sallow complexion, sitting in a booth with brown leatherette benches, inspected the newcomers. Leaning at the bar and watching the racing from Doncaster on Sky Sports, were three young lads, each one holding a pint glass nearly empty of lager. A solitary barman washing glasses at the sink acknowledged Murray with a slight flick of his head. He had a notion that his latest customers were from the law. Murray ordered two half-pints of lager, while Tara approached the muscular, shaven-headed man seated alone by a window and reading the *Daily Star*. Wearing a purple Liverpool away shirt, he had tattoos on both forearms and one on the left side of his neck, all symbols of his allegiances to Ulster Loyalism.

A gold ring through his left eyebrow set off his aura perfectly. He did not look the type of guy to be trifled with.

'Good afternoon, Mr Gracey?' said Tara in a friendly manner. The man lifted his head and squinted at his visitor through deep-set eyes. Without a word of acknowledgement, he lifted his pint glass of lager and drained the last few mouthfuls. He turned the page of his newspaper and continued with his reading. Tara, in no way intimidated, sat down on a low stool opposite.

'The name *is* Gracey, Tommy Gracey?' she asked.

'You lookin' for somethin', love? Only, I don't need to pay for a good time around here.'

Tara examined the smirk on his face. He was a man full of bravado and dull wit. She was well used to being overlooked as a police detective, not that Gracey would know.

'I'm not that kind of girl, but I am looking for something.'

'And what would that be?'

'The answers to some questions.'

At last, he raised his eyes from his paper but he did not look happy. Tara continued to study his face. His skin was smooth and tight with several scars; one in particular, ran below his right eye. Ginger eyebrows and green eyes seemed to shout the words, 'definitely not friendly.'

'I'm Detective Inspector Grogan, Merseyside Police and this' – she indicated Murray who was coming towards them carrying the half-pints of beer – 'is my colleague Detective Sergeant Murray.'

The man shrugged a 'so what'.

'Perhaps, for a start, you could confirm that you *are* Tommy Gracey?'

'Aye, so what?'

'Were you doing anything last Monday night?'

'Ask your ma?'

Tara smiled broadly. Here was a man intent on undermining the serious nature of her business with him.

'Nice one, Tommy, but I don't have time for your jokes. Just tell me what you were doing, please?'

'In here, all night, you can ask him.' He nodded towards the barman.

'OK, let's say you were in here. How much money do you lend at any one time?'

Gracey winced. For a moment, he seemed to consider the question but did not reply.

Tara persevered. 'I need to know about the kind of people you lend money to. Are they always able to pay it back? What if they can't?'

'What the hell is this? Who says I lend money? And why should I talk to you about it?'

Tara took a sip of her drink then scowled at Murray. She hated flat beer; it always tasted sour. She glanced at the barman. More than likely he'd just served Murray with two glasses of dregs. Gracey had returned to browsing his newspaper.

'Listen, Tommy,' Murray whispered. 'Early release licences can always be revoked, you know? Someone in contravention of the terms of their release might find themselves on a picnic to that prison in Belfast – Maghaberry, isn't that what it's called?'

The big man laughed with a deep growl and shook his head.

'Fuck do you know about anything in Belfast?'

'Just saying the way I see it, that's all.'

'Lending a few quid to a couple of mates won't land me inside.'

'Perhaps not, Tommy,' said Tara, 'but murder certainly will.'

'What the fuck are you talking about? Murder? I don't know nothin' about any murder.'

'Maggie Hull? You know her well enough, don't you, Tommy? You've lent her a few quid recently.'

'Never heard of her.'

'Still owe you money, does she? I can't see her paying you back though. Not now, she's cold and stiff.'

'You're off your head, love. I don't know fuck all about any murder.'

He rose from his seat, and for the first time, Tara noticed the walking stick that had been standing by his chair. She allowed Gracey to limp away.

'Think about your client list, Tommy,' she said after him. 'I'll call again in a couple of days and we can go through it.'

Gracey muttered something under his breath and hobbled to the bar. Tara took another sip of her beer and screwed her face in disgust.

'Bloody hell, Alan, are you trying to poison me?'

Murray, undaunted, had drained his glass.

They were just stepping through the swing door into the entrance porch of the pub when they met a hefty-framed man coming the other way. It was Murray, not Tara, who was first to recognise the face.

CHAPTER 23

'Ah, Beryl! Fancy meeting you here.'

Beryl grimaced and his face twitched nervously.

'Just calling for a pint, no law against that is there?'

'None at all, Beryl,' said Tara with a smile. 'You may as well enjoy it while you can.'

Beryl's reply was little more than a grunt as he barged past and into the bar. Tara turned to Murray as they made their way back to the car.

'Give it a minute, Alan, then put your head around the door and see if Beryl is in conversation with our friend Mr Gracey.'

'Dead right,' said Murray re-joining Tara a minute later.

'I thought so. Two bad eggs in the one dubious pub at the same time, there had to be some connection.'

'What are you going to do about Gracey?' Murray asked.

'Nothing for the time being. I reckon he probably lent money to Maggie at some point. He got shirty with me too quickly, not to be on his guard about something. Could be that one of his heavies, Beryl perhaps, went too far and hit poor Maggie over the head, although I'm not convinced. There was no struggle, Alan. Maggie Hull knew her killer, and if it had been the likes of Gracey then I imagine she would have put up a fight.'

'Not if she was taken by surprise. The killer might have been hiding in the house already, waiting for her to come in from work.'

'Trouble is, we can't prove that at the moment. We've no witnesses who saw anyone going in or coming out. My guess is that she probably knew her killer. Either he arrived at the house with her or she had no fears about letting him inside when he came knocking at her door. If Gracey came looking for money would she even have opened the door to him?'

'So where does that leave us? Another loan shark?'

'Maybe. We'll call with this Dempsey fella on the way back to the station. Also, Big Beryl might have something to tell us. We'll give it a day or so then pull him in.'

They arrived back at St Anne Street still in discussion over the murder of Maggie Hull and whether it had some connection to the suicide of Richard Andrews. So far, Murray couldn't believe it was anything more than coincidence. Tara retained the thought that the deaths were closely linked. Their meeting with Ray Dempsey, the final name on their brief list of loan sharks, had been fruitless.

Dempsey had described himself as a seventy-six-year-old 'businessman'. Nowadays, he claimed not to be in the cash-for-loan game. He'd ventured into the landlord business and was making more money from renting run-down flats to immigrant workers. Tara was content to accept his word for now. She, however, regarded Tommy Gracey with greater suspicion.

The operations room was awash with the news that several students were seriously ill, and that it was believed to be from another incident of poisoning. Although his squad was not currently involved in the investigation, Harold Tweedy had called a briefing to update his officers.

'Firstly,' he began, 'the latest case involves five students at Liverpool University, all seriously ill and presently being treated at the Royal Hospital.'

Already Tara's mind rushed to all manner of scenarios as to how these young people had succumbed to this latest poisoning event, and Tweedy soon confirmed one of her thoughts.

'This time,' he continued, 'we have a direct connection between the victims. It appears, with the exception of one girl, that all of them share the same student house. Most crucially, all five students spent yesterday evening together in that house. We have forensics and specialist hazard teams down there now looking for the source of the contamination.'

'A bad batch of drugs, sir?' Wilson called out.

'Very easy to jump to conclusions, John,' Tweedy replied. 'But that doesn't stack up with the other victims in this emergency.'

'Then it has to be food or drink,' said Murray.

'That seems the most likely, Alan, but let's wait and see what forensics turn up.'

'Has the poison been identified yet from the earlier incidents?' Tara asked.

'It seems to be more a case of they know what it isn't,' said Tweedy. There were a few scoffs from around the room. Tweedy was not put off. He referred to a file that he was holding. 'The use of a nerve agent such as that used in Salisbury has been ruled out. Items removed from the homes of David Leigh, Emma Whitehouse and Norman Forbes suggest that all three victims had consumed similar meals before falling ill. As for Marsha Ross and Kaley Watson, no such connection has been made although we cannot rule out the possibility that similar food was consumed away from home. This latest incident may shed light on the suspicion that food has been contaminated.'

'What type of contamination?' Murray called out, sounding frustrated. 'Is it like *E. coli* or horsemeat, or is some crazy-head going around deliberately adding poison to food?'

'We still cannot say, Alan. So far the lab has not been able to identify any substance.'

'Surely,' said Tara, 'that must rule out something like *E. coli*? The lab would have picked it up already. It has to be something peculiar that isn't easy to detect.'

'Let's wait and see, folks,' said Tweedy.

The meeting broke up, leaving Tara wondering when she was going to have an opportunity to work on this case. The investigation was already floundering, while more victims were appearing. Until the lab could identify the substance or source of the poisoning, the investigation was going nowhere.

CHAPTER 24

On her way home, Tara decided that a visit to her friend Kate was long overdue.

Tara parked her car close to the house on Canning Street where Kate occupied a ground floor flat. She was looking forward also to seeing her god-daughter. It had been nearly two months since they had been together. So much can change for a baby in that time.

'Hiya,' said Kate cheerfully when she opened the door. She hugged Tara, but it felt awkward for both women. 'What's new?' she asked.

'Nothing much,' Tara replied. 'I thought it was high time I called to see you.'

Tara examined her friend. Kate was the same age and of similar build to her. She worked as a cardiac nurse on a heart ward at the Royal Hospital. This evening, she looked tired and drawn, no worse than Tara was feeling, of course. She was so used to seeing Kate displaying her latest outrageous hair colour, but in recent months she had reverted to her natural shade, a dirty fair. It was much longer, too, falling below her shoulders, and in need of styling. It seemed that their frivolous days were over. Tara had lost her baby and Kate was now a mother.

Kate asked how she had been lately, and Tara recited a brief tale of the latest emergency for Merseyside Police. She could see that Kate looked disinterested in that aspect of her life. But what else could she talk about? Since Tara had miscarried, she had done little of interest. She told her about meeting Jez and even ventured to ask her thoughts on Jez having kissed her.

'You're not gay, Tara. You know you're not. Why would you even consider having a relationship with this woman? It's ridiculous.'

'I suppose you're right. It's just that after she kissed me I felt so confused about everything. And I'm feeling so alone these days.'

'Well, that is not going to solve your problem. It will only cause you more trouble, and heaven knows you've had enough of that in your life. You *do* still have me, you know?'

'Do I?'

'Of course, why do you even ask?'

'I know you must find it difficult, awkward because you have Adele and I…'

Kate hugged her again.

'You and me, next weekend,' said Kate, 'let's go out and have a blast. We're not getting any younger. Now go into the bathroom, clean yourself up and I'll put the kettle on.'

* * *

She left Kate an hour later but did not drive home. She couldn't wrestle thoughts of Jez from her mind. Kate was right; she wasn't gay and she was not going to have a romantic relationship with this woman. But she felt that she needed to see her; she felt something stir inside when she was with Jez.

Tara parked on the roadside outside the grounds of Jez's lavish home. There was another car on the drive next to Jez's Peugeot SUV. It was dark in colour, green perhaps, a Jaguar, and as she wondered who the visitor might be, the front door of the house opened and a man stepped out. She recognised him immediately. It had only been a few days since they had first met. It was the geriatric hippie.

'Hello, Inspector Grogan, isn't it? Just dropping off a few files to Jez.'

'Good evening, Mr McIntyre,' Tara replied.

She noted that McIntyre was quick to explain his presence at Jez's home. Jez then appeared at the doorway.

'Hi, Tara,' she said, cheerfully. 'Go on in, Skip was just leaving.'

Tara's mind raced to all manner of scenarios regarding the company director. Why was he here at this time of night? Was there something between Jez and him?

'Enjoy your evening,' said McIntyre with a cynical smile as he beeped his car open.

'So, what's Mr McIntyre like to work with?' Tara asked Jez, once she had seen her visitor off. The two women sat on well-worn armchairs in a smaller lounge that Jez used while watching TV. It was warm and cosy, well lived-in, with newspapers, books and magazines scattered on the sofa and an oak coffee table. Two empty coffee cups sat among the papers.

'Skip? He's all right. Mind you, he loves himself.'

'Has he been with the company for long?'

'Yes, I think so, he and Jimmy Ewing joined when Edward Harbinson took over from his father a long time ago.'

'Were Maggie and Richard close friends?'

This time there was a prolonged pause before the reply.

'Maggie was close to everyone. She treated Richard and Toby like a pair of kid brothers.'

Tara was suddenly conscious of sounding like a police officer again, and that was not the reason for her visit. She had decided to set matters straight with this woman. She was not looking for a relationship, but she wanted to remain friends.

'Sorry,' she said. 'I haven't come to interview you. I didn't mean to sound like a police detective.'

Jez's eyes widened and she smiled. 'So, why have you come?' she asked.

'To apologise for hurrying off the other night. It's just that...'

'I know. I'm sorry for pushing you into something that you don't want to do.'

'I would like us to be friends. I enjoy your company, Jez.'

Jez smiled warmly like she understood exactly what Tara was saying.

'Then that is exactly what we will be, Tara – good friends.'

Tara felt elated on the drive home. She and Kate had cleared the air and Jez now understood that she was not in search of a romantic relationship with her. The woman, though, remained a puzzle to her. What had her affair with Richard Andrews been about if she could so easily revert to seeking love from a woman? The sight of Skip McIntyre leaving Jez's house as she arrived also left her with a feeling of unease.

CHAPTER 25

The station was bustling with news and developments on the poisoning incidents in the city. Whilst no obvious connections had been identified between the first victims, the poisoning of the students had given the investigators an obvious link in the case. Of the seven students who had been in the house on the evening before the outbreak of illness, five of them were taken ill, while two had not shown any symptoms.

Tara and Murray listened as Tweedy gave an update on the situation. Both officers had maintained a keen interest in the case but remained frustrated by their lack of involvement in the investigation.

'Interviews have been conducted with the two males who were unaffected,' said Tweedy. 'Neither student noticed anything untoward on that evening. All those present had been drinking either bottled beer, and gin or vodka mixed with a variety of soft drinks. The seven students had eaten crisps and other snacks, however, the five who subsequently became ill had also, prior to the arrival of the other two males, consumed hot foods, namely chicken curry, chilli con carne and garlic bread. Samples of these foods have been retrieved from waste bins and sent for analysis.'

Tara relaxed slightly as her mind adjusted to the facts. It seemed now that the entire outbreak of illness and deaths was down to severe food poisoning and nothing more sinister such as a terrorist attack. Still, she would have preferred to be at the centre of the investigation.

'Any results from the lab?' Murray asked.

'Preliminary tests indicate a very potent toxin was present in the chicken curry. The exact nature of the toxin has yet to be elucidated,' said Tweedy.

'I assume, sir,' said Tara, 'that the contaminated food product is being removed from shops and all items already in circulation are being recalled?'

'That's correct, Tara.'

But it was the murder of Maggie Hull that required the attention of Tara and Murray. The case of poisoning, whether deliberate or accidental, was not for them to dwell upon. DC John Wilson had one development to report in the Hull case when Tara returned to her desk.

'Ma'am, we have a possible murder weapon. Uniform found an adjustable spanner inside a plastic bag. It was picked up on some waste ground a quarter of a mile from Bartlett Street.'

'Can I see it?'

'It went directly for analysis. Seems there was some blood on it. Also, it was not an ordinary spanner.'

'How so?'

'Part of a set, a toolkit. An expensive kit like those that used to come with an expensive car.'

'Good. Maybe we'll get some prints as well.'

Contrary to Tara's thinking, most of the evidence suggested that Maggie Hull had died at the hands of rogue moneylenders. The story from Jez seemed to back up such a theory, and Tara knew that she had not yet finished with Tommy Gracey or with Big Beryl.

* * *

It continued to niggle with Tara that the relationship between Jez and Harbinson Fine Foods was a little bizarre. She and Andrews had an affair which resulted in the collapse of his marriage to the daughter of the company chairman. Any right-thinking individual in the chairman's shoes, surely, would have found it difficult to maintain a working relationship with Jez the moment Andrews was dismissed and subsequently committed suicide. Edward Harbinson, on the contrary, had retained her as his secretary. It seemed as though the man had cornered the biblical market on forgiveness. Tara realised that so far Jez was her solitary link to the brutal slaying of Maggie Hull. Jez had known Maggie well enough to rescue her from unscrupulous moneylenders, well enough to give advice and to assist in sea changes within Maggie's lonely existence. Jez had been a rare friend to Maggie and yet that friendship had, at some point, turned sour.

Tara picked up her phone, checked the number in her notebook and dialled. From the receptionist at Harbinson Fine Foods, she was put through to Mr Harbinson's secretary.

'Hi, Jez.'

'Hello, Tara,' said Jez in a telephone voice. 'Don't tell me you've managed to get hold of tickets for the Foo Fighters already?'

'I'm afraid not. This is more of a professional call.'

'I see. How can I help you?' Tara noted her change in tone.

'I wonder if you could answer a few more questions in connection with Maggie Hull.'

'I'll try,' she replied.

'Firstly, do you know the name of the loan shark that you paid off on Maggie's behalf?'

For a moment there was silence.

'I'm afraid I don't. I was at her house the night they came to collect the money but they were only a pair of young lads. It seemed to me that they were the messenger boys who had either come to collect the payment or to dish out punishment for not paying.'

'How well did Maggie seem to know them?'

'Not well. She was very frightened of them. On that occasion, I told her to hide upstairs while I paid them off. They looked disappointed when I handed over the cash; I got the impression they were hoping to give her a beating.'

'In the time that you and Maggie were friends, did you ever meet anyone else that she knew well?'

'No one except for the others who work here. She was a very lonely person, Tara.'

'I realise that.'

'Not having much luck then?'

Tara sensed Jez's return to a lightened mood.

'We haven't got far, no,' she replied. There followed a brief pause in the conversation before Tara thought of another question.

'Did you give Maggie any of your paintings?'

'Give, no, but she did insist on buying one.'

'From your environmental collection?'

Jez laughed heartily at the phrase. 'Yes, that's right, my environmental period.'

'Two kids peeing a waterfall?'

'That's the one. Did you like it? Maggie thought it was hilarious, the idea of two young boys piddling in the forest, so natural and yet quite cheeky. She wanted to pay my normal asking price, but I'd spent months encouraging her to be more careful with her finances. I wasn't about to accept any money off her for one of my old paintings. I told her that if she kept herself out of debt that would be payment enough.'

'And did she?'

'Of that, I can't be certain. As I told you before we seemed to drift apart shortly after I paid off the loan shark.'

'Why was that exactly?'

'We never discussed it, but I suppose it had something to do with my affair with Richard. She was very fond of him and his wife, too. She was also very old-fashioned. In her view, men and women married for life and straying from that path was a mortal sin.'

'Was she religious?'

'Not particularly so. She never mentioned going to church. I think she simply had a strict upbringing and retained an old-fashioned outlook.'

As she set down her phone Tara noticed the clock on her wall showing five to five. She'd had enough and breathed a deep sigh, relieved also that her call to Jez had been successful.

In the furthest recesses of her mind, however, was an embryonic notion that if Richard Andrews were still alive then so too would Maggie Hull.

CHAPTER 26

Incessant rain and a bracing wind were the perfect foil for a cemetery set in the south-east of the city. Nature's cold storage – Tara didn't believe there could be a more weather-beaten place to be laid to rest. She was too late in leaving the office to make it to the funeral service in what had been Maggie Hull's local parish church at Wavertree. Instead, she arrived at Allerton Cemetery just as the hearse drove through the gates, continued out to the right and halted at a quiet corner bordered by low hedges. One funeral limousine and six other cars, including her Focus, had followed behind. Murray had offered to accompany her, but she asked him instead to go over the notes gathered so far on the case, particularly concerning the lead they had on loan sharks.

The men from the funeral home bore the coffin to the open grave. A man and woman stepped from the black limousine and walked, arm in arm, behind the pallbearers. The vicar from the Holy Trinity Church in Wavertree, frail and elderly, climbed from his Vauxhall, already dressed in his vestments, the wind taking its toll as he struggled against it.

Tara, reluctantly, stepped into the elements but remained a little way off, out of earshot of the proceedings but close enough to get a look at some of the mourners. Most of them were familiar faces, recently encountered in connection with Harbinson Fine Foods. Edward Harbinson was accompanied by his daughter, Nicole Andrews who looked pale and delicate, although most of her petite frame was well wrapped in a heavy coat and scarf. The funeral of her husband, Richard, had taken place only two days earlier. The company chairman appeared very withdrawn and reacted only to instructions from his daughter. Close beside them, a man battled to hold his umbrella against the wind, his face for a time obscured from Tara's view. Within a few seconds, the umbrella succumbed as spokes bent in the wrong direction. Only then did Tara recognise Skip McIntyre, wearing a dark suit and his long hair tied into a ponytail.

Several others had more luck with their umbrellas but it was difficult to make out other faces from the food company workers. Tara assumed that among the huddle of six people standing by the grave, opposite the principal mourners, one of them was likely to be Jez. She recognised also, one of two men standing with their backs to her, as Toby Ewing. The other man appeared much older and rather stooped.

As the vicar performed the committal ceremony Tara edged closer, looking from one mourner to another. The man and woman who had arrived in the limousine were middle-aged and well-dressed but looked tired, although, in the turbulent weather, many of the mourners appeared uncomfortable. Tara assumed that the man was Maggie's brother who had flown in from Toronto for the funeral. This was confirmed when she introduced herself after the vicar had concluded the ritual.

'Mr Hull? I'm Detective Inspector Grogan, Merseyside Police. May I offer my sympathy for the loss of your sister?'

The man, grey-haired with a leathery face, offered his hand.

'Thank you, Inspector,' he replied with only the slightest waver in his Scouse accent, even though he'd spent nearly thirty years of his life in Canada. 'This is my wife, Eileen.'

Tara shook her hand, and the woman smiled without speaking. Her cheeks were red, more from her make-up than the biting cold, her lips bold and drawn with scarlet lipstick to a false pout. Her eyes betrayed her; that she did not want to be there; they kept looking beyond Tara towards the sanctuary of the waiting limousine.

'I'm sorry that we haven't yet made any significant progress in catching your sister's killer.'

Kenneth Hull shrugged. What could he say to that?

A queue of mourners developed, all waiting to offer condolences to the brother of Maggie Hull. Tara moved away to a discreet distance to observe. Only then did she realise that Jez was not among those people shaking hands with Kenneth and Eileen Hull. The closest link to Maggie, for a brief period, it seemed, her only true friend and yet she hadn't attended her funeral. Maybe these sombre occasions were not for her? There couldn't be too many souls who enjoyed them, but usually, those closest to the deceased were the people who made the greatest effort to be present. The friendship between Maggie and Jez had perhaps cooled a few degrees more than Jez had so far admitted.

None of the mourners prolonged their conversation with Kenneth Hull. The people from Harbinson Fine

Foods shook hands politely and moved quickly to the sanctuary of their vehicles. Tara watched all of them depart and was surprised to notice just how slow Edward Harbinson was on foot, relying upon his daughter to guide him over the soggy lawn and back to his car.

McIntyre dumped his umbrella in a waste bin at the junction of two paths and stomped to his dark-green Jaguar. Toby Ewing accompanied the older man with whom he'd been standing, past the hearse to a silver BMW parked directly behind the limousine. As he opened the passenger door for the old man, he noticed Tara watching him. They didn't hold eye contact for long. Instead, Ewing glanced towards Harbinson and his daughter, then dropped his head as he made his way around to the driver's side. He stole another glance at Tara who had continued to observe him, then ducked into his car.

Kenneth Hull and his wife remained at the graveside for several minutes, and it was with some reluctance, it seemed, that he eventually obeyed his wife's desire to leave. Tara had decided that she needed another word.

'I'm sorry to bother you, Mr Hull, but I wonder if you would mind answering a few questions about Maggie? We could sit in my car if you like?'

Hull instructed his wife to wait in the limousine while he spoke with Tara.

'How can I help you, Inspector?'

'Perhaps you could tell me when you last spoke to your sister?'

'Gee, we usually spoke on the phone every couple of weeks,' he said thoughtfully. 'We took turns to call, but you know how things get out of sync and maybe three weeks would pass before she called me to give off stink about how I had forgotten all about her.' It was enough to raise a tear in the man's eyes which he tried to control with a hefty sniff. 'I suppose it was Thursday, two weeks ago when she last called.'

'How did she seem?'

'All right, the usual Maggie, bright and cheerful, after she'd given me an earful for not calling her on Mum's birthday.'

'Did she sound worried about anything? Or did she mention anyone who was causing her trouble?'

'Trouble? No, nothing like that, Inspector. I know she was lonely after Mum died. I asked her how work was going, but she didn't sound too enamoured with that. She told me about some guy from her office who'd killed himself. She was very upset about that. She said she needed a break. I've been going on at her for years to come and live in Canada but she wouldn't do it. She came over a few times for a holiday and loved it, but she told me that Liverpool was her home and home is where she belonged. Could be stubborn at times, our Maggie. If she had her mind set on something there was nothing anyone could do to change it. We used to have some rare fights when we were kids.'

He shook his head jovially at the thought.

'Truth be told, Maggie always wanted things. If I got a new football for my birthday, she wanted a new doll. When I got a new bike, she cried until Mum bought her a new pram. Dad gave us 50p on a Friday night for pocket money. By Tuesday I would still have 20p, while she'd spent all of her money in the sweet shop within the hour and was asking to borrow more from me.'

'Do you know of any reason why someone would want to kill her?'

Kenneth Hull shook his head, this time, in despair, raising his hands to his eyes. He drew a deep breath, and his body quivered nervously as he exhaled.

'Did she ever mention anyone who had threatened or assaulted her?'

He looked horrified at the idea.

'Why do *you* think she was murdered, Inspector?'

'At the moment we have no steadfast reason, but I believe that Maggie knew her killer well, or was at least acquainted with him.'

'She never mentioned anyone to me. The only people she ever talked or wrote about were those she worked with and the Baileys who've lived next door since we were kids.'

'Well, Mr Hull, thanks for your time, and once again I'm very sorry for your loss.'

'Thank you, Inspector,' he replied, shaking Tara's hand with a firm grip. 'I hope to hell you catch the filth that murdered my sister.'

'If you give me a contact address in Canada, I'll try my best to keep you informed of any developments.'

* * *

The day had taught Tara little except that Allerton Cemetery was best avoided, even in death.

When her unsettled mind returned to matters of police business, Tara began once again to wonder why Jez had not attended the funeral. As soon as she was back in the office, had some tea and dried off, Tara called Jez's work number.

'I'm sorry, Miss Riordan is not in the office today,' said a young man, sounding nervous.

She put down the phone. That explained it – Jez had been out all day on business, or perhaps was at home, sick and maybe tucked up in bed.

She called at the house in Woolton on her way home. The Peugeot SUV was not in the drive. There were no signs of life about the place, no lights on and the curtains were open. Tara pushed a hastily scribbled note through the letterbox just to let Jez know that she'd called. As she drove home to Wapping Dock, she continued to think it strange that Jez had not attended Maggie Hull's funeral.

CHAPTER 27

'Miss Riordan is not in today,' said the same young voice as the day before.

'When are you expecting her?'

'I'm not sure.'

'Well, is there anyone else who knows when she is due?'

'I… I don't know,' the boy stuttered.

'Would you mind asking someone?'

There was silence as the kid went in search of the answer. Tara wondered how on earth this lad managed to get through the day.

'No one is sure when Jez, I mean Miss Riordan, is likely to be here.'

'Do you have a number where I might contact her?'

'Hold on.'

Tara could scarcely contain her frustration, firstly, at having to spell everything out for this dodo and secondly, being unable to speak with Jez.

'You can call her at home,' said the listless voice.

'Right, thanks. You've been a big help.'

She slammed the phone down. She needed coffee, strong and hot to match her temper. The morning was even worse than she'd envisaged: a dull headache, feeling cold and overcome with drowsiness. She hadn't managed to get any sleep and had left home without showering or picking up a change of clothes. Her first call was in search of Jez Riordan. Right now, she wasn't sure if that was for professional or personal reasons. Murray approached her desk.

'Morning, ma'am,' he said cheerfully but with some tact. 'How are you?'

'Bloody awful!'

'That good?' he said, smiling conspiratorially. 'Big Beryl is here.'

'And what does he want?'

'It's his time for checking in – his bail conditions. But I thought you might like a word.'

Murray had remembered their intention to ask Big Beryl about his association with Tommy Gracey. At that particular moment, Tara was miles away from the idea.

'Yes, OK,' she sighed. 'Bring him into an interview room. I'll be right down.'

* * *

A few moments later, Big Beryl sauntered in bumptiously. Tara and Murray were already seated in the room.

'Mornin', Inspector,' he said. 'Before you start, I haven't done nothin'.'

He squeezed himself carefully into a plastic chair, his large behind only just slipping between the armrests. Tara had not yet lifted her delicate head from the papers in front of her. She thought she'd stay there for a while just to hear how much Big Beryl had to say before he was asked a question.

'I'm too busy workin' now, you know. You wouldn't be interested in ordinary work, would you? What I mean is that I'm straight now, Inspector, honest to God. I promised the wife, no more dodgy jobs, honest. Not fair on her, know what I mean?'

Murray could hardly contain himself, while Tara couldn't bear to see and hear such a giant of a man squirming in his juices.

'My heart's pumping custard for you, Beryl,' said Murray. 'I'll be handing around the Kleenex in a minute.'

'Just lettin' you know, Inspector, that's all.'

'It's all right, Beryl,' said Tara, looking up at last from her notes. 'I only want to ask you a simple question.'

The cockiness returned instantly if only to conceal his fear.

'My brief says I don't have to tell you nothin'.' He folded his arms defiantly, but his chest was so broad they barely met in the middle.

'What kind of work have you been doing for Tommy Gracey?'

'I'm sayin' fuck all.'

Tara rose from her chair and paced around the room, halting by the window. She stood behind the big man and smirked at Murray.

'You know, Beryl, if you could help us out with Tommy Gracey, we might be able to make those burglary charges go away.'

Tara had been thinking about this for a couple of days now, ever since Big Beryl had managed to win bail. She could see problems ahead if they took this case the whole way. They had not yet recovered any of the stolen property. A conviction rested solely upon Mrs Henshaw having identified Big Beryl as the man who was making off with her TV. Tara knew well that a good defence barrister would dispute this on the basis that Mrs Henshaw had recognised Big Beryl from working at the Speedy-Klean car wash, thereby casting doubt on the validity of the formal identification process. The defence would simply claim that Mrs Henshaw had successfully identified a man who worked at a local car wash and was confusing that image with a man who had broken into her home. If they weren't going to pursue the case, Tara could at least use it as a stick to beat a few answers out of Big Beryl.

'Then again,' she continued, 'if you can't help us, I might have to pass on some information that would be detrimental to your continuing bail.'

'Like what?'

'Like the fact that you are associating with convicted criminals who are themselves only free under licence. So, tell me about you and Tommy.'

Sweat broke across Big Beryl's forehead and he looked at Murray in hope of a friendlier face.

'C'mon, Inspector, you'll get me a bullet in the knee if I tell you anything about Tommy.'

Tara grinned to herself before turning to face the big man. When her eyes met Beryl's, they were deadly serious.

'Your choice, Beryl,' she said coldly.

* * *

After a light lunch of tea and buttered toast, she felt herself slowly returning to normal. She was in more of a mood to try Jez at home once again, however, there was still no answer from her telephone. She was beginning to think it very strange. Jez had told no one of her whereabouts or when she was likely to return home. If Tara cared to admit it, she was worried about her new friend.

She and Murray spent some time with Tweedy in the afternoon. The Detective Superintendent filled out several more pages on his flipcharts with the information they had reported to him concerning their interview with Big Beryl. By the time they'd finished, they were ready to bring in Tommy Gracey for questioning regarding the murder of Maggie Hull.

Tara again called at the house in Woolton on her way home. There was nothing different from the night before. Jez was not at home and, it seemed, had not been there since Tara's last visit. There were not too many places Tara could imagine Jez having gone to. A holiday? Perhaps, but why didn't they know about it at her office? Maybe she'd gone to London, something to do with her painting – to visit an exhibition? Again, was there a need for her to keep it a secret? That was about it, unless some harm had come to her. Tara didn't dare contemplate it.

When she arrived home, she tried Jez's number again but without success. A few minutes later her telephone rang. She rushed from the kitchen and made it before the third ring.

CHAPTER 28

There was no measurable success in the questioning of Tommy Gracey. Information extracted from Big Beryl had given them grounds to believe that Maggie Hull had been a client of Gracey's at some time in the recent past. Big Beryl had remembered collecting payments from her two years previously. What Tara needed most was proof that Gracey had done business with Maggie Hull close to the time when she was murdered. A search of his home provided evidence that he was a loan shark, but his books were either written using the Enigma code or else the guy conducted his business by the seat of his pants. They were unable to decipher much of his accounts. Jez had described the debt collectors who she'd paid, on Maggie's behalf, as mere youths. Neither Big Beryl nor Gracey was forthcoming with names of any youngsters who did their dirty work.

Tara was losing interest with this line of the investigation. It had been their only possible lead, but she'd been sceptical from the outset. Her suspicions lay somewhere closer to Harbinson Fine Foods. With days going by and no sign of Jez Riordan, she began to imagine scenarios of how the two incidents could be related. It was uppermost in her thinking now and she'd decided to run the matter past Tweedy.

A week had elapsed since Tara had last spoken with Jez. She had thought it had been Jez a few nights ago when she raced to answer the telephone, but it was Kate calling to ask her to babysit for Adele. This evening, as her god-daughter slept beside her on the sofa, Tara thought it strange that there was no news forthcoming from Jez's office on her whereabouts. She failed to understand their lack of concern, and she had now reached the point where she would be the one to report her officially as a missing person. That, of course, would have consequences for her. Tweedy was bound to ask why she had such a close association with a woman who might well be a suspect in a murder case.

A miserable Wednesday morning was spent in the office pondering all of the possible connections between Jez's disappearance, Maggie Hull's murder and Richard Andrews' suicide. Her theorising did not encompass what she was soon to learn when Tweedy entered the room and called for everyone's attention.

'Right folks, I have some news concerning the spate of poisonings.'

Everyone in the office stopped what they were doing to listen to their superintendent.

'Laboratory results have confirmed that in the case of the student victims the source of the poison was confined to a chicken curry ready meal. The nature of this poison remains unconfirmed. As you know, all similar products have been removed from sale in shops, and a general product recall is in force. Similar items retrieved from the homes of the other victims are still being tested. The manufacturers of the food product are now helping with inquiries. A team of environmental health officers are already on-site at the factory and carrying out an investigation.'

Tara suddenly felt she already knew the answer to the question she was about to ask.

'Sir, what is the name of the supplier?'

'Harbinson Fine Foods.'

In a fleeting second her investigation into the murder of Maggie Hull, the suicide of Richard Andrews and the apparent disappearance of Jez Riordan had taken on a whole new meaning. Tara now found herself in the middle of the biggest police emergency on Merseyside that she had ever faced.

CHAPTER 29

None of the senior executives from Harbinson Fine Foods were available at the company's head office in the Liver Building. Edward Harbinson, CEO, and Toby Ewing, director in charge of primary production, were both at the factory in Speke assisting investigators in trying to locate the source of the poisonous contamination. At the firm's other Merseyside factory in Birkenhead, Skip McIntyre was doing the same. Tara and Murray, upon instruction from Tweedy, had hurried down to the factory in Speke. She was eager to speak with the company chairman, and she and Murray had to battle their way through a posse of media vying for the latest on this crisis. When they reached the reception desk, they flashed their warrant cards and marched directly towards the factory floor. Immediately, there were shouts from a man standing above them on a mezzanine.

'Oi! You can't come in here dressed like that!'

Tara looked up at the man who was clad in white overalls and a hat.

'Merseyside Police,' she replied.

'I don't care if you're the bloody CIA, you can't come in here without the proper protective clothing! We're in the middle of a major safety incident here.'

Tara looked at Murray, who merely shrugged. A set of double plastic-flap doors to their right were suddenly thrust open, and a woman dressed in white overalls and wellingtons entered.

'Put these on before our Nigel has a heart attack,' she said.

She was a red-faced woman in her fifties with bright eyes and a bemused grin. Murray and Tara each took a pair of disposable coveralls, removed the polythene wrapping and began to put them on. The clothing was similar to the forensics suits they used when attending a crime scene. Next, the woman handed them a disposable elasticated cap and a pair of disposable overshoes.

'Now you can go wandering wherever you like,' said the woman.

'Thanks,' said Tara, 'I would like to speak with Mr Harbinson, do you know where I might find him?'

The man who had continued to look down on them as they dressed finally strolled away. He had no interest in engaging with the police detectives.

'Follow me,' said the woman.

She walked briskly through the largely empty hall, through another set of flap doors and into an area filled with machinery, overhead conveyors and stainless-steel benches. Approximately thirty workers were dotted around, some clustered in groups of four or five. The machinery was silent; there was no work going on, food production at a standstill.

Tara felt the coolness of the air and there was a pervading smell of disinfectant. They were led through the rows of benches and at the end of one conveyor platform, a group of people were deep in conversation, whilst one woman leaned across a bench and wiped a swab over its surface. When they drew closer, Tara saw that Edward Harbinson and Toby Ewing were listening to another man who was pointing at various places within the factory floor.

'Sorry to interrupt,' said Tara, 'Mr Harbinson, may I have a word?'

Harbinson turned to face Murray and her; he did not look happy. His face was strained, his complexion was deathly white.

'Inspector Grogan,' he said with a forced smile, 'would you mind waiting a few minutes? In the meantime, Jean can show you around.'

The woman who had guided them thus far smiled warmly. 'I'm Jean, follow me.'

Without another word, she led them from the building, across an open yard and into another shed which was dimly lit but open on one side. Two articulated wagons were parked in loading bays. Tara heard noises from within the trailers, the clucking and muttering of birds. She saw that both vehicles were full of plastic crates, packed with live chickens. Jean suddenly launched into a spiel of information.

'This is our loading bay where the birds come in. Each bird is removed from the crate and hung on a hook.' She indicated a line of steel hooks above them. 'In less than a second, it meets the rotating blade where the head is removed. We keep this area dark so as not to stress the birds as they are unloaded.'

'I think you'd be fairly stressed anyway if you were about to have your head chopped off,' said Murray.

Jean smiled thinly at the comment.

'Stress in the birds affects the quality of the meat. Follow me,' she said. She continued to speak as she walked them into another area of the building. 'Once the birds have been placed on the overhead line, no human hand touches them again until the product is ready to be shipped.'

'Where do you think the contamination might have occurred?' Tara asked.

'We don't know yet if any contamination happened at this factory,' she said, frankly.

Tara glanced at Murray who seemed amused by Jean's rather defensive attitude.

'This is where the feathers are removed,' Jean continued.

They stood before a long line of stainless-steel troughs where the overhead conveyor with its headless chickens on hooks descended for each bird to be immersed in hot water.

'The baths are maintained at sixty degrees and the water is agitated by rollers. By the time the birds emerge at the far end, the feathers have been removed.'

Jean walked a few yards beyond the troughs and stood by another machine, the mechanism of which was suspended from above. She held up a metal spike that resembled a large drill bit.

'This is automatically inserted into the carcass and is used to remove the insides of each bird. The innards are dropped into a tray beneath the carcass. Every carcass remains directly above its innards for the remainder of processing.'

'I'm sure the birds are pleased about that,' said Murray.

Tara nudged him in the ribs, while Jean again could only offer a dry smile of tolerance.

They were taken inside a control room on the mezzanine above the factory floor. There was a large square window that seemed to look into a dark blank space.

'When the line is running,' said Jean, pointing into the darkness, 'behind this window each bird passes in front of a camera which is linked to the computer. The carcass is graded depending on its shape and size. Class A birds go for sale as a whole chicken or breast fillets, drummers, etcetera. Class B meat goes to Birkenhead and is used in our cooked ready meal products.'

'How many chickens are processed each day?' Tara asked.

'Two thousand an hour, and with 24 hours running, considering shift changes and down-time, we process around 42,000 every day.'

'Do we really eat that much chicken?' Murray asked.

'And then some,' Jean replied. 'That's just the local produce, we also import already processed product from the Far East and Brazil for our factory in Birkenhead.'

A few minutes later they were back in the hall where they had first encountered Edward Harbinson.

'This is where the meat is packaged ready for shipping. The meat has not been touched by human hands from the time it was placed on the line until this point. Unfortunately, by this afternoon this area will be full of the recalled product.'

'What will happen to it?'

'It will go to cold storage until all the testing is complete. Then, I imagine, it will be incinerated or go to landfill.'

'Thank you, Jean,' said Tara. 'You've been very helpful. If there was a source of contamination in this factory where do you think it would come from?'

Jean shook her head. It was clear that she had already been briefed not to comment on such questions.

'I'm sorry, I can't say, but between you and me, Inspector, I don't think you'll find anything like that poison in here or in any of our factories.'

'How can you be so sure?'

'All the poisonings we've seen on the news have happened in Liverpool. There haven't been any cases in other parts of the country. But Harbinson products are distributed nationally; our products are in all the main supermarkets. If the contamination originated here in Speke, or at Birkenhead, then surely people in other parts of the country would have taken ill by now.'

CHAPTER 30

When the tour of the factory was over, Jean took them to an office in the main building of the complex. They found Edward Harbinson, now in his business suit, standing by a window that overlooked the main road. He seemed to be staring vacantly into the distance, yet he was aware of his visitors.

'How can I help you, Inspector?' He remained with his back to them. 'There isn't much more I can tell you about Maggie. As you saw earlier, we're up to our eyes with this health and safety inspection.'

'Mr Harbinson, don't you think it's time we discussed your staff turnover figures?'

It wasn't difficult to notice his fuming temper. She and Murray both sat down in matching wooden armchairs while Harbinson remained by the window.

'Inspector, I trust you have a good reason for asking that question? I don't think you appreciate what is happening here today. We have already lost two clients, and I have a meeting with our biggest customer this afternoon, during which I will have to explain how this damn crisis is not of our making. My company is at risk of going under and hundreds of people will lose their jobs. Meanwhile, Merseyside Police have failed to find the cause of this poisoning outbreak.'

'Fuck your clients, Mr Harbinson. I want you to tell me why your staff numbers are declining with such tragic regularity?' It was stronger language than she needed, but her frustrations had found a sudden release. She was convinced there was something sinister going on within this company.

Having, at last, turned to face them, the chairman's face had developed a rosy hue, affronted by the strong language blowing his way.

'I assume you're referring to Maggie? Has there been a development?'

'There's been a development all right. Let me ask you something, Mr Harbinson, why have you not reported Miss Riordan as missing? I've been trying to reach her at your head office for the past few days, but no one can tell me where she's gone or when she is likely to return.'

There was an acid change in the man's complexion, his face was now grey-white and decidedly agitated. He seemed to be considering his answer carefully, choosing the right words before responding.

'I wasn't aware that she was missing, Inspector. She said nothing of where she was going or what she was doing, but I had no reason to think it particularly strange. She goes to London quite often, business, I believe, related to her painting. Between such occasions, I am not Jez's keeper.'

'But you are her employer; didn't she request a period of leave?'

Murray had a blank look on his face. Tara had not shared her concern over Jez Riordan with him.

'Believe it or not, Inspector, we are quite flexible with our employees, particularly those who work at head office. I trust Miss Riordan to organise cover when she is on leave.'

'And when did you last speak to her?' Tara asked teeth gritted, she didn't much care for this man's attitude.

'I'm not sure precisely, early last week I think.'

'Was that before or after Maggie Hull's funeral?'

'Before. Look, Inspector, are you going to tell me what's wrong? Is Jez all right?'

Too late with that question, my friend.

'Do you know of any reason why she did not attend Maggie's funeral?'

'I can't think of one.'

'And you have no idea where she spent the past week?'

'None at all. What is going on, Inspector? If something has happened to Jez, I insist that you tell me.'

'Forgive me for being so blunt, Mr Harbinson, but at the moment we are dealing with the deaths of two of your employees, the apparent disappearance of another and your company is now at the centre of a major food scare that so far has caused the deaths of four people. Coincidence? Maybe, but I think Ladbrokes would make it odds-on that there is a connection between them. So far, that connection points to this company. Now's your chance to tell me something I don't already know.'

'I'm afraid that I can't help you, Inspector.' He looked Tara straight in the eyes. She didn't baulk.

'Do you know if there is anyone else around here who can?'

'It's been a very trying time for all of us at this company ever since Richard's passing. I don't know of anyone here who can help you, Inspector. Now, if you have no further worthwhile questions, I suggest you continue with your enquiries elsewhere and leave me to get on with saving my company from closure.'

Tara rose from the chair but before leaving, placed both hands on Harbinson's desk and leaned forward.

'I'll tell you this, Mr Harbinson, there is a stinking smell around here and it isn't the chicken. Someone knows what is going on, and I will keep coming back until I find out. Do you know what strikes me most about this company? The management doesn't seem to give a damn about the deaths of two employees and the disappearance of another. A bit too cold for my liking. I'll be seeing you, Mr Harbinson.'

CHAPTER 31

'That was a bit strong,' said Murray on their way back to the car.

'Believe me, Alan, I could have said a lot more. I'm done with pussy-footing around people, particularly those who are suspects in a murder. How the hell does that man not see a link between the deaths of his employees and this poisoning case? What is he hiding? How can he not know whether his secretary is on leave or whether she's just taken off somewhere? We need to find out what's going on before we have any more victims.'

They were on the road back to the city when Murray next ventured to speak.

'So, how are things, ma'am?'

'What do you mean – things?'

'I mean, how are you, how are you feeling at the moment?'

'Am I holding it together, is that what you want to know?'

'In a way, yes. You haven't been the bright and buzzing woman I'm used to working with.'

Tara didn't reply. She had no sensible answer. Her life had changed irrevocably, she knew that much. She didn't feel the same about anything: her work, her relationships, her hopes for the future.

Deep within, she felt a determination to get things done, and quickly, as if there may not be a tomorrow. She wiped a single tear from her eye as Murray drove in silence. He was simply showing that he cared, but she couldn't bring herself to open up to him. Right now, she didn't think she could open up to anyone.

At St Anne Street, Tara was secretly pleased to now be included in the main briefing on the poisoning cases. She was asked to report on her investigation into the murder of Maggie Hull and the possibility that this might be linked to the main enquiry. She and Murray sat together listening to Detective Superintendent Richard Myers from Admiral Street station update the staff involved. He, like Harold Tweedy, was a sound detective of more than twenty years' experience, originally from the Met and particularly accustomed to dealing with emergencies. He had a strong physique, a confident face and a South London accent. He spoke in a manner suggesting that he was very well used to taking charge.

'The good news is that we have no further incidents or casualties to report,' he said. 'Forensic analysis is now centred on the factories in Speke and Birkenhead of Harbinson Fine Foods. Initial test results should be available shortly. We now have information from some of the victims who were taken ill, namely the students, as to where the food product was purchased. Similar traces are in operation for the other food products retrieved from the earlier victims. The stores and supermarkets concerned have been contacted and will be subject to forensic examination. Any questions?'

Tara raised her hand. Myers spotted her and pointed in her direction.

'Inspector Grogan,' he said.

'Sir, it might be useful to examine the CCTV footage from these stores.'

'And why is that?'

'I believe that the source of this contamination originates from an individual or individuals from the Merseyside area deliberately applying the poison to a food product. I don't think you will find anything in the factories.'

Myers seemed a little surprised by her suggestion. Tara had taken on board the comments made by Jean at the factory in Speke.

'Harbinson products are distributed nationwide but the cases of poisoning have occurred only on Merseyside.'

'It may simply be down to a particular batch of a product originating at the factory and that batch having gone only to stores in Liverpool,' Myers replied. He moved on to another question.

Tara winced, not having thought of that possibility. Her face flushed red. She had not made a good first impression upon the Chief Investigating Officer.

Following her embarrassing participation in the briefing, Tara's afternoon quickly went downhill. Not wishing to publicly disagree with Superintendent Myers, she tried to figure out how best to initiate an investigation into CCTV footage from those stores identified as a source of the contaminated foods. She could not go over his head, so perhaps it was best to wait and see what results came from the Harbinson factories. If a source of the poison was located within the food production facility, then it would indicate contamination on site, either deliberate or accidental. If no poison was found in the factories, then Myers would have to think again. Maybe then he would consider looking at the CCTV from the shops for a potential culprit.

Tara also wondered why it was taking the labs so long to identify the poison. She had heard during Myers' briefing that several laboratories across the country were now testing food samples. How difficult could it be?

CHAPTER 32

With little to show for her day, apart from the frustration in dealing with Harbinson Fine Foods and embarrassment during her first encounter with Myers, she contemplated her evening. As was usual these days, she would spend it alone in her flat at Wapping Dock, a book or television for company, a frozen ready meal for nourishment and a bottle of wine for comfort.

Murray snapped her out of the darkening thoughts of self-pity, but it wasn't to be anything to induce a lighter mood.

'Ma'am, you'd better take a look at this,' he said, and without invitation began navigating her browser to the relevant page.

It was a bulletin posted by police in Birkenhead. She read the brief notice, and instantly her heart beat faster.

'It could be anyone, ma'am, but just in case I thought we should get more information.'

Tara couldn't summon words. Somehow, she felt it was the news she had feared. She allowed Murray to make the necessary phone call. Ten minutes later, they were making for the tunnel under the Mersey. By the time they arrived at the entrance to Royden Park, near Caldy, darkness was descending. Under the canopy of trees, it was already a dim and gloomy setting.

Several marked police and emergency vehicles were on site, including a forensics van and an ambulance. Murray pulled to the side of the lane. There was a small parking area ahead, but it had already been cordoned off. A white incident shelter had been erected and arc lights were being set up a little way off the car park and into the woods.

Tara and Murray got out of the car and made their way towards the group of uniformed officers gathered by the police vehicles. There were tall trees all around, and the forest paths ran off on either side into the dense undergrowth.

Already, Tara felt sick. Her body trembled, and she felt cold despite wearing a padded anorak, jeans and boots. She feared she was about to encounter the inevitable, the loss of a friend, albeit someone she had known for only a short time. She stood back and allowed Murray to make contact with the detectives from Birkenhead. She didn't feel capable of conversation. A plainclothes officer, however, approached her.

'DI Grogan,' he said, 'I'm DS Tom Lydiate. DS Murray tells me that you may know the victim?'

He was a tall, very slim man, unable, it seemed, to fit into his jacket very well. It hung off his narrow shoulders. His hair was cut in a traditional short back and sides, his face was pinched, and his Adam's apple protruded as he spoke. Tara did little more than to shrug in response.

'The description seems to fit,' she replied eventually. 'A friend of mine has recently gone missing.'

'There is no ID on the victim, but if you wouldn't mind taking a look, ma'am.'

Never particularly strong at a crime scene, she felt her knees go weak. The thought of stepping inside that tent forced her to momentarily shut her eyes.

'You OK, ma'am?' Murray asked. She nodded.

'Stay with me please, Alan.'

She allowed him to lead the way. As they approached, she saw that the tent was positioned off the rough parking area and sat several yards into the undergrowth. They stepped over a low wooden boundary and the ground fell away steeply. The shelter was perched at an angle ten feet down the slope. A uniformed officer, seeing them approach, lifted the flap of the tent. Tara remained behind

Murray as they ventured inside. She gripped his arm tightly when she caught a glimpse of the body.

CHAPTER 33

The vision made her stomach heave, and she continued to hold on tight to Murray's arm. He sensed her discomfort and put his arm around her shoulders and drew her body close to his. Tara's hand went to her mouth as her mind adjusted to the reality before her. Jez had been such a recently acquired friend, and yet Tara felt that they could have become close. In a short space of time, merely within a few occasions, they had come to know each other quite well. But now there was such mystery. Why was Jez dead?

Murray attempted to guide her out of the tent and away from the scene, but Tara forced herself to look, to take in as much detail as her mind would allow. Jez lay on her back and a dried trickle of blood ran from the side of her mouth into the earth. Mud and a few dead leaves were stuck to her beautiful face. There were no obvious signs of what had transpired here. There were no bruises or cuts on the face, and as far as she could see there were no signs of strangulation. The flesh was darkened and already in decay. Tara noticed also that her friend was dressed similarly to the night they had gone to the Philharmonic. She wore a long black, tailored coat which lay open revealing a black silk blouse and black slim-fitting trousers. On her feet were a pair of black ankle boots with gold studs around the heels. Her face still showed traces of substantial make-up with dark eyeshadow and a dark-coloured lipstick. Her clothes, however, were muddied and stained with blood.

The medical examiner, despite looking a young age, was rather stooped in posture as he stood at the head of the body. He was passing on his initial findings to DS Lydiate.

'I would say she has been here for several days,' he said in a loud voice. 'No obvious signs of sexual activity. The clothes are mostly intact. Both legs are broken and there is severe trauma to the upper torso. Crush injuries. My guess is that she has been run over by a vehicle of some description. Judging by how far she is away from the lane and the parking area I would say that either she was thrown this far by the impact or else someone dragged her here after the collision.'

Tara had seen and heard enough. She managed to make it close to their car before, out of sight of everyone but Murray, she threw up. Murray supplied the tissues for her to wipe her mouth. Now, she was cold and trembling. With Murray's help, she climbed into the car and he drove them to the first pub he could find.

'Drink this, ma'am, it'll warm you up if nothing else.'

'What is it?'

'Brandy.' Murray placed the glass with a double measure of Rémy Martin into her hands.

'Ughh! I hate brandy.'

'Drink, that's an order… ma'am.'

She sipped at the warming liquid and attempted to smile at her colleague.

'Thanks, Alan, I couldn't have got through that without you. I feel as though someone has taken a knife and gouged out my insides. I feel so bloody useless.'

The pub near the town centre of Birkenhead was quiet. To anyone who cared to notice, Tara and Murray looked like a couple enjoying an early evening drink. Their surroundings, however, were far from salubrious, Formica tabletops, wooden bench seats and a TV blaring out a helping of *Hollyoaks*.

'What's happening to all of us, Alan? We're old before our time and it's all because of this damn job. I don't think I can stand much more of it.'

'Life is tough, Tara, it's just that sometimes we're right at the coalface.'

Murray saw that Tara was crying, sobbing like a child.

'Hey, come on, Tara love, we'll get through this one, we always do.'

'And then what? Another case? Another murder, another killer for us to track down?'

CHAPTER 34

'The post-mortem is at ten-thirty,' said Murray. 'I thought you might want to be there.'

Tara nodded before gulping some orange juice. She'd just let Murray into her flat, and now she stood in her kitchen trying to ease the effects of several double brandies from the night before. Her head throbbed and her eyes felt as though they'd been wide open in a sandstorm. She remembered Murray driving her home, opening her door and helping her inside. He may well have helped her to bed, but that's where her mind was blank. Murray was still talking, but her head suddenly filled with the vision of her coming on to him, trying to kiss him and then asking him to her bed. God, what had she done?

'Tweedy was trying to get a hold of you, he wants a word.'

She nodded acknowledgement.

'Make yourself some coffee. I need a shower,' she said. 'Help yourself to anything you can find to eat.' She traipsed past him then stopped and turned around. 'Alan,

I'm really sorry about last night. Whatever I did or said, I can't remember.'

He smiled, trying to look sympathetic but it seemed to her that he was enjoying her unease.

'God, this is so embarrassing,' she said, retreating to the bathroom.

DS Lydiate appeared to have been waiting for them as they walked into the bare entrance hall outside the post-mortem suite of the Royal Liverpool Hospital. He looked tired and drawn, the events of the previous day had taken its toll. His face was heavily lined and he hadn't shaved properly, leaving blotches of red on both cheeks and scattered areas of stubble. He was too old for late nights and early morning starts.

'Ah, morning, ma'am,' he said with his hand outstretched. 'I'm glad you could make it. At the moment you're the only person who can identify the deceased.'

'I'll arrange for one of Jez's work colleagues to come along. It might be more appropriate.'

'Right, well, maybe, if you don't mind, you could at least confirm that the deceased is Miss Riordan?'

Lydiate led Tara and Murray through a set of double doors and into a post-mortem room. Tara was well used to this place, but this morning her experience was of no comfort. Her embarrassment and her hangover had not subsided, and now she was trembling already at the sight of her friend covered by a green theatre sheet and lying on a stainless-steel bench awaiting the pathologist's knife. Tara glanced around the room in need of something else to focus upon, something other than the shape of this once stunningly beautiful woman. A cold echoing room with its array of clinical aromas was no place for a woman with a hangover and, orange juice and coffee aside, an empty stomach. Come to think of it, she would not wish to be here with a full breakfast in her either.

The pathologist's assistant wasted no time in pulling back the sheet to reveal the head and shoulders of the woman's body. Tara drew back. She saw the woman with whom she'd had the briefest of friendships. What lay before her now was a lifeless frame, the beauty and the warmth had gone. Lydiate spoke softly but matter-of-factly, simply doing his job.

'Can you confirm this woman's identity as Miss Jez Riordan?'

Tara gave a single nod.

'I can,' she replied. Lydiate then indicated to Murray that he should lead his DI from the room. As he did so, the pathologist moved in to begin his work.

The pair of them were grateful for a bright crisp morning, such a transformation from yesterday, a smattering of frost covering those pavements sheltered from the sun. Tom Lydiate joined them outside.

'Thanks for that, ma'am. Are you feeling all right?'

'I'll be fine,' she lied. 'Not used to seeing a familiar face on the slab, that's all.'

Lydiate seemed to understand her feelings.

Murray drove Tara to the station and once there she sat listlessly at her desk, with a strong coffee and two paracetamol. When she felt a slight improvement in her mood, she again pulled out all the information she held concerning Maggie Hull, Richard Andrews and now Jez Riordan. Maybe the link between their deaths would rise from the folders lying before her. She certainly hoped so.

Tara viewed the unfinished note found in Andrews' car. What did he have to say to Toby Ewing and why had he not finished it? Fool was the word most obviously missing from that incomplete sentence. "I've been such a... fool?" Ewing had been a close friend to Andrews. She had learned that much from her inquiries over Maggie Hull. The two men had been like a pair of mischievous brothers. Was there perhaps a warning for Toby Ewing in this note? Or was it some kind of apology?

She flipped the folder closed and sifted through the notes compiled to date on Maggie Hull. A loan shark demanding payment, or a motiveless killing? Both scenarios were an understandable conclusion until the death of Jez Riordan. Now, everything pointed toward Harbinson Fine Foods. She was getting nowhere, and she didn't need anyone to tell her so.

What had Jez been doing in Royden Park? She was hardly dressed for walking in the woods, more like for an evening out. Had she been waiting in the park to meet someone, and if so whom? The most bizarre question was: how were these deaths linked to the cases of poisoning that now so obviously centred around Harbinson Fine Foods? Someone within that company knew the answer. Tara was convinced of it.

CHAPTER 35

Kate called to see her in the evening. Her showing up with little Adele was a welcome relief for Tara. She desperately needed a friendly face and something to take her mind off the case. In seconds, she was down on the floor playing with her god-daughter.

'I'm so sorry to hear about Jez,' said Kate, who was enjoying a moment's peace and a cup of coffee.

'You would have liked her. I think we could have had a lot of fun together. Kate, I've been thinking that when this case is finished, we could take a holiday together.'

'Sounds great, but it would have to be a time when Adam can look after Adele.'

'Yes, sure. I was thinking also that I would pack my job in, do something else.'

'Oh, Tara, love, that would be great. I can see what this job has done to you. I want the Tara back that I grew up with, the shy and fun girl instead of the dark-thinking woman you've become since joining the police.'

Tara wiped tears from her eyes.

'I just can't do it anymore, Kate – the murders, the horrors and the hateful people I have to deal with.'

She invited Kate to stay for the night. Adele went to sleep in Tara's spare room, and the two friends shared a pizza, two bottles of chardonnay and watched a couple of rom-coms on Netflix.

* * *

For the second day in a row, Tara was suffering from her over-indulgence. She sat with Tweedy, Wilson and Murray in a briefing room while Superintendent Myers brought everyone up to date on the poisoning case. She'd had little sleep, chatting with Kate into the early hours and now, in the stuffy room, she fought to stay awake. Myers didn't seem to have much to say that was new. Tara was the one making connections now, trying to figure out how the food company was linked to the poisonings and why three employees had lost their lives. She hardly noticed when a man, sitting at the front of the room, got to his feet and Myers introduced him.

'I'd like to introduce Dr Sean McCush from the Agri-Food and Biosciences Institute in Belfast. Dr McCush is a food safety analyst, and he is here this morning to explain his findings on the tests carried out on the food samples linked to the cases of poisoning. For the time being, folks, please regard the information as highly confidential. We cannot have anything leaked to the press until we are sure of how to proceed.'

Myers stepped to the side and stood with arms folded as McCush lifted a remote control and brought up a PowerPoint slide on the screen behind him. He was a slight man in his early forties with sandy hair and a freckled face. Casually dressed in a plain blue open-neck shirt and chinos, he spoke, not in a Belfast accent but more akin to a rural area of County Armagh. He began by explaining his work background and why a laboratory in Belfast had come to be testing the samples collected on Merseyside.

'Our work is centred upon the chemical analysis of food at the primary production level, that is, we test samples collected from abattoirs, on-farm, from the sea and food products imported to the UK from outside the EU.'

Tara listened intently as McCush went through the list of samples he had tested in connection with the poisoning cases in Liverpool.

'We use several techniques for testing, based on liquid chromatography-mass spectrometry.'

McCush presented several slides showing pictures of the equipment used for analysis and he went on to explain the scientific principles behind the tests. Despite his attempts to dumb it down for the layperson, for Tara, with little scientific background, it was still quite a difficult concept to grasp. Tara just wanted to know what kind of substance was responsible for causing the deaths of four people.

'Liquid chromatography allows us to separate those substances that may be of interest from those that are not significant, such as proteins, fats, sugars and other materials that would be present naturally in food. Mass spectrometry then identifies chemical compounds based on their molecular mass. We can further elucidate their identity by subjecting a specific compound of interest to further mass spectrometry where the molecule is split into several fragments, the nature of which is largely dependent upon the parent molecule's structure. Overall, we have then produced something akin to a fingerprint for the substance being analysed. The presence of a specific compound in a sample of food may then be confirmed by analysing a standard material, if available, for this compound. The quantity of the substance present in the food can be calculated against the concentration of the standard material.'

Tara found herself staring at several diagrams of chemical structures and graphs, but she longed for McCush to get to the crux of the matter. What the hell was responsible for killing four innocent people and making several others seriously ill?

'From two of the samples of chicken korma, one of beef lasagne and another of lamb hotpot we identified the same toxin to be present. Gastric content removed from each victim also gave high concentrations of this toxin. The substance is called palytoxin or PTX. PTX is a non-proteinaceous marine toxin which is mainly produced by marine soft corals of the genus *Palythoa*. Initially, they were found only in waters surrounding Hawaii and Japan but the occurrence of PTX and its analogues has now been reported worldwide. PTX is also produced by dinoflagellates and found in other species, including fish.'

'Hold on, please,' Wilson said. 'Are you saying that this poison comes from the sea?'

'Yes, that's correct,' replied McCush.

'Then how come the stuff was found in chicken curry and lasagne? None of the victims ate seafood?'

'I'm sorry, but we can only speculate at the moment on how this toxin got into such foods.'

Superintendent Myers interjected.

'Fish and other kinds of seafood are processed by Harbinson at their Birkenhead factory,' he said. 'They also have a separate fish processing facility near Dundee. Dr McCush's team will be testing samples collected from both sites.'

'Are you saying that this toxin occurs naturally?' Tara asked.

'Yes,' said McCush. 'It's just one of many so-called marine bio-toxins. Many of them, in low concentrations, can cause food poisoning when someone eats seafood, particularly shellfish such as oysters, scallops and mussels.

Palytoxin causes intoxication called clupeotoxism which is due to the consumption of clupeoid fish, such as sardines, herrings and anchovies.'

'How much fish would you have to eat to become ill?' Tweedy asked.

'Very difficult to say exactly. We can't even be sure how much toxin was present in the samples we have tested. Usually, we measure the amount present against a standard material of known concentration. In the case of palytoxin, there is no pure standard material available. We have to make estimates based on measurements taken of previous positive materials that have been analysed several times to set a mean value.'

'The symptoms experienced by the victims,' said Murray, 'are they consistent with poisoning by this toxin?'

'Yes, absolutely,' said McCush. 'Symptoms of the PTX-group of toxins include vasoconstriction, haemorrhage, myalgia, ataxia, muscle weakness, ventricular fibrillation, ischemia and death. Rhabdomyolysis syndrome is the most commonly reported complication after a poisoning incident with PTX. This consists of a loss of intracellular contents into the blood plasma, causing injury to the skeletal muscle. The toxin's previous worst cases resulted in renal failure and disseminated cardiovascular coagulation.'

'If the food is cooked or heated,' Wilson asked, 'would that destroy the poison?'

McCush shook his head.

'I'm afraid not. Many of these toxins are not degraded when food is cooked.'

Tara had one last question for the scientist.

'If this toxin did not get into food by accidental contamination, might someone have put it there deliberately?'

McCush gestured with his hands wide apart. Myers gazed towards her but didn't appear troubled by her remark.

'I suppose it could happen, but I would have difficulty believing how someone might have got their hands on so much of the material.'

At that point, Myers thanked Dr McCush for sparing the time to brief his officers.

'For now, while Dr McCush's team continue with testing samples, we are to be stood down from the investigation. It is solely a matter for the environmental authorities and the Food Standards Agency.'

Tara thought differently as she made her way back to her office and her desk. Three people were dead, not from poisoning and yet very much linked to Harbinson Fine Foods. The answers to this mystery lay with that company.

CHAPTER 36

In the afternoon Tara set Murray and Wilson to work on gathering as much CCTV footage as they could find from the stores identified as having sold products from Harbinson Fine Foods, particularly those associated with the samples that tested positive for palytoxin. It was conceivable, she thought, that if the poison had not been added at one of the Harbinson factories then it might have been added to the food within the supermarket stores.

She received a call from DS Lydiate concerning a car found abandoned in Royden Park, near the spot where Jez's body was discovered. Lydiate wondered if Tara would care to look over it. Several items were found inside that might be of interest to her. She left Murray to his work on footage from the CCTV and drove herself to Birkenhead police station.

DS Lydiate showed her to a silver Peugeot SUV. It had been brought into the station yard and was covered by a dust sheet. A full forensic examination had already been conducted.

Tara helped Lydiate to remove the sheet. He handed her the keys.

'Feel free to have a look around. Some items have been removed. I have them in the office. You can see them when you're finished here.'

'Thank you.'

'No problem, ma'am. We can go back inside when you're ready.'

Tara opened the driver's door and climbed inside. At first glance, the car was clean and tidy. There was nothing that stood out which indicated that Jez had even been the owner.

'No prints lifted other than the victim's,' said Lydiate.

Tara switched on the sound system. As she might have expected, the radio was set to Classic FM. She glanced behind into the rear seats but they were clear of anything that might have belonged to Jez.

'Any damage to the outside?' she asked.

Lydiate shook his head.

'Not a scratch. The car is pristine. I checked with a Peugeot dealership; the car is less than a year old, bought from new by Miss Riordan. No finance involved – paid in full.'

At Lydiate's desk, the DS displayed the items that had been removed from the car by the forensics team. Each item had been placed in a separate evidence bag. Tara lifted one from the desk. Inside was a pink slip of paper, a delivery note or an invoice. Mattson's Art was the company name printed in bold at the top of the page. Five items were listed, three of which were various types of paper and the other two were presumably paints or dyes, noted by a reference number followed by the colours, yellow and crimson. In the next bag, there was a till receipt from Tesco for the sum of £27.95 and dated 11 October. Another bag contained a plain white envelope, along with a card from the Silverstein Gallery in Kensington inviting Jez to a forthcoming exhibition of '*Inner City*' painting entitled, '*Decline and Fall.*' The card was dated 19 September. She passed over the latest programme for the Philharmonic Hall and the dates of the winter season for the Royal Liverpool Philharmonic Orchestra, pausing for a second to recall their first outing together, a night which seemed to point towards a future friendship.

Stuck to the outside of a brown envelope was a Post-it with a number written upon it. It appeared to be a mobile number. She took a note of it and would try it later. In the last evidence bag was a note taken from the brown envelope. It seemed to have been written in some haste, the handwriting untidy and sitting askew on the page. It read, 'Jez, please don't do this to me. I thought we meant more to each other. I'll see you tonight, we'll talk.' There was no signature, and the absence of a date was all the more frustrating. If it was recent then she could be looking at the words written by Jez's killer. Or perhaps, it was a final plea from Richard Andrews before he threw himself off the Liver Building. The thought of Andrews brought her to think about the location of Royden Park where Jez's body had been found.

CHAPTER 37

Tara had already decided to pay another visit to Jez's home as she drove away from Birkenhead station. She intended to search for anything that would be a clue to finding who killed her friend. Aside from the mysterious note and a telephone number, there had been little found in Jez's SUV. She also felt an inclination to be close in some way to the woman whom she had quickly grown to like, despite

Jez having been somewhat of an enigma. She still wondered about those two occasions when Jez had kissed her and what she had been intending.

The gates to the house were open, but police incident tape had been strung across the driveway. She left her car on the street, ducked beneath the tape and strode uneasily to the front door. A set of house keys had been retrieved from Jez's Peugeot, and Tara had asked to borrow them from DS Lydiate. The house was in darkness as she turned the key in the lock. She found a switch and lights came on in the hallway and on the landing above. Such a large house for one person, she thought, wondering if Jez had lived a lonely life. In the short time they'd spent together, she never spoke of friends or family except to mention that both her parents were dead. Tara didn't know if Jez had ever been married. Did she have children? Friends in London, perhaps?

She nudged open the first door on her right into the sitting room where she had first spoken with Jez. The room was in disarray. Cushions from the sofa were scattered on the floor, books had been pulled from a shelf next to the fireplace and some of the pictures on the walls had been knocked to crooked angles. Tara assumed that police, in performing a search, had not been concerned about causing upset on the premises. She didn't feel right about leaving the room in such a state. She replaced the cushions and the books and straightened the pictures on the walls. As she did so, she looked out for anything to help her discover what had happened to Jez.

There was nothing obvious but, for the first time, she wondered why a mobile phone had not been found at the crime scene, either in the car or close to Jez's body. During the time she'd spent in her company, she didn't recall Jez ever using a mobile. She made a mental note to have Wilson check with the phone companies for any reference to Jez Riordan. From the sitting room, she wandered into the extensive kitchen at the rear of the house, the result of a major extension to the original building. Several cupboard doors were ajar and a few items of packaged foods had been removed and set upon the workbench beneath. Several drawers lay open, but she found nothing of interest. For a few moments, she leaned her back against the island and tried to picture her friend working in this space. She felt an emptiness inside consummate with the room. It was a peculiar feeling of sadness, regret and foreboding. She heard a noise. It shook her from her thoughts. A thudding sound came from upstairs. There was someone in the house. She stepped to the door that led into the hall and called out.

'Hello? Police, who's there?'

As she placed her hand on the door handle, the door suddenly swung inwards and slammed into her face. She reeled backwards. Her feet stumbled on the tiled floor and she went down. The back of her head thumped against the edge of the island as she crashed to the floor. For a few seconds, all was hazy. She heard footsteps. Running steps. Then the front door slammed. Instinctively, she put a hand to the back of her head. She felt it warm and wet, and when she brought it down it was coloured red with blood. The pain, however, came from her forehead and tentatively she raised her left hand to the wound. There was no blood this time, but already she felt a swelling.

Neither injury stopped her from scrambling to her feet and rushing to the front door. She was way too late. Whoever the intruder was had vanished in the darkness. She ran along the drive to the gates colliding with the stretch of incident tape, tearing it in two. The road outside was quiet. There was no sign of anyone and no sounds of a car starting up and racing away. They had been quick on their feet.

Breathing hard and trembling, she walked slowly back to the house, peering at times into the hedges and shrubs in case the intruder had simply hidden in the garden. Tara closed the front door behind her and leaned against it for a while, trying to steady her breathing. The back of her head was still bleeding. She found some tissues in the kitchen and pressed a wad of them against the cut. She didn't dare look again to see how bad it was. Instead, she continued with her inspection of the house.

The bedroom to the rear of the house in which Jez slept had been ransacked. Duvet and pillows had been dragged to the floor and the contents of an enormous built-in wardrobe had been pulled out and dumped on the carpet. Jewellery was scattered across a dressing table and items of make-up discarded on the bed. Two guitars, one acoustic, one electric, had been pulled from their housing on the wall and, it seemed, had been thrown across the room to lie next to the wardrobe. The intruder had been searching for something. Tara wondered if they had found it, or had she interrupted the search?

Her head throbbed as she circled the room. She should call for help. Already, by coming here alone she had put herself in danger. It was too late now, she thought and moved on to what was supposed to be the master bedroom but which Jez had used as her studio. Again, the room had been ransacked. Paintings had been thrown around, some ripped to pieces. An easel was upturned and tubes of oil paints scattered on the floor. Tara felt such sadness at seeing the work of a talented woman damaged beyond repair. The so-called 'environmental' picture depicting the herd of cows queuing outside a McDonald's had been sliced with a knife. Tara thought again of the relationship between Jez and Maggie Hull, Maggie having had one of these paintings on the wall of her living room. Who had taken against these women? Did they even have the same killer? How in the hell did it relate to the deaths of four innocent people from food poisoning?

As she was about to switch off the light, she noticed what looked to be a painting wrapped in brown paper. It sat on the floor against the wall with several other canvases. She lifted it free from the others and held it up.

There was a small card attached, and the reading of it brought heavy tears to her eyes.

For Tara. Thank you for the memory of a wonderful day. Love, Jez x.

She pulled some of the brown wrapping paper away and examined the picture within. She recognised the scene straightaway. Llanberis and Llyn Padarn. She couldn't bear to take it with her as she left the house in tears and pain, still bleeding.

The remainder of her evening was spent at A & E in the Royal Liverpool Hospital. Whilst there, she sent a text to Kate in the hope that she might be on duty and could pop down to see her. Kate appeared within two minutes, in tears to see that yet again Tara had been in the wars and it was down to the bloody life she was leading.

'I'm all right, Kate, honest. It was partly my fault. I stumbled backwards and hit my head on the bench.'

'Oh, Tara love, when are you ever going to get out of that damned job? Look at your face. I've spoken to the triage nurse, you won't have much longer to wait.'

'I'm sure there are people here who are a lot worse off than me.'

'That's as may be, Tara, but you are going to have to take better care of yourself. What are we going to do with you?'

Tara squeezed her friend's hand. At that point, she was called into a treatment room, and an hour later she was driving home with two staples in the back of her head and a developing black eye. On the drive to Wapping Dock, and as she left her car and walked slowly to her flat, a question occurred to her as to why she still had Royden Park on her mind.

CHAPTER 38

Before Murray got into explaining that he'd so far seen little of interest on the CCTV footage, Tara asked him to drive her out to Caldy on The Wirral. She realised the previous night that Royden Park was not far from a house she had visited quite recently. The day was cold and damp; once crisp brown leaves by the roadsides had become soft mulch from overnight showers.

'If you don't mind me saying, ma'am,' said Murray as he stopped the car, 'you look a bit of a sight to be calling at someone's house.'

'Yes, thank you, Alan. You certainly know how to make a girl feel good about herself.'

Make-up had done little to conceal the purple bruise on her left cheek and across her eye. She could hardly see from the swelling. In a final desperate effort to look more presentable, she had brushed her hair so that it lay across the left side of her face.

'And why are we here, exactly?' Murray asked as he held the car door open for her.

'I need another chat with Andrews' widow. She does have a motive for killing Jez. Put that with the proximity of this place to the crime scene, and I think we have a right to ask questions.'

'What about killing Maggie Hull? How does that fit? Not to mention the poisonings.'

'Too late, you already did. Let's just see what we get from here this morning, shall we?'

When they reached the driveway of the house, two young children, a boy of about eight and a girl of not more than five, were playing on a brightly-coloured adventure playground toward the rear of the house. Nicole Andrews must have spotted them as they walked from the car because she emerged rather speedily from the back of the house and called to her children. She did not acknowledge her visitors until the boy and girl were by her side. The electric gates lay open and Tara and Murray strolled into the drive.

'Mrs Andrews,' said Tara, 'you may not remember me, I'm Detective Inspector Tara Grogan, and this is my colleague, Detective Sergeant Murray.'

Andrews gave a cursory nod, glanced at their warrant cards but said nothing.

'I wonder if you would mind answering a few more questions.'

'About what?'

Tara looked towards the children in the hope of expressing tactfully that they should not be present. Nicole Andrews took the hint.

'Off you go, children, Mummy needs to speak with these nice people.' Both children returned to the slide and climbing frame. 'You'd better come in, I suppose,' she said coolly. 'I have to organise lunch for the children. It's half-term and we're going swimming this afternoon.'

Tara hadn't noticed much change in the woman from their first meeting. Her clothes were dark, jeans and a woollen sweater, her manner somewhat distant, even stand-offish. Perhaps it was the ordeal of police investigations and the recent traumatic events in her life, but Tara wondered why she seemed to lack warmth or charm.

They followed her inside to a spacious kitchen which opened onto a family room where a television was playing a relocation-in-the-sun programme. She invited them to sit at the breakfast bar then, and using the remote, muted the sound on the television.

'Can I get you anything, coffee or tea?' she asked from the far side of the kitchen.

'Coffee would be great,' Murray replied.

Tara glared at him sternly although she, too, did not refuse the offer.

'I assume, Mrs Andrews,' Tara began, 'that you have heard about the death of Miss Jez Riordan?'

The woman ceased all movement and for a moment glared icily at her visitors. Tara knew fine well that she was striking a nerve, but she needed to witness her reactions.

'Her body was found in Royden Park on Wednesday. We believe that she had been missing since the previous Thursday.'

Nicole Andrews' face was ashen. She had a tight grip on the kettle that she'd just filled with water, but she stood motionless, staring vacantly at Tara.

'You did know of Miss Riordan's death?'

'Yes, my father told me,' she replied at last. 'I wish that I could say I was sorry, but at the moment I don't feel anything.' Her eyes filled with tears but she busied them away, placing the kettle on its stand and fetching three mugs from a cupboard.

'I was wondering, perhaps, if she had paid you a visit recently, last Wednesday or Thursday, for instance?'

'Certainly not. She would hardly have received a warm welcome.'

'And you had no arrangements to meet with her elsewhere?'

'Again, Inspector, I had no desire to ever set eyes on the woman.'

'Her car was found close to her body,' said Murray. 'Royden Park is not far from here. You didn't notice her in the area?'

'I'm afraid not.'

'Did you ever meet her?' asked Tara, suddenly struck by the thought that Nicole may never have set eyes on the woman she held responsible for destroying her marriage and, ultimately, her husband's life.

'Yes. Once,' she replied. 'She came here to tell me that she and Richard were having an affair. Apparently, he hadn't the nerve to tell me himself.'

'And when did this visit take place?'

'About eight weeks before Richard finally left us.' Again, she returned to the task of preparing the refreshments, placing a spoonful of coffee into each mug, fetching some biscuits from a tin on the bench, using the silence to recover some composure.

'Do you mind if I ask you some questions about your husband, Mrs Andrews?'

The woman shook her head in submission and tried ever harder to speed the coffee preparation along.

'What was the relationship like between your husband and Maggie Hull?'

'Maggie? She was like a big sister to him. She was a big sister to all of us, Richard, Toby Ewing, me and every other fresh face that ventured into the office.'

'So, you work for your father also?'

'Used to, B.C.' She set two mugs of coffee and a plate of Penguins and Kit Kats on the breakfast bar. 'Before Children,' she added with a hint of a smile, the first Tara had noticed. 'I worked in the office during summer holidays from school and university. Richard came to work there the year I finished A-Levels. We married the week after I graduated from York. Maggie used to keep all of us in order. Richard and Toby were a couple of jokers. They used to keep her going all the time. But she never got angry. Always threatened to tell Dad about their antics, but she never did. They used to invent clients, make them sound really important and very rich. Maggie had to spend half her time screening people whenever they called just in case it was a prank. If Dad had ever found out he would have hit the roof; sacked the pair of them probably. She was a good person, Inspector, and a good friend to me.'

'Had you seen much of her recently?'

'Not really. She came to see me once, a few days after Richard left us. As always, she was well aware of what had been going on. She was certainly disappointed in Richard and very angry with Jez. And she wasn't afraid to tell them so.'

'Did she have any specific reason for coming to see you?'

Nicole shook her head and took a sip of coffee.

'I don't think so. She was just concerned for me and the children.'

'Was that the last time you saw her?' Murray asked, joining in between mouthfuls of chocolate biscuit.

'Yes, I believe so.'

'I'm sorry for bringing this up again, Mrs Andrews,' Tara began in a more compassionate tone. 'I was wondering about a letter that Richard had begun to write on the day he died. It was intended for Toby Ewing. Can you think of any reason why he would have something to say particularly to Mr Ewing?'

'No, I can't,' she replied rather curtly.

'As far as you know, were Richard and Toby on good terms at that time?'

'Yes, as far as I know. They were best friends, Inspector. They played golf, went sailing; both our families were close. Heather, Toby's wife, and I are good friends. We used to go on holiday together, shopping trips, girls' nights out, that sort of thing.'

'Seems as though the arrival of Jez Riordan at your father's company upset a rather blissful lifestyle for you and Richard.'

Nicole Andrews glared at Tara with a degree of incredulity. The remark was at best a statement of the obvious, at worst, sarcastic. Either way, it failed to solicit a reply. Tara, however, had intended it, not as a question but more a prelude to her final comment.

'I have to say that I was curious as to why your father kept Jez on as his secretary in the company after Richard's death.'

'You're assuming that Richard was sacked over his affair with Jez.'

'Isn't that the case?'

'You should address that question to my father, Inspector. Now, if you don't mind, I will have to get on with preparing lunch for the children.'

'Thanks for your time, Mrs Andrews.'

'And the coffee,' added Murray.

They rose to leave and had reached the door when Tara remembered something.

'One more thing,' she said, pulling her mobile from her pocket. She had taken some photographs of the evidence removed from Jez's car. She opened up the phone and selected the first picture and showed it to Nicole. 'Do you recognise the phone number, by any chance?'

Andrews inspected the image carefully before handing it back.

'No, I'm afraid not.'

Tara wasn't finished. She swept her finger across the screen to reveal another image. 'Do you recognise this handwriting?'

Nicole's face reddened when she looked at the photo of the handwritten note. Suddenly the back door swung open, and the little girl came charging in.

'Mummy, Simon won't push me on the swing,' she cried.

'Chloe, Mummy is busy.' The child stopped in her tracks and clung to her mother. 'Go and tell Simon that it's time to come in now.'

Off she ran, calling to her brother across the lawn.

'So, the writing's not familiar to you?'

'Sorry. I've never seen it before.'

'Thanks again, Mrs Andrews.'

Murray was prepared for Tara's habitual question as they walked back to the car.

'Well, Alan, what do you think?'

'She's not the friendliest of people, although she's had a hard time of it lately, I suppose.'

'Certainly keeps her distance. I was getting a bit fed up having to speak across that enormous kitchen. The only time she came close was to serve the damn coffee.'

They stopped when they reached the car. Tara turned around and gazed at the house they'd just left.

'A shrewd cookie that Mrs Andrews,' she said. 'She got very prickly when I asked her about Jez staying on as Harbinson's secretary after Richard Andrews died.'

'Understandable.'

'And she lied about the handwriting.' She climbed into the car.

'Do you think she had anything to do with Jez's death?' Murray asked, starting up the engine.

'Nicole Andrews certainly has a strong motive for killing Jez. Firstly, her marriage was destroyed and then she had to stand by and watch as her father keeps his secretary in her job. Even a saint would be tempted to wring the woman's neck. But Jez knew who she was meeting on the day she disappeared. She was dressed for a night out or a date. With whom, I don't know. I don't believe she would have dressed that way if she was intending to meet Nicole Andrews. Besides all that, Alan, Nicole Andrews has no apparent motive for killing Maggie Hull, except perhaps to deflect the attention from the killing of Jez Riordan.'

'Assuming, of course, that Jez and Maggie were murdered by the same person?'

'Had to be,' said Tara.

'Then it has to be someone else in that food company?'

'Or maybe just someone who was acquainted with both women.'

CHAPTER 39

Tara had spent the previous afternoon going through the report on the post-mortem for Jez Riordan. It did not make for pleasant reading. The main points confirmed much of what had been said by the medical examiner at the crime scene. Jez's body had been dumped in the spot where it was discovered. She had probably been lying there for at least five days, and it was likely that she had been run over by a vehicle of some description. The pathologist believed also that in addition to an initial collision it was likely that the vehicle had run over the body while it lay on the ground. The driver or other persons unknown had then dragged or carried Jez's body to the place where it was discovered. The fact that Jez's car was found nearby suggested that the killing had taken place within Royden Park.

For Tara, the question remained – why had Jez been there in the first place? She was a long way from home. Who was she planning to meet? She had been well dressed as if for an evening out or possibly for a date. Had Jez even realised that her life was in danger?

Tara stood in front of the full-length mirror in her bedroom. She wanted to look her best but couldn't think why. Jez was dead. It was her funeral. Who was going to care about how she was dressed? She wore her best black skirt, jacket and silk blouse. Her tights were fine denier black and her shoes were patent black with three-inch heels. She would have preferred to pin up her hair, but the bruise on her face was still unseemly. She brushed it forward to conceal the worst.

Today was about paying her respects, but it was also about observation. She wanted to see who turned up at the church to mourn Jez's passing. She wanted to look into the faces and eyes of those who had worked with Jez and Maggie Hull. She wanted to find answers.

First thing on Monday morning she had telephoned the mortuary to check if Jez's body had been released following all post-mortem examinations. She was informed by the female receptionist that a firm of undertakers from Woolton, Headie and Sons, had collected the remains on the previous Friday. A woman with a tranquil voice answered Tara's call at the funeral home.

'Good morning, Headie and Sons. My name is Maureen, how may I help you?'

'Good morning, Maureen,' Tara replied, attempting to match her pleasant yet appropriately sedate tone. 'This is Detective Inspector Tara Grogan, Merseyside Police, I wonder if you can help me? I believe that you are in charge of the arrangements for a friend of mine, a Miss Jez Riordan?'

'Yes, we are, Inspector. I am very sorry for your loss. She was quite a young woman, I believe?'

'Yes, she was,' Tara agreed, although she had not learned Jez's true age of forty-one until after she was dead. 'I would like to assist with the funeral expenses. I know that she had no close relatives, and I assume that her former colleagues are taking care of the arrangements?'

'Em, no, I don't think so,' said Maureen, sounding puzzled. 'All arrangements concerning the funeral of Miss Riordan are being taken care of by a Miss Anne Gibson.'

'Oh, I see.'

'I believe she is an aunt of the deceased.'

'Oh right,' Tara said surprised. 'I didn't realise.'

'The funeral is on Wednesday, two-thirty at the Parish Church, here in Woolton.'

'Thank you, Maureen. You've been very helpful.' She put the phone down.

Tara tried to shake off that particular piece of hitherto unknown and startling information by launching into a third call of the morning. She dialled carefully, checking each digit from the photo on her mobile. The phone rang twice before she heard a loud, male voice.

'Hello?'

'Ah, hello. Who am I speaking to?' She employed a jovial manner for the second time.

'Who is this?' A gruff voice, even with such few words, antagonistic.

'This is Detective Inspector Grogan, Merseyside Police–' There ended the conversation. Tara looked gleefully down the receiver as if to delight in making someone's day.

She noticed Wilson beavering away at his desk.

'John? If you're not too busy this morning, I'd like you to do a few things for me.'

'No problem, ma'am,' replied the young detective. He joined Tara at her desk.

'First of all, I want you to run a check on this mobile number.' She handed over her mobile for him to make a note of the number from the image on the screen. 'Secondly, find out from forensics if they have any more information on where the spanner came from that was used to clobber Maggie Hull. Also, I want you to make a list of the cars belonging to the staff at Harbinson Fine Foods. Just the head office people for now. Oh, and while you're there, try and rustle up a sample of the handwriting for each of the directors. Include Richard Andrews' writing from his suicide note in that.'

'Is that everything?'

'That's all for now, John. If you happen to set eyes on that Murray bloke, tell him I'm off to a funeral this afternoon. He's late.'

* * *

The Parish Church in Woolton was a brownstone building surrounded by a low wall and with a lych gate. A parish graveyard lay to the rear of the building. She realised as she parked her car close to the graveyard that Jez's home was not far away. She wondered, too, about Miss Anne Gibson. The thought of her existence intrigued her, if only because she wondered if she might resemble her niece in any way. Tara felt a certain twinge of excitement at the idea of meeting her. Hopefully, Anne Gibson would be able to provide her with a background to her niece and just maybe there would be something in it that would lead to the apprehension of her murderer.

Tara was early, it being only ten past two, but several cars were already parked, and the hearse sat outside the church door.

Two men wearing dark overcoats were standing by the arched doorway as Tara approached. They nodded politely, stepping back for her to enter. Once inside, the sound of her footsteps echoed on the stone floor as she moved along the aisle, one or two heads turning or looking up to put a face to the steps. She chose an empty pew halfway along on the left. Tara's eyes were diverted immediately to the coffin, resting upon trestles directly below the sanctuary. A single spray of white lilies sat on top, with a little rectangular card just visible in the centre. Tara exhaled deeply then dropped her head. It wasn't a prayer, certainly not to any god, but she filtered a few tender and sad thoughts through her mind, pondering life, any life, and where it takes us.

When she had raised her head once more, she gazed at the ten or so faces dotted around the church. Only two were familiar, Toby Ewing and Skip McIntyre, seated together, a couple of pews in front of her. Both heads were bowed slightly. Three women sat in the pew directly opposite. Tara assumed they were Harbinson's head office staff but could not recall having met any of the women during her visits to the Liver Building.

A tall woman, with short reddish-brown hair, wearing a knee-length, black overcoat sat down in a pew at the front and within seconds was kneeling forward in prayer. A door at the front opened and the vicar of the Parish made her entrance. Immediately, she took to the pulpit and a service of thanksgiving for the life of Jessica Riordan began.

As the coffin was wheeled from the church a song played over the sound system. The vicar announced it as being Jessica's favourite song, *The Daring Night*. Tara listened to the words as she and the other mourners filed from the church.

In a corner of the churchyard, furthest from the road, Jez Riordan was laid to rest in a grave already occupied by her mother and father. The surname on the headstone, however, was Gibson; Paul having died on 24 March 1994, aged forty-eight. His wife, Eleanor, died on 7 October 1980, aged thirty-two years. Seeing a surname other than Riordan set Tara thinking again on the mystery surrounding her friend.

CHAPTER 40

McIntyre looked on impassively as the coffin was lowered into the grave. Toby Ewing appeared more upset, his face pale and drawn. If she had been standing close to him, Tara thought, she would have felt the man trembling. The three women from Harbinson's head office looked saddened and dabbed at their eyes with tissues. Miss Anne Gibson stood close to the Reverend Upritchard as she said a final prayer and committed the body to the family grave. Judging by the number of people assembled, Anne Gibson might well have been the last of that family circle and at that moment, perhaps for only a fleeting moment, she pondered her demise and stole a preview of her future resting place.

When the vicar had finished, Anne Gibson, tears in her eyes, tossed a small bunch of pink roses into the grave. Reverend Upritchard shook her hand, offered comforting words and they embraced briefly. Several others, two men and three elderly women, moved forward to offer their sympathies to Anne Gibson. Most of them appeared to be her friends rather than Jez's although the staff from Harbinson's took their turn in shaking the woman's hand as they filed past.

'I see your chairman couldn't make it,' said Tara to Skip McIntyre as he attempted to make his way around the gravestones towards Anne Gibson.

'Prior engagement,' he replied without conviction, then proceeded to greet the woman.

They embraced warmly and Anne Gibson seemed to listen intently as McIntyre spoke. Tara got the impression that they were already well acquainted. It did not seem like the first conversation between them. Tara couldn't help pondering the connection. She watched Toby Ewing who had followed behind McIntyre. His manner was nervy, although he didn't look at all different from Tara's first encounter with him, the day after Maggie Hull was murdered. Unlike McIntyre, Ewing did not appear as well acquainted with Anne Gibson, but still, Tara got the feeling that they had at least met before. The two executives nodded and smiled weakly as they passed by Tara on their way out of the churchyard. The Reverend Upritchard smiled, too, and came to shake Tara by the hand.

'Very sad occasion,' the vicar said, more softly than she'd spoken in the church where her voice, even for a funeral service, had bellowed. 'I'm sure that Anne very much appreciates your support this afternoon. Were you a friend of Jessica's?'

'In a way, Reverend,' Tara stumbled, unsure of whether to reveal that she was a police officer. 'Although I hadn't known her for long. My name is Detective Inspector Tara Grogan, Merseyside Police.'

The vicar's face flushed and, instinctively, she shook Tara's hand for a second time.

'I suppose that your interest here is professional, Inspector? Jessica's death was tragic in itself without the knowledge that it was at the hands of another.'

How well suited was this woman for the church, thought Tara. The briefest mention of police and she comes over all thunderstruck.

'Reverend, would you mind introducing me to Miss Gibson?' she asked, having decided it best not to prolong the conversation with the well-meaning but rather interminable vicar.

'Yes, yes, of course, Inspector.'

Anne Gibson, however, had overheard the mention of Tara's title, her lips already tightening with concern.

'Anne, this is Detective Inspector Grogan from Merseyside Police.'

'Hello, Miss Gibson, I'm very sorry about Jez.'

The woman nodded acknowledgement, although she did not appear too impressed by the referral to her niece as Jez. She refrained from answering, preferring instead to wait for Tara to state her business. She was an attractive woman, although Tara was not immediately struck by any resemblance to Jez. She had smooth skin except for developing crow's feet and yes, her eyes were powder blue, just like her niece's. Tara's overriding impression was that this woman could, at some time in her past, have been every bit as elegant and striking as her niece, and yet she appeared to be someone who for some time had not taken the trouble to impress.

'I was wondering if you could tell me a little about your niece.'

'What would you like to know, Inspector?'

There was a gentle air in her voice, but Tara had rather expected an accent similar to Jez's. Instead, she spoke in the manner of a woman born and bred on the banks of the Mersey, a true Scouser.

'Jez died in mysterious and terrible circumstances, Miss Gibson. I need to find out more about her background, the people she knew, her friends, family, anything that might shed light on why she was killed.'

'Oh, I see,' she said quite shocked. 'If you fancy a cuppa, my place is just around the corner.'

'A cup of tea would be great.'

'Follow me then, I have plenty to tell you about our Jessica.'

CHAPTER 41

It was as Anne Gibson had said, just around the corner on Allerton Road. She led Tara inside a quaint terraced cottage in a row of three, nowadays, squeezed between a solicitor's office and an estate agent's.

The front door opened directly into a lounge where a narrow staircase sat to the left. It was a cosy-looking room, a mix of modern and dated furniture, a well-worn sofa and TV chair, an antique occasional table and a large-screen television. Within the reveals to each side of the chimney breast were a collection of framed photographs of various sizes. Some were in colour, others in black and white. To one corner and below the pictures were shelves crammed untidily with books, records, CDs and DVDs.

'Please make yourself comfortable, Inspector. I'll put the kettle on.'

Anne Gibson slid open a door to reveal a bright galley kitchen, while Tara remained standing looking around at the pictures and photographs on the walls. There were a pair of oil-painted landscapes of places she did not recognise, although she dared to assume that they had been painted by Jez. On the wall above the sofa was a collection of black and white photographs, depicting groups of young people. She did not immediately recognise anyone but wondered perhaps if a younger Anne Gibson was featured. The fashions displayed looked as though they came from way back, the sixties maybe, but she wasn't sure.

Within a couple of minutes, Anne, still wearing her overcoat, entered the lounge carrying a tray with two cups of coffee, a jug of milk, sugar bowl and a plate of shortbread. She set the tray on the occasional table then pulled off her coat.

'Help yourself to some shortbread,' she said, handing Tara a china cup.

'Thank you, Miss Gibson.' Tara was feeling hungry and lifted one of the biscuits from the plate.

'You can call me Anne, love, no need for formalities here.'

She took her coffee and sat down in the chair opposite Tara who had placed herself in the middle of the sofa.

'And I'm Tara,' she reciprocated.

'So, what would you like to know about our Jessica?'

'As much as you can tell me, Anne. I'm investigating her murder, but I was also friends with Jez... with Jessica for a short time.'

'I see. Well, there's not much I can tell you about her recent past. We haven't been that close since she came home to Liverpool. If you ask me, I think she had changed greatly in the time she was away. I suppose we all do as we grow older.'

'Was there anyone close to her, a boyfriend, or had she been married?'

Anne shook her head. 'Not that I know of, although she might well have been at some point while she was living in London. Relationships were not something she ever spoke about to me.'

Tara felt she had to know the reason for the difference in surnames between Jez and her parents.

'Can you tell me why Jessica used the surname of Riordan, since her parents were Gibson, like you?'

'That was a puzzle to me too, the reason for the change. Riordan was her mother's maiden name, but Jessica only started using it after she came home to Liverpool. She may have used it while she was in London, I suppose, in connection with her painting. Maybe she thought it suited her as an artist. She never discussed it with me, but I would guess that was the reason behind it.'

Tara couldn't help herself from reaching for another piece of shortbread. She was starving.

'I noticed from the gravestone that her parents died at an early age.'

'Eleanor died when Jessica was only three.'

'What happened?'

'Overdose of drink and drugs. She had a problem for years. Paul, my only brother, drank himself to death. Two wasted lives, Tara, and Jessica was left on her own when she was just seventeen. She came here to live with me for a while until she went off to university in London. The house she had lived in, here in Woolton, belonged to Paul. She inherited the place, though I never thought she would ever move back in.'

Anne shook her head, staring into space or the depths of family memories.

'Jessica spent her entire childhood looking after her dad. He was seldom ever sober. Not since the end of The Moondreams.'

'The Moondreams?' Tara asked.

Anne Gibson's eyes seemed to ignite at the sound of the words.

'You've not heard of The Moondreams?' Anne smiled. 'No, I don't suppose you would. You're much too young.'

She rose from the chair and went to the bookshelves. After a few moments of searching, she pulled out what looked like a scrapbook. The cover was a jazzy array of colour with 'Moondreams' written in black felt pen across the top. She sat down next to Tara on the sofa and opened the book. The first page had a single black and white photograph stuck with Sellotape to the manila page.

Tara stared at the image of two young men with mop-top haircuts and smart suits. She could have been looking at two of The Beatles.

'That's our Paul on the left with the fag in his mouth and the other lad is Roddy Craig,' said Anne. 'They were best mates those two, a right pair of jokers.' Anne turned the page to reveal several more photographs and cuttings from newspapers. 'That's me,' she said with a slight laugh. Tara gazed at a very beautiful girl, a teenager, huddled with three other smiling girls all wearing the same school uniform. 'Those were the days.'

Tara attempted to read some of the newspaper cuttings, but Anne quickly turned to another page in the scrapbook. Next, there was a picture of Anne, her brother and two other young men.

'That's Paul and me with two of The Hollies when they used to play The Cavern. That's Alan Clarke and the other one is Graham Nash.'

On the next page was a small poster, glued in place. It advertised a show featuring The Merseybeats, Dave Dee, Dozy, Beaky, Mick and Tich, The Mojos and, at the bottom of the line-up, The Moondreams. They were all on the bill for The Cavern Club in Mathew Street, made famous because The Beatles had played there so many times.

'I used to sneak in on my lunch break to see all the different bands. I was a bit young when The Beatles played there although I saw them a couple of times. But when they became famous it was like we had lost them from Liverpool. We girls soon moved on to other groups. Paul and Roddy's group, The Moondreams, were headed for the big time, too.'

Anne turned yet another page of the scrapbook to reveal several cuttings all displaying a similar message: 'Roddy Craig drowns in the Mersey.'

'What happened?' Tara asked.

Anne Gibson shook her head and her eyes immediately filled with tears. She reached over the side of the sofa and pulled several tissues from a box, using them to blow her nose. Tara looked on; she could see that Anne had been a very pretty girl and still was an attractive woman, now in her early seventies.

'Roddy and I were an item for a while, for a couple of months anyway. He was lovely, so full of life. He had everything, good looks, a sense of humour and – boy – could he sing.'

Anne jumped up from the sofa and went to the shelf that held her record collection. She had no difficulty extracting the disc she wanted, and within a few seconds it was on her turntable and she was adjusting the volume. Soon, a strong yet smooth voice filled the room. For Tara, it could have been any song from the sixties, but she realised that the voice of the singer was indeed special.

'That's Roddy,' said Anne. 'It was his voice you heard at the end of the funeral, singing *The Daring Night*.'

They sat in silence for a while listening to the record until the second track began, the heavier-sounding music quite different from the opening song.

'The Cavern was like heaven and hell rolled into one,' Anne continued. 'It had the best music, the best groups you could hear anywhere, but it was the most cramped space and had the worst toilets on the planet. You could hardly move in the place when a good band was playing, packed shoulder to shoulder with the condensation dripping like rain from the brick ceiling. But we wouldn't have swapped it for anything. It was ours; it belonged to Liverpool and everyone who played there knew that, too.'

Tara read the newspaper clippings on the death of Roddy Craig as Anne told of her experiences back when she was a teenager. From what she read, there did not seem to be any definitive story on how the singer had come to drown in the Mersey.

'The Moondreams were going to be as big as The Beatles,' said Anne. 'Everybody who went to The Cavern knew it. Paul and Roddy were special; they had star written all over them, Roddy singing and Paul on guitar and harmonising with Roddy. The others in the group were all right too, but they were just along for the ride. Paul and Roddy were the geniuses. By the time Roddy died, they had progressed from playing The Cavern and Liverpool. They had moved to London and recorded their first album. Again, just like The Beatles, at Abbey Road Studios. I suppose in a way, like The Beatles, by that stage we had already lost them to the big wide world. I went down to visit Paul a couple of times in London. All the lads were living the high life, going to parties, beautiful women baying for them, and then there was the drink and the drugs. I don't think I ever saw Roddy sober after he left Liverpool. Most of the time he was stoned. Paul wasn't much better, but by then he had met Eleanor Riordan and for a while, she held him in check. Eleanor was gorgeous, a fashion model, she moved in the same circles as Marianne Faithful, Jean Shrimpton, and Twiggy. I used to see those types at every party we went to. Of course, I was completely spellbound by it all. It was a world away from Liverpool. Paul and Roddy fitted right in. I was so proud of them both and a little sad that I was no longer Roddy's girl.'

Anne paused as another track on the album began. It was *The Daring Night*, and now Tara was hearing it for the second time that day.

'This was Jessica's favourite. She always said it summed up her parent's life: full of life and hope yet destined to fail.'

'What happened the night Roddy died?'

Anne looked at Tara and shrugged.

'No one seems to know,' she said. 'At least no one in the group ever talked about it, including Paul.' Anne rose from the sofa and stopped the LP on the player. 'The Moondreams had just released this LP, and they were about to go off around the world to promote it. Paul had the idea that first, they should play The Cavern one last time to thank the fans who had been with them from the start. I was there watching with Eleanor. That night The Moondreams were fabulous. The entire audience just stood there in awe at their playing. When the show finished we all nipped across to The Grapes for a pint before closing time. The boys were all high, whether it was just the excitement of the night or whether they were all popping pills, I had no idea, but they wanted to move on to somewhere else. I went home with my girlfriends. I never heard anything until Monday morning. My friend phoned me at work to tell me that she'd heard that Roddy had been pulled out of the river on Sunday morning. When I checked the morning paper, the headline said that Roddy had drowned.'

'Roddy's death was also the end for The Moondreams,' Anne continued. 'Although Paul never spoke of it to me, there was a rift between him and the other lads in the group. Besides, without Roddy, they were never going to have the success they'd dreamed of. He was one half of the songwriting talent. Paul tried on his own for several years, but by then he had a serious problem with his drinking. He and Eleanor had moved to the house in Woolton, the house where Jessica was raised. But Eleanor, having given up her modelling career for Paul, had developed a drug habit. Even when Jessica was born, Eleanor was already on a downward spiral. She died of a heroin overdose when Jessica was three. Paul was devastated, but it just made his drinking worse. By this time, he had given up on his musical career and lived off his share of the royalties for *The Food of Love* LP which continued to sell all over the world.'

'Who looked after Jessica?'

'I did, although Paul was adamant that she should continue to live with him. So I went round there every day, made sure that Jessica was fed and dressed, got her off to school, made her tea and helped her with homework. By the time she was a teenager, Jessica was taking care of herself and her father. Paul passed away when she was seventeen. She came to live with me for a year before she went off to university. When she eventually came back home, three years ago, she decided to open up her old house again and she moved in. But I haven't seen much of her these last three years.'

Tara decided she had taken enough of Anne Gibson's time, but she asked one final question.

'Did she ever mention why she moved back to Liverpool?'

'Not to me. She came back here all of a sudden, and as far as I know, settled into her new job at Harbinson's. She never told me why she left London.'

'At the church, you seemed to be well acquainted with Mr McIntyre?'

'Skip? Another of my beaus from the sixties. He was in The Moondreams with Paul and Roddy. He played the organ.'

Anne Gibson reacted to the expression of surprise on Tara's face.

'Oh, I should have said. Eddie Harbinson, Skip McIntyre and Jimmy Ewing were the other lads in The Moondreams. Jimmy played drums and Eddie, the bass guitar. When they broke up Eddie went back to work in his father's food business. Jimmy and Skip had worked there too before they were in the band, and they all ended up back where they started. Eddie has made a big success out of the company.'

Tara stood up, suddenly eager to leave.

'It was a pleasure to meet you, Anne. Thank you for sharing your story with me.'

'I hope it's of some help to you in finding who killed Jessica, but somehow I don't think her past life has anything to do with it. Some madman, off his head on booze, ran her over and couldn't face up to it. That's what I think.'

Anne stood by her front door as Tara stepped outside.

'One thing troubles me though,' said Anne. 'I can't think why Jessica ever took a job with Harbinson's. She was better qualified than to be a secretary.'

'You mean with her degree in art and her painting?'

'No, no. Painting was never more than a hobby for Jessica. She didn't study art at university. She studied chemistry.'

CHAPTER 42

Tara decided to call at the station on her way home. She thought that if Murray was still there she could run her fresh theory past him. If she was right, then they might be close to explaining why four people had been fatally poisoned with a strange toxin. Her mind swirled with theories. She was trying hard to reconcile the impression she held of Edward Harbinson, company CEO, with the idea of him as a pop star of the 1960s.

Wilson was first across to her desk as she sat down.

'Ma'am, the telephone number that you asked me to trace? It's a mobile phone registered to a Thomas Gracey.'

Tara smiled. It was exactly what she had been expecting to hear.

'Okay, Alan. Arrange for Mr Gracey to come in for a chat in the morning.'

Murray was nowhere to be seen, so she made for home.

* * *

She fetched a microwave dinner from the freezer, gave it the requisite time in the oven and sat down to eat in front of her laptop. The Thai green curry was much too hot and she burnt her tongue with the first mouthful. She set her plate to the side and opened up Google. Among several references to the Norman Petty song *Moondreams*, and to Buddy Holly, there was plenty of information on the short-lived Liverpool band. Much of it referred to the death of lead singer Roddy Craig in 1968, the consensus being that he had drowned in the Mersey after a night of partying in Liverpool's city centre.

There were downloads available for the album *The Food of Love* including several links to Amazon and Spotify. She clicked on a link to images of the band and was presented with a large array of photos, mostly black and white with a few pictures in colour dotted around the page. Roddy Craig was no doubt a handsome young man, dark hair, fire in his eyes and devilment in his smile, Tara thought. Paul Gibson, too, had an attractive face, a little more serious in expression and more deliberate in his pose. Eddie Harbinson bore hardly any resemblance to the man she had already met as CEO of a large food company. His face was full of laughter; he appeared a carefree young man. Conversely, Skip McIntyre looked no different from the man she last saw at Jez's funeral: a thin face, much younger, of course, and long hair hanging in all directions. Jimmy Ewing, the drummer in the band and father of Toby, had an inconspicuous face, a man easily forgotten, easily missed in a crowd. He sported the fashion of the period but didn't have the looks to go with the clothing.

She found pictures also of various band members in the company of other famous people. Roddy standing with John and Yoko Lennon, Skip McIntyre enjoying champagne in the company of Princess Margaret, and Eleanor Riordan in the arms of Jimi Hendrix. They were heady times, she thought, and yet life was to change dramatically and tragically for the young men in The Moondreams. She clicked on a link to YouTube and sat back to listen to a rare live recording of the band performing for BBC Radio. As the music played she attempted another mouthful of chicken curry before going to her kitchen and tipping the entire meal into the bin. She removed a half-full bottle of chardonnay from her fridge and finally slumped on to her sofa with a full glass as the song *The Daring Night* played in her head for the third time in a day.

CHAPTER 43

'Morning, Mr Gracey,' Tara said jovially as she joined the thickset Belfast man at the table. Murray had come along to observe the proceedings. 'I'll try not to detain you for too long. We're very busy at the moment, and I'm sure there are things that you could be doing also.'

It was as though Tara had not uttered a single word. Gracey sat motionless, staring straight ahead at the blank wall. Tara knew the stance well, she'd seen it a hundred times before. It came with the breed. These guys had perfected the technique in the days when the right to silence for a terrorist suspect in Northern Ireland was sacrosanct. If that was the way the game was to be played, then she would proceed until she got the desired reaction.

'OK, Tommy,' she began. 'As you know, this interview is being recorded and one of the advantages of this is that I only have to ask the question once and you only have to answer once. That way we save time all around because we don't have to repeat ourselves.'

Still no movement from across the table.

'Right then,' Tara continued, maintaining her calm and friendly manner. 'Can you tell me where you were on the evening of Monday, 21 October?'

There was no reply, no reaction at all.

'Can you account for your whereabouts on Wednesday, 23 October?'

Gracey glared resolutely at the wall.

'OK, maybe you can remember what you were doing on Thursday, 24 October?' Tara did not expect an answer. She removed the slip of paper from a buff-coloured file on the desk. 'Is this the number of your mobile telephone, Mr Gracey?'

No attempt was made to even look at the note.

'For this recording, the telephone number on the note reads; 02477 768873.' She paused for a few seconds. 'I know this is the number of your mobile telephone, Mr Gracey. I can show you the details of your registration if you wish? A written note of this number was found inside a car belonging to a Miss Jez Riordan. Would you like to comment on that?'

None of Tara's questions had so far posed any threat or exerted any real pressure on Tommy Gracey. A continued silence could not be made any easier.

'Miss Riordan is dead,' she continued. 'Her body was found in Royden Park on Wednesday, 30 October.' Tara thought for a second that she detected a slight twitch on the man's face. 'Would you care to comment on that? Perhaps you would like to suggest a reason why Miss Riordan would have a note of your telephone number?'

Tara paused again to pour herself some water from the jug on the table. She took a welcome drink and a few long, calming breaths of air, while she gathered her thoughts for another round of questions. If these did not achieve a response then she would be struggling. She would then have to decide on whether or not she could detain Tommy Gracey for a longer period without placing charges.

'Let's change the subject for a while, Mr Gracey. You admitted to me recently that you are engaged in moneylending, isn't that correct? You lend money, with a very high rate of interest, to helpless people and you get very annoyed with clients when they have trouble paying it back? Did you lend money to a Miss Maggie Hull on one occasion? Or was it two or three occasions? She had difficulty paying you back, didn't she? You sent someone round to her home to threaten her, to frighten her into paying it all back, isn't that so, Tommy? And she did, every last penny. A friend of hers helped her out, but it wasn't long before Maggie was up to her eyes in debt again and she came back to you. Except, on this occasion, there was no friend to pay you back.'

Tara paused again just in case Gracey was about to open his mouth. But Tara didn't want him to speak, not yet. In a few seconds, yes, but not right now. Instead, she sat back and watched the sweat begin to seep from Gracey's shaven head.

'So what happened next, eh, Tommy? Well, here's the way I see it. Firstly, Maggie tells you that she can't pay up, so you send a couple of your boys round to her house. Threaten her, rough her up a little, leave a bruise or two and she'll be so frightened that she'll do anything to pay you back the money. But one of your boys goes a bit too far and poor Maggie gets thumped on the head. Now you have no money and you have no client. How does that sound, Tommy? Accurate is it?'

Tara was warming to her task, her voice rising, her tone gathering a hefty punch.

'Of course, the one person who knows of the mess that Maggie got herself into also knows about you because she's already paid you off once. She has your phone number. Jez Riordan knows exactly who you are and she can tell us what's happened, isn't that right, Tommy?'

Gracey shifted in his chair, pulling his gammy leg in close, his gaze to the far wall broken at last.

'So, you decide that it's wise that Miss Riordan doesn't live to tell her tale? On a stormy night, let's say Wednesday, 23 October, you arrange to meet her, or else you follow her and it all becomes so easy. This time you don't have to clobber anyone. Just run her over in your car.'

'I was at home, you can ask my girlfriend,' Gracey protested.

Tara smiled with glee.

'So, which question are you answering Tommy?'

'I was at home all those nights you're talkin' about. I never did nothin'.'

'I see you have a slight problem with your leg. How did that happen?'

'How do you think? I fell down the stairs.'

'Ah right. I thought for a minute that someone did it for you. A comrade in arms, a comrade from Belfast who perhaps didn't like the fact that you'd overstepped the mark. What is it they call it, nowadays? A punishment shooting? But anyway, what I mean is that you're not likely to go chasing after poor defenceless women looking for money, not in your condition. You'd send one of your gofers, wouldn't you?'

'I told you, I don't know nothin' about any women or any murders.'

'Just a name, Tommy, that's all. How's about Big Beryl?'

'Never heard of her?'

'Ach, Tommy, credit me with a bit of sense, will you? It's common knowledge that Big Beryl and you are acquainted. You met with him on the same day that I spoke to you in The Hallowed Turf, remember? Is that when he came to tell you about Maggie? That he didn't mean to hit her so hard? That now you'd no chance of getting paid? C'mon, Tommy, just a name? Who handled the dirty business for you?'

'You're talkin' bollocks, cop.'

'Then maybe you can explain why Jez Riordan had a note of your telephone number?'

'I was givin' her one, wasn't I?'

'She liked a bit of rough, eh, Tommy?'

A self-satisfied smirk crept over the face of Tommy Gracey in celebration of his little victory. Tara didn't care. She was sure that within a few minutes that smirk would be well and truly wiped from the hard man's face.

She allowed Murray to deal with the formal closing of the interview and had instructed him to bring Gracey through the station reception area before releasing him. Tara made sure also that she was standing by the desk as Gracey passed by. She wanted to see the look on his face.

'Tommy!' called the loud, high-pitched voice. 'What the hell are you doing here?'

Gracey stole a glance at Tara who had her smug grin at the ready.

'Hey, Tommy!' Big Beryl called again. His weekly report to the station as part of his bail conditions had been neatly orchestrated to coincide with Gracey's departure. Not that Tara required any proof that both men were acquainted, and not that it had any real bearing on the case, but she never liked a hood like Gracey getting one over on her. Big Beryl looked rather perplexed as Gracey limped by without uttering a word. No doubt, a few severe words would soon be exchanged.

CHAPTER 44

Tara was shown immediately into Edward Harbinson's office at the Liver Building, not that anyone would have prevented her entering. She was on a mission, determined that someone in this company would finally tell the truth. Harbinson seemed intrigued by her appearance. Firstly, she had made no effort to impress: jeans, white trainers, T-shirt and denim jacket. Secondly, the bruise across her eye remained prominent. Tara would not have struck anyone as being a Detective Inspector in the Merseyside Police. At that moment, she didn't care. Neither did she care about how the conversation began.

'Good morning, Inspector, what can I do for you?'

'Did you know?'

'I'm sorry, did I know what?'

Tara, with Murray beside her, dropped into a chair and slammed her hand on the chairman's desk.

'Did you know who she was when you hired her?'

Harbinson feigned a blank stare.

'Jez Riordan, did you know she was Paul Gibson's daughter?'

Murray's face also was bathed in confusion. Tara had not briefed or updated him on what she had learned the day before from Anne Gibson.

'Not straight away,' Harbinson replied, looking concerned, 'but it didn't take me long to realise. I don't see what that has got to do with you, Inspector. Paul was an old friend. I was more than happy to have Jez working for me. What has that got to do with you solving this poisoning crisis?'

'Didn't you notice her qualifications? She was a chemist, Mr Harbinson. Do you think it possible that she may have been behind this poisoning?'

'No, I don't, Inspector. That is completely ridiculous. Besides, nothing has been found at any of our factories. Were you not aware of that fact before barging in here this morning? Those cases of poisoning, tragic as they are, have nothing to do with me or my company. We have been given a clean bill of health, so I suggest that you go and look elsewhere for your terrorist.'

Tara got to her feet but couldn't help pointing her finger at Harbinson as she spoke.

'Four innocent people are dead. Another six are still recovering from that stuff in your products, Mr Harbinson. Richard Andrews, Maggie Hull and Jez Riordan, all worked for you and now they are dead. How dare you suggest it has nothing to do with this company? I will get to the truth. There is something rotten here that involves you or some of your employees. Have the decency to tell me what you know before someone else is killed.'

'If that is all, Inspector, I think you should leave. I have a business to run, trying to regain the customers that this nonsense has lost me.'

Tara stood fuming, her eyes bulging in wild anger. Only Murray's discrete hand on her arm persuaded her to leave well alone. She felt like giving the man a good slap.

'What was all that about?' Murray asked on the way down in the lift.

Tara was still agitated, her face red, the skin of her neck in red blotches. She cupped her face in both hands and tried to breathe more slowly.

'Something is going on with that man and his company, Alan. I know it. Don't try to tell me that all of those deaths are not linked. It can't be a coincidence that while random people are poisoned by Harbinson food, two of its employees get themselves murdered and a third commits suicide. I mean, what the fuck?'

Murray drove them to a Starbucks and, sitting over coffee, Tara related the story she had been told by Anne Gibson. As she spoke, however, the story seemed to have less and less relevance to the current situation. Tara wondered if she had gone off the deep end with Edward Harbinson. Murray wasn't helping.

'Harbinson are clear of any wrong-doing at their factories as far as the poisonings are concerned,' he said. 'Strange as it is, the murders of Maggie Hull and Jez Riordan could be down to loan sharks and have nothing to do with the company.'

She glared at Murray over the rim of her coffee cup.

'You're nearly there, Alan, except for this.' She pointed at her black eye. 'Who did I run into at Jez's house? What were they doing there? What were they looking for?'

CHAPTER 45

At St Anne Street, Wilson and several other detectives were painstakingly reviewing the CCTV data gathered from the supermarkets, food stores, restaurants, cafés and other public places where an individual might have had an opportunity to tamper with the food products. Tara was bored and frustrated by it all, but she did suggest to the team that they concentrate on searching for a forty-something female behaving suspiciously. Murray disagreed, and when Tara was out of earshot, he hinted to those slaving over their PC screens that they should keep an eye out for any individual acting strangely.

Tara sat at her desk trying to concoct a motive for Jez to have acted as a poisoner. The story of The Moondreams clawed at the fringes of her thinking. Anne Gibson had mentioned a rift between the band members after Roddy Craig died. Had Jez been told the story by her father? Were there grudges held, and therefore was revenge a possibility? Seemed like a long shot. What could have been so terrible between members of a sixties pop group to give rise to so many innocent deaths fifty years later?

Murray was right, she thought. Harbinson's were not to blame for the poisonings. None of this toxin stuff had been found on any of their premises. According to Dr McCush, it was more likely to have been cross-contamination of some kind. A tragic but accidental occurrence. Palytoxin was such a rare substance, and it came from the sea. She decided that she needed to look elsewhere for the killer or killers of Maggie Hull and Jez Riordan. For now, Tommy Gracey and his kind would remain in the frame.

She switched off her computer and went home.

Unable to switch off her thinking in the same manner, at various times in the evening she decided that she would speak with the other surviving members of The Moondreams.

* * *

DC Wilson, working long into the night with two colleagues, examined tape after tape of CCTV footage of car parks, shop doorways and supermarkets, every aisle in every store. His eyes were tired, his eyelids having lost the ability to move, stayed partially shut or completely open. Like all such matters of diligent searching and sifting through evidence, it only takes a second to make a huge discovery. It was after eleven o'clock when Wilson isolated a figure on screen, a figure acting strangely in the aisle of a major supermarket. This was no shoplifter. Wilson hoped he was looking at the person responsible for the deaths of four people.

CHAPTER 46

'I would have thought you had enough on your plate, Inspector, without asking questions about something that happened fifty years ago.'

Skip McIntyre stood in the lounge of his penthouse apartment in Beetham Tower. He had a clear view of the city centre, the Mersey and the Irish Sea beyond. Tara and Murray sat on ivory leather, swivel armchairs, both officers unable to resist taking in the opulence of the surroundings and the magnificent view from the 28th floor.

'In the past few days I have had reason to wonder if the recent events concerning Harbinson Fine Foods are connected in some way to those of 1968,' Tara replied.

She had decided that McIntyre still looked the part of an ageing pop star. His jeans, shirts and shoes would be more associated with a younger, trendier gentleman. His home was fit for any musician. Through an open door, she noticed a grand piano in the next room. From where she now sat, she had a clear view of an acoustic guitar and an alto saxophone resting on floor stands and, to her right, hanging on the wall, were three commemorative discs: two gold and one platinum. She couldn't make out the detail but she presumed that all three related to The Moondreams. Completing the image of the pop star lifestyle, McIntyre's girlfriend, an attractive redhead about Tara's age had answered the door when they called.

'Why do you think that?' McIntyre asked.

'Firstly, Jez Riordan was working at your company. She is the daughter of Paul Gibson, your former companion in The Moondreams. Secondly, the mystery surrounding her recent death and that of Roddy Craig in 1968.'

'Is that it?'

'Did you know when Jez came to work at Harbinson's that her father was Paul Gibson?'

'Not at first,' said McIntyre, 'but then I had little contact with her. She was Eddie's secretary.'

'And yet I met you one evening coming out of Jez's house.'

'That was nothing. Like I said at the time, I was just dropping off some files.'

'What happened to Roddy Craig?'

'He drowned in the river.'

'Is that all you know about it?'

McIntyre grinned sardonically.

'You sound like a reporter from *The Sun*, Inspector, digging for something that isn't there. Roddy's death was the end of The Moondreams. There is nothing more I can add on the subject.'

'My dad liked your music,' said Murray.

Tara glared at her DS.

McIntyre responded with a smile. 'A lot of people liked us,' he said.

* * *

Tara seethed in the car as Murray drove from McIntyre's apartment, out of the city, to the home of the fifth member of The Moondreams.

'Is it just me, Alan, or is everyone associated with that company acting very blasé regarding the deaths of four people by poisoning and the murders of Maggie Hull and Jez Riordan? At the very least, you would think they might display shock, disbelief or dismay at such tragedy. Instead, they all behave as if the worst is over, that they know exactly who is behind it all and they no longer have any need to worry.'

'Do you think that they have solved a problem by killing Hull and Riordan, or are they struggling to protect a secret?' Murray asked.

'You mean do they have something to hide over what happened to The Moondreams?'

'Or maybe you're making too much out of what Anne Gibson told you.'

'Thanks, Alan, I appreciate your support.'

'Has to be said, ma'am. There's more evidence for Gracey and Big Beryl having killed the two women than it having something to do with a pop singer who died fifty years ago.'

'Stop talking, Murray. You're not helping.'

CHAPTER 47

Jimmy Ewing, former drummer with The Moondreams, could hardly lift a teacup these days never mind keep a beat on a drum kit. At home he spent half his day attached to an oxygen mask, the other dozing in his armchair or asleep in his downstairs bedroom. A life of excess: cigarettes, alcohol and, for a time, dependence on prescription pills, accounted for a steady decline in his health. He suffered now from arthritis, poor circulation, diabetes and COPD: chronic obstructive pulmonary disease.

Tara rang the doorbell of the house in Hesketh Road in Southport, an extensive building with a high pitched roof and Tudor style architraves. The house was remarkably similar in style to the one in Woolton where Jez Riordan had lived. Tara and Murray had said little more to each other on the drive from the city.

The door was opened by a wrinkle-faced woman with long silver-grey hair and penny glasses, who was wearing jeans and a grey T-shirt with 'I "heart" LA' in red lettering stretched across a full but sagging bosom. Tara introduced herself and asked to speak with Mr Ewing. In the brief exchange with the woman she learned that she was Molly Ewing, the long-suffering wife of Jimmy, she joked, although Tara thought it was probably not far from the truth. Molly Ewing led them down a bright hallway, lined with several framed photographs of what Tara presumed were family members, and into an equally bright lounge. There they found Jimmy Ewing asleep in his chair facing a television with a cookery programme showing.

'Jimmy!' shouted Molly. 'Police are here to see you.' She tapped his foot and he jumped awake.

When Ewing noticed he had company he pulled down his oxygen mask and eventually sat up straight in his chair.

'I'll make some tea,' said Molly. 'Sit yourselves down.'

She left the room, while Tara and Murray both sat in a large cushioned sofa to Ewing's left and facing a tall fireplace with a dark wood mantelpiece. A modern log burner sat on the hearth but it wasn't lit.

'What can I do for Merseyside's finest?' Ewing croaked as slowly he perked up. His Scouse accent had not diminished with his age, although there was little strength in his voice. His hair was long and silver, he was unshaven and his abdomen looked distended. He wore brown slacks without a belt and a red plaid shirt stretched across his tummy, straining several buttons.

'Would you mind telling us how well you knew Jez Riordan?' said Tara. As she spoke, she noticed for the first time a large framed picture above and behind Ewing. It was a photograph of The Moondreams in performance. Ewing's extensive drum kit was most prominent, the face of the young drummer relishing his playing.

'Jez?' said Ewing. 'She was Eddie's secretary.'

'Did you know when she first joined the company that she was the daughter of Paul Gibson?'

'I soon found out.'

'Anything you want to add about that?'

'What can I say? The lass had a rough life. We were glad to see her making a go of things, unlike her old man.'

'Did you have much to do with her?'

Ewing shook his head.

'Did she cause you any trouble?'

'Trouble? What kind of trouble?'

'How did you feel about her having an affair with Richard Andrews?'

'That was none of my business.'

Molly Ewing appeared with a tray of cups and saucers and a pot of tea. She set it on a coffee table in front of Tara and Murray then proceeded to serve as Tara continued with her questions. So far, she had learned nothing from the old drummer and swiftly moved her inquiry on to the subject of The Moondreams.

'What can you tell me about the break-up of your group back in the sixties?'

'A shame that it had to happen,' Ewing wheezed then coughed. His wife passed him a cup of tea containing a lot of milk. 'We were on the verge of making it big when Roddy died.'

'What happened that night when he drowned?'

There followed a bout of prolonged coughing and Molly had to take the cup from her husband in case he spilt his tea. Tara and Murray sipped at theirs.

'He fell in the Mersey. Pissed as a fart.'

'Is that it?'

'It's all that I know,' said Ewing taking his cup back again.

'Where were you when it happened?'

'No idea. I was pissed, too. We'd just finished playing The Cavern. Then we made it to The Grapes for a few before closing. Somebody slipped us some bottles of gin and vodka, maybe a few pills. Next thing I know, it's the following day and I got the news from our manager that Roddy was missing. Then they pulled his body from the river.'

'So none of the other members of the group were with Roddy when he died?'

Ewing was now sipping his tea and more concerned with the cookery programme on TV than in answering Tara's questions.

'Not that I know of,' he replied.

They left the house with Tara concluding that she was not going to get to the bottom of the story of what happened to Roddy Craig in 1968, at least not from any of the surviving Moondreams.

'Doesn't that strike you as odd, Alan?' she said as they climbed into their car. 'None of them have anything to say about what happened to their lead singer.'

'Maybe there isn't anything, ma'am.'

'I know you think that, but don't you also think it strange that not one of them asked me why I was interested in what happened to Roddy Craig?'

* * *

As Murray pulled onto the road from the driveway of the house, another car, with headlights already on in the fading daylight, slowed down to let them out. The driver recognised both officers as they drove away and wondered what their business had been within the Ewing household. That pretty detective was doing too much snooping for his liking.

CHAPTER 48

Arriving back at the station in the early evening, Tara and Murray encountered a small gathering, including DC John Wilson and Superintendent Tweedy, around a PC monitor in the office. None of the group seemed to notice Tara and Murray as they arrived.

'Watch it again,' Wilson was saying. 'Look at the right hand.'

'What are we looking at, folks?' Murray chirped.

No one responded as everyone continued to study the screen. Tara had a clear view and looked on in horror at the figure displayed. The person was holding something in their hand, but she couldn't make it out.

'What is it?' she asked. Wilson paused the screen.

'Ma'am, I think this is our poisoner,' said Wilson. 'This is CCTV taken at a superstore in Bootle. We have more footage of the same bloke.'

'Bloke?'

'Yes, ma'am.'

If anything, Tara had been expecting to see a woman. Somehow she still thought it possible that Jez Riordan had been the poisoner. Now she was staring at a screen that showed evidence that the possible Liverpool poisoner was male. She didn't dare look at Murray. She knew he would have a smug grin stretched across his face. She looked on, mystified, as Wilson ran through the evidence he and his colleagues had uncovered.

'Firstly, we have three shots of the same guy at three different stores in the city on the same day.'

Tara watched the short video pieces showing a man walking through a store entrance wheeling a shopping trolley. On each video he wore a loose-fitting waist-length coat, a baseball cap pulled down to cover his face and a pair of sunglasses.

'This one,' said Wilson, referring to the third section of footage, 'is the store in Bootle where David Leigh's wife did her weekly shopping. Leigh, the man who died in Williamson Square.'

Tara continued to examine all the footage that Wilson had assembled. Next, she saw what presumably was the same man entering a high street convenience store, this time minus a trolley.

'This is the shop where the students did their shopping.'

'Is there anything to identify him or that shows him tampering with food?' Murray asked.

Tara didn't acknowledge his question. Wilson clicked the mouse of the computer and another set of files appeared. He clicked on the first tab at the bottom of the screen.

'This piece clearly shows him doing something to a package that he lifted from the frozen food section.'

Tara looked on as the man removed what appeared to be a frozen ready meal and slipped the outer cardboard sleeve away to reveal part of the film-covered plastic tray. He took a careful look around him then something appeared in his right hand that he seemed to press against the food package. Just as quickly, his hand returned to his coat pocket then re-appeared to slide the outer packaging back over the plastic tray. Then he replaced the carton in the freezer and moved on, out of shot of the camera.

'We were lucky with that shot,' said Wilson. 'Apparently, the store was in the process of re-aligning their cameras to suit a new shop layout. A week later, the freezers were moved and a clothing area was put in place in front of this particular camera.'

'Which store was that?' Tara asked.

'It's in Speke,' Wilson replied. 'Emma Whitehouse bought two cartons of vegetarian lasagne from that very freezer a day later. Norman Forbes, also from Speke, was shopping in that store on the same day that the food was tampered with. We haven't yet found out what he bought.'

'What did the perpetrator use to spike the food?' Tara asked.

'We think it is a syringe of some kind, with or without a needle. We are not sure. If you zoom in on this shot from

Bootle, I think he is wearing some type of glove, latex maybe.'

'And there's nothing you have that shows his face?'

'No, ma'am, but we're still searching. We still have loads of street cameras and car park stuff to look at.'

* * *

Tara sat alone in her car ready for home, but she had not yet started the engine. Her mind tried to process the information just learned in the office, real evidence on a screen, not some concoction of a theory she had invented. It seemed easy now, and also ridiculous, to have placed Jez Riordan at the centre of this mystery. She was a chemist, and she had endured a tough upbringing in a household devoured by tragedy. It seemed to Tara reason enough for Jez to embark on a plan to get back at the people she blamed for ruining her life. Now, though, Tara decided that she must look elsewhere for the answers.

CHAPTER 49

With her job as a police detective, it might have been expected that Tara was always cautious when out alone after dark, even if she was only making her way home from work. But it was so easy to become complacent, thinking that nothing was ever going to happen to her. Driving from the station, she was oblivious of the car following behind. It was the same car that had slowed to let Murray emerge from the driveway of the Ewing home three hours earlier. She was unaware that it made every turn that she made, and she took no notice of it when it piggy-backed its way through the barrier into the parking area beneath her building.

She wandered away from the kitchen and sat on her sofa, nursing a glass of cool white wine, her prawn salad abandoned on the counter. She had taken note of Anne Gibson's number, on the day they'd met following Jez's funeral, and called it up. The woman's chirpy voice answered a few seconds later.

'Hello, Anne, it's DI Tara Grogan here. I wanted to ask you a few more questions if you don't mind.'

'Fire away, Inspector.'

'Can you tell me which university Jessica attended in London?'

'Oh, love, they all sound the same to me. I think it was Imperial College. Would that sound right?'

'Yes, that seems likely. You told me that she studied chemistry. Did she ever do any research or specialise in any particular field?'

'I wouldn't have a clue about that, love. She was Dr Gibson, but she never seemed to use the title and, as you know, she had started going by the name of Riordan by the time she came back to Liverpool.'

'Thank you, Anne. You've been very helpful. Sorry to have disturbed you.'

'No problem, love, anytime.'

Still holding her phone, she did a quick Google search for the name, Jessica Gibson, Imperial College. There were quite a few relevant hits with Jessica's name.

The first referred to an exhibition of paintings held at the college two years earlier, but Tara was looking for a mention of science, chemistry, or possibly a reference to food or poisons. It didn't take long to find it. There was sufficient information in the titles of the scientific papers for Tara to realise that she had been correct in her thinking about Jez. Many of the articles in the list had Jez designated either as the first-named author, as a co-author, or as the corresponding author, that is, the person who was the direct contact between the scientists and the publishers of the journal.

Safety perspectives of seafood in the food supply chain.
Detection methods for ciguatera food poisoning.
Identification of ciguatera poisoning cases in Puerto Rico.
The effect of cooking upon concentrations of marine bio-toxins in seafood.
Phycotoxins in marine shellfish: occurrence and effects on humans.

Tara recognised enough terms and phrases to realise that Jez could well have been responsible for the cases of poisoning in Liverpool. If she had mentioned the name to Dr McCush she was certain he would have been familiar with Jez Riordan, or Jessica Gibson as it appeared now on the screen and was directly associated with research into food toxins. If Jez had been involved in poisoning people in Liverpool then who was the man Wilson had found on the CCTV, and who had murdered Jez?

There was an abrupt knocking on her door. Her mind was elsewhere, dealing with confused thoughts. Tara didn't think it odd that the caller had not buzzed the intercom from the main entrance of her building.

Still deep in thought, she went to her door and pulled it open wide.

CHAPTER 50

He rushed forward. Both his hands grasped her neck. She made it easy for him by reeling backwards. Deftly, he kicked the door closed behind him and forced Tara further inside the room. She could do little to resist him. He swung around behind her and placed his gloved hand over her mouth.

'Now, let's see what we have,' he said, sounding confident, yet Tara could feel his agitation, the trembling in his hands as he kept hold of her.

He pulled a roll of duct tape from his coat pocket and, with Tara wriggling in his grasp, he still managed to pull the end free and stick it to her face. It wasn't neat, but he gripped her hair tightly as he wound the tape several times around her head. When he'd finished, he noticed that both Tara's mouth and nose were covered. She couldn't breathe, her hands reaching desperately for the gag. Quickly, he pulled down on the tape so that her nostrils were exposed. Tara continued to struggle, but he maintained a firm grip on her arm as he dragged her to the bedroom. He found her dressing gown lying on the unmade bed.

'This will do,' he said, tugging the belt free from the garment.

He shoved Tara's face into the mattress and pinned her to the bed with his knee pressing into her shoulder blade. Again, she struggled for breath as her attacker fumbled then managed to tie her hands behind her back. When he released his hold on her she found it difficult to right herself. Not only was the belt tied around her wrists but it was also wound around her neck. The more she struggled, the tighter the belt was upon her throat. Her cries were lost as she drew a breath through her nose and her face coloured a deep red. He wasted no time in dragging her back to the lounge where he thrust her onto the sofa and she landed on her back. Despite her struggling to breathe, her mind tried to deal with the shock of seeing this man standing before her.

'Now, Inspector Grogan, any more nonsense from you and I'll pull that tight around your pretty neck.'

Toby Ewing didn't have the look of a villain. He didn't appear strong enough, although Tara now knew differently. Despite his air of confidence, his voice maintained that wimpish quality she'd observed on their first meeting. He had never struck her as a successful company executive and certainly never as an accomplice to Jez Riordan. She had so many questions for him, but she feared that soon they would be of no consequence. There was no doubt in her mind that Toby Ewing intended to kill her.

She watched him pace around her living room, a man running on his nerves.

'You're a very clever lady, Inspector,' he said. 'I saw you talking to Maggie's brother and Jez's aunt. Do you specialise in attending funerals? Then you ask my father about his past, about The Moondreams, of all things. How the hell did you arrive at that? A real super-sleuth, although you're certainly a lot prettier than Miss Marple, and much younger, too. But you really should stay out of things that don't concern you. My father is not a healthy man. He doesn't need the police asking him questions about stuff that happened fifty years ago. And for what?'

Tara looked pleadingly at him, towering over her as she languished on her sofa. The slightest movement of her hands behind her, or of her head, and the belt tightened around her neck. It was hard enough breathing through her nose; she felt like she could pass out at any moment. What did Ewing want with her? What had he come to tell her? She looked on helplessly as he wandered around her flat. Why not kill her straightaway?

'Ah, prawns! How appropriate and how convenient, too.' He helped himself to a prawn, dipping it into the dish of seafood sauce on the counter then popping it into his mouth and licking his finger. 'Wonderful. I love prawns, especially spicy or with loads of garlic. Come and join me.'

She didn't move, but Ewing came towards her and gently helped her to her feet. In doing so, he knocked over her glass of wine and it spilt onto her mobile phone.

'Oops! Careful,' he said.

Gripping her tightly by the arm, he led her to the kitchen and stood her before what was supposed to have been her evening meal. She drew a strong breath through her nose as her fear caused her slight body to tremble and her knees to buckle. Ewing produced a small, clear plastic vial from his pocket. Tara could see that it contained only a few drops of a clear liquid. But the realisation of what it might be had her whimpering, and she tried to pull away.

'Now, now, don't make a fuss, Inspector.'

He tugged on the belt and she began to choke. While she gasped for breath, Ewing unscrewed the cap of the vial and dribbled the contents over her prawn salad.

'Jez told me that there is a risk of various natural toxins in almost every food. It's just that seafood is riskier than most. All sorts of nasty things in shellfish. You see, many of them, like mussels and oysters, feed on plankton in the sea. They filter seawater and extract all manner of weird stuff. Then all the nasty things accumulate inside them and dumb people like you and me come along and eat the buggers. Next thing you know, we have a gippy tummy or we're throwing up all around the place. Some aren't quite as lucky, though, and they die. Did you know that Jez was something of an expert on seafood toxins? I bet you didn't.'

CHAPTER 51

Murray did not go home. He was in no hurry to return to an empty flat. Wilson, also, had no reason to leave the station early. He wanted to get through more of the CCTV recordings they had amassed at St Anne Street as part of this enquiry. Both detectives were convinced they had found the poisoner, but neither one had identified the culprit. Murray realized that Tara was adamant that the perpetrator was linked to Harbinson Fine Foods, but he wasn't convinced. For instance, why hadn't the poisoner planted the poison at one of the Harbinson factories if they were connected to the firm? Surely, this would have been the best way to discredit the company. Instead, the perpetrator had visited several food stores, putting themselves at greater risk of being caught directly, or on CCTV. Murray reckoned this could simply be a case of a nut-job acting alone, wanting people dead just for kicks. Or maybe it was a disgruntled customer, taking his complaint to the extreme by attempting to blacken the name of the company.

As both detectives studied the video images well into the evening without further success they were beginning to think their luck had run out.

Murray sat back from his computer, yawning and stretching his arms in the air. Wilson had nipped out of the station and brought back some fish and chips with lots of salt and vinegar and a couple of cans of fizzy drink. Just the stuff to keep you on the job for another hour or two.

'They didn't have cod,' said Wilson, 'so I got haddock.'

It didn't matter. Murray could seldom taste the difference.

'I'm bloody starving,' said Murray. 'Staring at all that food in the supermarkets has given me an appetite.'

'Find anything interesting?'

Murray shook his head, his mouth full of battered fish.

'I was wondering about a car,' Wilson continued, 'before I went out.' He logged into his screen and called up an image of a vintage sports car. Then he turned his screen for Murray to see. 'It's a Triumph Stag. Don't know the year, but the same car appears several times in various car parks around the city.'

Murray shrugged, so what. He was enjoying his meal.

'I was just thinking,' said Wilson, who had yet to eat even one chip. 'That spanner, the one used to kill Maggie Hull. We reckoned it came from a toolkit or a set of tools, you know, like the ones you used to get when you bought a new motor. My dad bought a Toyota in the seventies and he still has the tool roll that came with it. It's got spanners, screwdrivers, pliers, a spark-plug spanner and a hammer.'

'So what's your point?' Murray asked before taking a slurp of his drink.

'If we can identify the car used by the poisoner, and if it's a classic like this one then maybe the spanner will be missing from the toolkit.'

'Jeez, Wilson, you sound like Tara linking the murder of Maggie Hull with the poisoner again. And then you go off on one about a nice motor you've spotted in a car park.'

Wilson grimaced and finally took one of his chips.

'Well, I think I'll keep an eye out for this car, just in case.'

CHAPTER 52

'One squeak from you, Inspector Grogan, and I'll pull the belt tight until you're dead, understand?'

Ewing removed the tape from Tara's mouth. It snagged painfully in her hair and she cried out. The sound died in her throat as Ewing tugged hard on the belt fastened to her wrists and around her neck. Tara's face turned red. She gagged. Ewing stood behind her, his knee pressed into the small of her back, his hands holding the belt tight like a pair of reins. Her legs could no longer support her, but Ewing released his grip and she collapsed to the floor. Before she caught a decent breath, he hauled her to her feet again and stood her to face him. He held her steady, grasping her by the arms, pinching at her skin. His pale face was a picture of hate.

'What do you want from me?' she managed to croak as she struggled to catch a deep breath.

'You should have stayed out of it.'

'I'm a police officer. Innocent people are dead because of what you've done.'

He grinned a remorseless sneer in response to what she'd said.

'Have a prawn, Inspector!'

He picked a single prawn from the plate and pressed it to her mouth. Despite the pain in her neck, she managed to turn her face away. Ewing scooped a handful of food from the plate, pulled Tara closer and pressed his hand to her mouth. She tried desperately to keep her mouth closed, but Ewing, with his free hand, jerked her head back by pulling her hair. Still, her mouth stayed shut. He stepped behind her and held the food tight against her mouth and nose. She had to breathe. Suffocate, or die from the toxin in the food. Her reflexes finally succumbed and Ewing pushed lettuce, prawns and seafood sauce into her mouth. Holding her from behind, he reached to the plate for another helping.

Tara struggled at the most inopportune moment for Ewing. His hand missed the plate, and as Tara thrashed back and forth, choking on the mouthful of food, the plate swept off the counter and smashed on the floor. With all her strength, she backed Ewing against her fridge and tried to wrestle free. She spat out the food from her mouth, praying that she had not swallowed any of the poison. Before Ewing could catch hold of the belt that still was choking her, she scurried away.

'Come here, you little bitch!'

Her mobile rang. Despite the wine spill, it was still working. She scrambled to reach it on the coffee table. Ewing chased after her and tackled her to the floor. Falling short of the phone, she at least saw the caller ID. It was from Wilson.

'No, you don't, Inspector. I haven't finished with you.'
Ewing grabbed the ringing mobile and threw it across the
room. It clattered against a wall.

'Let me go! That's my colleague; he's at the front door.'

'You're lying!'

'Stay and find out. While you're here, you can give
yourself up.'

She saw the nervous expression return to Ewing's face.
This man was no hardened killer. He rolled her over so
that she lay face down on the floor, Ewing sitting astride
her lower back. Suddenly, her head felt as though a ton
weight had just dropped upon it. Ewing had thumped her
across the back of her head. He yelled frantically and
rained punches into her head and back. He pulled tight on
the belt around her neck. Then he struck her hard to the
side of her face. She was vaguely aware of him rising from
her. She thought she would never again draw breath. All
went dark and silent.

CHAPTER 53

Murray was first to react when he saw the broken plate
and prawn salad scattered over the kitchen floor. Wilson
was already calling for an ambulance. Tara was groggy but
conscious.

'The food, Tara, was it poisoned?' asked Murray.

He unfastened the pink towelling belt from around
Tara's throat and wrists and noticed the deep red imprint
on her skin. He saw also the remnants of food smeared on
her cheek. There was blood smudged over her face where
Ewing had inflicted his panicked blows. Tara's eyes were
open, there were a few uttered groans but she couldn't
speak coherently.

'Ambulance on its way,' said Wilson, helping Murray to lift Tara onto her sofa.

The detectives had reacted after their second call to Tara's mobile. With no reply, Murray decided, from previous experience with his DI, that something was amiss. Tara seldom ignored calls. Once Ewing had fled, Tara finally managed to answer the third call from Wilson by pressing her nose to the call answer symbol on her screen. Beyond that, she was incapable of anything more. With no response to his questions, Wilson decided immediately that Tara was in trouble. They had to hope that they would find her at home.

* * *

At the Royal Liverpool Hospital, Tara was treated in the same manner as the other victims of poisoning had been. Her stomach was flushed, and she was placed on a high intake of fluids. Murray had gathered some of the food from the kitchen floor and it was sent immediately for testing. Both detectives stayed with Tara until her parents arrived. By then, Tara was fully awake and slowly regaining some strength to her voice. She couldn't help a slight giggle when she noticed her two police companions standing over her bed in the A & E department.

'It was Toby Ewing,' she muttered.

'We know, ma'am. That's why we were calling you,' said Murray. 'John made a brilliant discovery.'

'Yes, ma'am,' said Wilson. 'We couldn't get a face of the poisoner on the CCTV, but I noticed a car in the car park at several stores. Sometimes it was just a glimpse of it coming and going, but we managed to get the licence plate. It's a classic car, a Triumph Stag, 1972, royal blue convertible, registered in the name of Toby Ewing. I thought it was too big of a coincidence for his car to be at several of the stores affected by the poisonings.'

'Well done, John, very good job,' said Tara with a sigh. 'I knew it had to be someone in that damn company.'

At that point, Tara's parents and Superintendent Tweedy arrived. Murray and Wilson stepped outside to catch some fresh air. It had been a long night.

After a few minutes listening to her mother's concerns for her well-being, Tara soon had the urge to be out of the hospital and alongside her colleagues working to bring an end to this case. Even as her mother issued plans for her convalescence at home in Caldy, Tara was dealing with questions still unanswered. Was Toby Ewing the sole perpetrator? Had she been wrong about Jez? If Ewing was the poisoner, why had he done it, and was he also the person who had murdered Jez and Maggie?

She had to get out of the hospital. Surely, if she were to be affected by the toxin it would have already taken its toll. She ached all over and had no strength in her voice but that was not going to stop her.

CHAPTER 54

Following a restless night on a ward where she had been transferred, finally, at three-thirty in the morning, she was relieved that she didn't seem to have any ill-effects from the food that had been forced down her throat by Ewing. At least, she didn't believe so. Her head pounded, her eyes were puffy and her back was so stiff she felt like a woman three times her age. Once the junior doctor had done his morning rounds and the nurse had checked her blood pressure and temperature, Tara wasted no time in asking to use a telephone. She was allowed the use of a desk phone at the nurse's station. She called Murray.

'Come and get me out of here,' she whispered when he answered the call.

'Ma'am?'

'I said, get me out of here. We have work to do.'

'But you should be resting, Tara. You can't just up and walk out of hospital.'

'Yes, I can and don't call me Tara. It's ma'am to you. So get your ass over here now!'

She put the phone down. The young nurse seated at the desk looked open-mouthed at her. Tara smiled demurely as if all was well and limped back to bed.

She was dressed and waiting in the ward when Murray arrived.

'Ewing's done a runner,' he said, as she carefully eased herself into the front seat of his car.

'Can't say I'm surprised. Have you been to his home?'

'Not yet. A patrol car was despatched there late last night. No one at home.'

'Right then. Let's get out there now. And afterwards, I want Harbinson brought to the station for questioning.'

'Harbinson?' Murray drove into the morning traffic.

'Yes, Harbinson. That man knows exactly what has been going on the whole time. We'll make do with him until we get our hands on Toby Ewing. Talking of whom, where exactly does he live?'

'Barnston.'

'Wow, not that far from Royden Park. He wasn't too concerned where he did his killing.'

Tara thought on about Toby Ewing as Murray drove to The Wirral. She had to admit that on the first meeting with the man, despite his rather anxious manner, he was not someone she had in her mind for any of these killings. She regretted now, not having done enough background checks on him.

* * *

The Ewing house was a renovated stone cottage that sat on a quiet road not far from the centre of Barnston village. The area was probably well-suited to the lifestyle that Ewing enjoyed, Tara mused. Murray parked the car on the gravel drive. A double garage, both doors open, was separated from the house by a wide farm-style gate that led to extensive gardens at the rear. Murray alerted Tara to the vehicle inside the garage.

'Ma'am. The car that Wilson identified on the CCTV.'

Tara looked briefly at the well-maintained classic. Murray, thinking the same thoughts as his boss, had gone straight to the bonnet.

'No signs of any damage if it was used to run down the Riordan woman,' he said, inspecting the front bumper.

Tara shivered at the thought.

'I'm sure he has at least one other vehicle.'

Murray joined her as they approached the solid oak door of the cottage. There was no bell, so Murray used the heavy knocker to summon whoever might be at home. A moment later a woman's face peered out from the quartered window of the kitchen. Tara glared back until the face disappeared.

'Who is it?' said a distorted female voice. Only then did Tara and Murray notice the intercom, fixed to a wooden post to their left and partially obscured by a potted palm.

'Detective Inspector Grogan and Detective Sergeant Murray, Merseyside Police,' Tara replied into the speaker.

'How can I help you?' said the voice.

Tara puffed in exasperation. Were they going to conduct the entire interview through this bloody machine?

'We would like to speak with Mr Toby Ewing,' said Murray. 'Is he at home this morning?'

There was no immediate reply until, a few seconds later, there came the sound of a bolt being released and the heavy door edged open on a chain. Tara stepped forward, taking command.

'Morning, Mrs Ewing, is it?' She didn't let her answer. She presented her warrant card for the face to inspect. 'Is your husband at home this morning?' she asked.

'I'm afraid not,' said the face. The voice was soft but concerned, the accent typical of a soul who has spent more years in the south than on Merseyside. The face looked thin, rather bony and sported a pair of dark-framed glasses. That was as much as could be seen through the partially open door.

'Then maybe you could help us, Mrs Ewing?' said Tara, keeping patience.

The door closed momentarily as the chain was slid off.

'You'd better come in,' Ewing said nervously as she opened the door wide.

Tara didn't find the woman at all pretty, slim yes, wearing a dark skirt, cream blouse and a pair of pink fluffy slippers but not attractive. She looked more like someone, an academic, for instance, who cared more for her work than her appearance. Her mousey hair, resting on her shoulders, was straight and unadventurously styled, her pasty face devoid of make-up. Considering also the curt tone of the woman, as far as Tara was concerned, she seemed to lack any charm at all.

She led them through a chilly and dim hall with several coats hanging from hooks and several pairs of wellington boots standing on the stone floor. The kitchen felt much warmer, an Aga was doing its job and there was a rich smell of coffee percolating. Mrs Ewing did not invite them to sit; it was unlikely therefore that they would be offered any of the coffee.

Tara had been right on one score. Several heavy-looking books were open on the kitchen table.

'How can I help you?' Mrs Ewing said. She seemed to inspect the bruised face of the young officer who had limped into her home.

'Doing a spot of work, I see,' Tara commented and nodded towards the books, her attempt at being friendly.

Ewing winced more than smiled but offered no further information.

'My husband will not be home until late tonight, Inspector. What is this about?'

'You're certain of that?'

'Yes. I'm not sure of his plans exactly, but I do expect him home tonight.'

Tara snatched a glance around the room. A modern kitchen with all the gadgets, the coffee maker, microwave, double fridge-freezer, an enormous wine rack, well-stocked, a plasma television in one corner beside a comfortable sofa and a computer workstation close by. Mrs Ewing had watched Tara carefully as she scanned her room.

'When did you last speak with him?'

'Yesterday afternoon, why? Please tell me why you wish to speak with him, Inspector.'

'Did he come home last night?' Tara asked, ignoring, for now, the woman's plea for information.

'I refuse to answer any further questions, Inspector, until you tell me exactly what this is all about.' Defiant, but looking more like a fuming schoolgirl, Catherine Ewing folded her arms and glared at Tara.

'We wish to speak to Mr Ewing in connection with the murders of four people. You may have heard about them in the news. They were poisoned.'

Ewing's arms dropped to her sides. She looked like someone who had just seen a boulder crashing through her kitchen.

'But I thought Harbinson's had been cleared of any blame. The poison did not come from the factory.'

'I'm not talking about Harbinson's. Our enquiry is focussed upon your husband.'

'But this is ridiculous! Toby would not be involved in anything like this.'

'Can you tell me where he is right now?'

Ewing's face grew even paler, her eyes darting with nerves.

'At work, I suppose… but…?'

'Thank you, Mrs Ewing. Some of our officers will be here later. They will have a warrant to search this property.'

'I don't understand. You must be wrong about this, Inspector.'

'Please remain here until your house has been searched. If you are in contact with your husband, please suggest to him that he calls us.'

Tara and Murray left the woman dealing with news she could never have imagined. She watched through her window as the detectives drove away.

'Seems like she hadn't a clue what her husband was up to,' said Murray.

'Yes, but I don't think that will stop her from trying to warn him off. Although I expect he is already out of the country by now.'

CHAPTER 55

DC Wilson showed Tara through the CCTV footage they had isolated that pointed to Toby Ewing as the main suspect for the poisoning of food in several supermarkets around the city. The young detective, however, had still not produced a clear image of the man pictured, apparently spiking food with the deadly toxin. The evidence was more circumstantial. They had recordings of a man, unidentified, acting suspiciously in several stores. They had a clear image of a 1972 Triumph Stag, its licence plate linked to Toby Ewing and the vehicle recorded in the car parks of the same stores around the time the man had spiked the food. They could not say unequivocally that the culprit was Toby Ewing. Considering, however, his attack on Tara, it left the police in little doubt over who was responsible.

Tara, of course, was desperate to establish why Maggie Hull and Jez Riordan had been killed. She still suspected that Jez had had some involvement in the scheme. Jez's career history suggested that she would have been the person who had supplied the toxin to Ewing. While the search continued for Toby, the CEO of Harbinson Fine Foods, Edward Harbinson had been brought to St Anne Street. Tara hoped that he would now be prepared to explain a lot more about the affair than he had so far revealed.

When Tara and Murray entered the interview room, a seething Edward Harbinson was seated next to his solicitor, Geoffrey Forbes, a man of similar age and stature to his client but with a shiny face and bald head. For some reason, he had cause to smile at Tara when she sat opposite him. She assumed he was bemused by her battered appearance. She did not return the smile; she was hardly ecstatic at how she looked or felt.

'This had better be worth my while, Inspector,' said Harbinson. 'Merseyside Police have caused enough trouble for me and my company. I need this mess cleared up as soon as possible.'

In consultation with Tweedy, Tara had decided that Harbinson should be interviewed under caution. She smiled weakly then explained to both men what was to happen. To her surprise, Harbinson did not offer any further protest although his face maintained a pained expression.

Tara did not exactly feel full of the joys. She was dealing with a deeply depressing situation, the murder of six people, and she had been lucky to survive an attack by the chief suspect in the whole affair. It was still morning, but she felt she'd been on the go for days without rest or sleep. Before entering the interview room, she had taken two paracetamol to fight off yet another headache. She had little patience for antics. Harbinson would answer her questions, or she would drag him screaming and shouting all the way to the bloody cleaners.

'Mr Harbinson,' she began, 'how long was it after you employed Jez Riordan before you realised that she was plotting against your company?'

Harbinson looked in horror at his solicitor, while Murray gazed at Tara. The question seemed to have startled everyone.

'How long, Mr Harbinson?' Tara was not prepared to wait for any hesitation. She wanted an answer in order to move on. She watched the company chairman as he looked for guidance from his solicitor.

'I'm not sure I can answer that question,' Harbinson replied.

'OK. Let me re-phrase it for you. Did you know that Jez Riordan was intending to harm your company's reputation?'

Again, the man looked for guidance from Forbes.

'No comment.'

Tara winced. She felt a pain in her lower back from the scuffle with Ewing, but she also fought to suppress her anger.

'What were your thoughts when the poison was linked to your food products?'

The man shrugged. Tara, once again, felt like slapping him.

'Did you not think it strange? It seemed that someone had targeted your food products.'

'My company was found not to be the source of the poison, as you know, Inspector.'

'Perhaps not, but by then you already knew the identity of the perpetrator, didn't you?'

Harbinson made no reply. He and Tara stared at each other, neither one prepared to relent.

'Why did you not report to police that one of your employees was missing?'

'I told you last time, Inspector. I didn't know that Jez was missing.'

'You didn't attend Jez's funeral, why was that?'

'I had a prior engagement.'

'Did you kill her, Mr Harbinson?'

'What? That's ludicrous! Of course I didn't kill her.'

Geoffrey Forbes spoke up.

'If that's all you have, Inspector Grogan, I suggest you end it here and let my client get back to running his business. After all, this entire affair has not been of his making.'

Tara drew a long breath but it didn't soothe her temper.

'That is where you and I must disagree, Mr Forbes. And before your client walks out of here today, I will have the truth! Six people are dead, several others seriously ill. One of Harbinson's executives is currently on the run and is the main suspect for these murders. Your client knows much more than he has so far revealed to us. When eventually we bring Toby Ewing to book for these crimes, I promise you I will come after your client and have him for attempting to pervert the course of justice!'

Tara was on her feet, spitting the words into Edward Harbinson's face. Suddenly, he looked to be a man staring at an entirely different reality. His face paled and he became agitated.

'Toby? What do you mean, Toby is a suspect? This has nothing to do with him, surely?'

Murray discretely tugged on Tara's blouse and she resumed her seat. She took the tissue he offered her and used it to wipe her mouth and nose. There was hardly a spot on her face that didn't ache or wasn't bruised. While Tara composed herself, Murray supplied some information to the gentlemen sitting across the table.

'Mr Ewing is currently being sought in connection with the act of contaminating food at several stores in Liverpool. We have CCTV evidence to support the charge. He also attacked Detective Inspector Grogan at her home yesterday evening and attempted to poison her by forcing her to eat contaminated food. It is likely also that he is implicated in the murders of your employees, Jez Riordan and Maggie Hull.'

Harbinson looked drained of any resistance. His eyes settled on the battered face of the woman who had, a moment earlier, threatened to charge him over his involvement in the murders. Geoffrey Forbes attempted to respond to Murray's revelation, but Harbinson stopped him.

'Please, believe me, I knew nothing about Toby. His father is one of my best friends. Jimmy isn't in good health; this news will kill him. I'm sorry for your trouble, Inspector, really I am. I promise I'll help you in whatever way I can.'

CHAPTER 56

Murray brought in some tea in paper cups. Harbinson had loosened his tie, while both Tara and Forbes waited for the man to reveal all that he knew. Tara, for now, desisted from asking questions. She hoped that maybe Harbinson had, at last, come to his senses.

'When Jez started working for us I had no idea that she was Paul Gibson's daughter. She was simply a new employee, a stunningly attractive new employee. It was close to Christmas when she joined us, and I first met her at our Christmas party. You know how some of these things go. We got chatting over a few drinks, and before I knew it we were alone in a quieter place. One thing led to another…'

Harbinson looked at Tara, as if hoping for sympathy or understanding, but Tara concentrated on writing notes despite the voice recorder capturing every word.

'I'm married, Inspector. I am hoping that this will not get back to my wife. I have a young family.'

Tara offered nothing by way of reassurance. At this stage, she already knew that Harbinson was on his third wife: a forty-year-old named Elise, who had given him two young sons. Nicole Andrews was his daughter from his first marriage.

'After that Christmas, I continued to see Jez,' said Harbinson. 'At this point, she was not yet my secretary. We used to meet in my office, or at her place and on one occasion she accompanied me on a business trip. It was shortly after that trip to London that she told me who she was. I had no concerns, even then. We were enjoying each other's company, or so I believed. In a way, I thought it quite sweet that she should choose to come and work for me. I told her stories about her father when we played together in The Moondreams that she claimed not to know, and our affair continued. A couple of months later, she suggested that she should work directly for me. She wanted to be my secretary. It was difficult to say no to her, and it was equally as hard to move Maggie on to Toby. Maggie was the backbone of my company. She'd been my secretary for years. I relied on her. But Jez told me not to worry, that she could handle Maggie, and so I relented and Jez became my secretary. For a few weeks, it was wonderful; I saw her every hour of the day. We worked late, we ate together and we went on a couple more business trips, one of them to Amsterdam. To be honest, Inspector, I was nearing the point where I was going to leave Elise for Jez.'

'What happened that you didn't?' Tara asked him matter-of-factly, as if she'd just enquired about the weather. She had the man's co-operation, but he would never have her respect. Tara remained untouched by the emotion gradually overtaking the man's speech.

'One morning, she came right out and told me exactly what she thought of me. Can you believe that? We were staying in a hotel outside Edinburgh, getting dressed in our room. "Are you going to leave Elise?" she asked me. I said that I was thinking about it. She then said she had something that might speed up the process. I hadn't a clue what she meant. She switched on her laptop and showed me a recording of the two of us in bed together at her house. "Perhaps, you should show her this," she said. I was horrified, but all she did was laugh. "I'm only joking," she said, but suddenly I felt so ashamed. I realised that Jez had no real feelings for me. She had been playing games. When we got back to Liverpool I asked her why she had recorded us in bed together. "Why do you think, Eddie darling?" she said. "I am going to destroy you, your family and your fucking company." I asked her why, and then she spouted all this vitriol about how I had ruined her father's life and her mother's. She told me that if it hadn't been for me her father would have been a star, a successful musician. Because I had ruined the lives of her parents, I had also ruined hers. I tried to explain what happened between Paul and me – what had happened to The Moondreams. She wouldn't listen. She walked out of my office laughing. The next morning, she came in as if nothing had happened, although that was an end to our affair.'

CHAPTER 57

'Poor Richard,' said Harbinson, sniffing back his tears.

By this point, Tara could see that Harbinson was a broken man. She even wondered if he might get around to confessing to the murder of his former lover. He certainly had a motive. So far, she could not determine what motive Toby Ewing possessed for killing Jez.

'You mean your son-in-law, Richard Andrews?'

'Yes. At first, I didn't know about it, his affair with her, but then she came and told me everything. "You might want to warn your daughter," she told me. "Richard is going to leave her." I didn't know what to do. I was at my wit's end. I prayed that Jez would just clear off and leave us alone. But she didn't. Then Richard left Nicole and his children and moved in with her. Jez would come into the office every morning and tell me in great detail exactly what they had done together the night before. My God, she even tried to come on to me again. One day, I lost it completely and slapped her across the face. She just laughed. Within the month, though, she told me proudly that she'd thrown Richard out and that she wanted me back. First, of course, she insisted that I make sure that Richard was sacked.'

Harbinson broke into sobs. Murray was again the one to supply the tissues. Tara was now thinking she had never heard a story so fantastical, so absurd and yet tragic, in her life. That Jez could put together such a contrived agenda to ruin people she had never really known and all because of what she believed had been her father's misfortune. At that point, Tara would have liked Anne Gibson to be present. The woman had never alluded to such hatred existing within her family, all of it stretching back fifty years. Tara wondered if Anne Gibson was aware of the vendetta and whether she also had been a part of it. Had she, albeit unwittingly, helped to foster a need for vengeance in her niece?

'I'm sure you can put together the rest of it, Inspector. Once the blame for the poisonings was aimed at us, I realised that Jez was behind it. When I checked on her past I found out that she had been a scientist working with food contaminants. But you must believe me, I knew nothing about Toby.'

'Did you kill Jez Riordan, Mr Harbinson?' Tara asked again. He certainly had motive, she was thinking.

'No!' he cried before collapsing into heavy sobs. 'When she disappeared I thought I would go to her house to retrieve her laptop with the recording of the two of us in bed. But there was someone else in the house. I ran off. Anyway, I didn't find a laptop.'

'That someone was me, Mr Harbinson. I shouted a warning that I was the police. You chose to ignore it!' She raised her finger and pointed to her still bruised and swollen eye. Harbinson dropped his head.

Tara wasn't finished with the CEO. Surely, he could tell her what it was that had happened so long ago that caused Paul Gibson to feel so much resentment, a hatred that Gibson had also instilled in Jez.

CHAPTER 58

'Just before the release of our LP, *The Food of Love,* Skip suggested that we go back home and play The Cavern one last time before we became superstars. I was surprised when Paul and Roddy agreed to it because I believed that they had already forgotten their roots. As you are aware, Inspector, Roddy died the weekend we came back to Liverpool. None of us felt that we wanted to continue with The Moondreams after that, and Paul became very resentful towards the rest of us. We parted company with him calling us for everything. I'd lost all interest in being a musician and after a few months off, I went back to work for my father and I invited Skip and Jimmy to join me. Paul continued on his own for a few years, trying to make it big with various bands. His drinking and drug-taking meant that no one was prepared to invest in him. We never spoke or met again, but I know he blamed me for breaking up the band. I suppose, considering what has happened recently, he cultivated that resentment in his daughter Jez.'

At that moment, the door of the interview room opened and Wilson was there. He asked to speak with Tara outside.

'What's up, John?'

'Ma'am, we just got word. Big Beryl has been shot.'

CHAPTER 59

She left Murray to continue the interview with Harbinson. There were still a few answers she would like to extract from the company director. For instance, what had happened to Roddy Craig? Or was that a mystery that could never be solved?

On the way to Aintree Hospital, Wilson filled her in on the details of the shooting. The previous night, around ten o'clock, Big Beryl had been taken from his home at gunpoint by three masked men. According to Big Beryl himself, who had already been interviewed by uniformed officers, he had been forced into a car and driven near to Goodison Park where he was shoved onto the road. Before driving off, one of the men got out, pointed a pistol at Big Beryl's legs and fired a single shot. The bullet passed through his right leg just below the knee. Fortunately, for him, he was discovered within a few minutes by a courting couple on their way home from the pub.

A uniformed officer was seated outside the private room in a ward on the third floor of the hospital. Tara introduced herself and Wilson to the constable and, without knocking, proceeded into the room. There were two female visitors at Beryl's bedside. One of the women, looking worried, middle-aged with the countenance of someone who'd experienced an unhealthy share of life's troubles, rose from her seat when the two detectives entered.

'You're all right, love,' said Tara. 'We're from Merseyside Police, we just want to ask a few questions.'

At that, the woman resumed her seat.

'I'm his mam,' she whined. 'I hope to hell you get the bastards that did this.'

Tara nodded some acknowledgement, falling some way short of being charmed by such blunt language.

The second woman, large like Big Beryl, with a shy expression, was holding his hand.

'And you must be?' Tara inquired.

'I'm his wife,' she replied with an indignant twitch of her shoulder to emphasise the response.

Big Beryl, covered only in a blue patterned theatre gown, head propped up, his right leg sporting a huge square of thick gauze to cover his wound, had a sorry look on his chubby face. His tight eyes craved sympathy and not the barrage of awkward questions that Tara was about to fire his way.

'I never did nothin'. I swear ta fuck, Inspector,' he said, pitifully for such a big man.

'That's all right, Beryl, but you know that I'm going to ask you who did it?'

'What're you askin' him for?' his mother snapped. 'How the fuck does he know?'

Tara grinned to hide her annoyance at being spoken to in such a manner. She promptly neglected to answer the woman.

'Well, Beryl,' she continued. 'Start at the beginning and tell me exactly what happened.'

'He's already told the friggin' bizzies,' said the mother. 'How many times does he have to friggin' say it?'

Tara glared at her with a sarcastic smile.

'Maybe you could leave us alone for a few minutes, Missus? John, will you take these two… *ladies* for a nice cup of tea?'

The wife, her body squeezed into a pair of extra-large, red jeans, got to her feet willingly but the mother seemed determined to stay put.

'I wanna hear what the bizzies are gonna do about catchin' the scum,' she said defiantly.

'Mam, give us peace for a minute, will ya? Go and have some tea. Aaargh!' Beryl cried out in pain as he tried to ease himself further up the bed. 'The bastards!'

Both women trailed out of the room with Wilson leading the way. Tara looked down upon the stricken bulk of Beryl, puffing air through his cheeks.

'Who are the bastards, Beryl? Come on, you must have an idea who it is?'

'It isn't who you think, Inspector.'

'And who do I think?'

'Tommy. He'd never do this to me. We're good mates.'

'Then give me a reason why he might want to hurt you, Beryl?'

He seemed a little confused, out-manoeuvred by the question.

'Um, no reason. It's just that you think that he had something to do with it. Do you think it has something to do with that murder? That's why you're here, aren't ya?'

'Let me put it like this, Beryl. If you and Tommy had nothing to do with Maggie Hull's murder then you are probably quite right, Tommy didn't arrange your wee party last night. Then again, if you know something about the murder, or even if Tommy believes that you do and that it might implicate him, then he could have sent a few of the boys round to see you. Do you know what I mean?'

Big Beryl took some time to consider what Tara had said. He winced as he tried to shift his leg to a more comfortable position on the bed.

'I collected from her, that's all.'

'When?'

'Ages ago.'

'Weeks? Months? Come on, Beryl, help me out here.'

'I don't know, months I suppose.'

'And did she pay?'

'Yeah, but not all of it.'

'Was it for Gracey?'

'Yeah.'

'What did you do when she didn't pay all of it?'

'I don't remember.'

'Come on, Beryl. That leg must be getting sore. You need to take things easy.' Tara sat heavily on the edge of the bed. She was done playing the genteel girl cop. She demanded answers.

'Aaargh! Shit! I can't remember.'

Tara moved a hand towards Big Beryl's foot, threatening to tickle the sole. Instinctively, the big man pulled back.

'Aaargh! Bitch!'

'Tickly feet, eh, Beryl?' Again, she moved her hand slowly towards the stranded right foot.

'OK! I thumped her, that's all.'

'That's all! A big man like you thumped a defenceless woman?'

'It was only a smack in the mouth. Just to let her know I'd be back.'

'And that was all?' She waved her hand across Beryl's feet, just to let him know that she was still there.

'And I took her plasma screen with me,' he surrendered.

'You have a strange fascination for televisions, don't you, Beryl? So, where do you keep all this stuff that you collect?'

'Ah no, Inspector, that's not fair. I'm not doing that anymore.'

'All right, Beryl, let's get back to Maggie Hull. The next time you called, did she pay up?'

'I didn't have to. Tommy said that Maggie had some rich friend who coughed up for her. I never saw her again.'

'How long ago did this happen?'

'I'm not sure, but it was ages before she died, like April or May.'

'And Tommy never mentioned her again?'

'Nope, not until after we heard that she got killed.'

Tara reckoned that the big man was telling the truth but still she wondered if Gracey's involvement with Maggie had gone further. If Gracey wasn't the prime candidate for the murder of Maggie Hull, then he was certainly suspect number one for Big Beryl's misfortune.

'Right then, Beryl, tell me exactly what happened last night.'

The events of the previous evening were delivered in heart-rending fashion. The big man, no less a crook but likeable enough, played the victim to Oscar-winning proportions. By the time the two detectives left him to the dubious company of his vulgar mother and his tawdry wife, Big Beryl was calling for a nurse requesting another dose of painkillers. Tara had concluded that if Tommy Gracey was not involved in the shooting then they had little to go on and were unlikely to ever gather enough evidence to convict anyone else. It resembled a so-called punishment-style shooting favoured in the home city of Tommy Gracey. For now, she had an excuse for having another crack at the tough guy.

Tara, despite her questions for Big Beryl, did not now believe that loan sharks were responsible for the death of Maggie Hull. Far too much had happened since the woman's murder. Far too many things connected to Harbinson Fine Foods pointed to the murderer being the same person who had poisoned four people and killed Jez Riordan. What Tara still had not figured out completely was why Toby Ewing had become involved in the entire plot that seemed to have originated with Jez Riordan.

On their way back to St Anne Street, Tara was feeling the effects of her ordeal the previous night at the hands of Toby Ewing. Suddenly, she was overcome by the need to lie down and get some sleep.

'Would you mind driving me home, John?' she said. 'I've had more than enough for one day.'

Wilson took her home to Wapping Dock and insisted upon seeing her safely into her apartment. Toby Ewing was still at large; he had attacked her once; they could not be sure he wouldn't try again.

'Thanks, John, stay and have some coffee.'

'Thank you, ma'am.'

He sat down on her sofa and absorbed the view across the old dock to the ultra-modern edifice of the Liverpool Exhibition Centre, while Tara made the coffee. When she set a tray on the table in front of him, Wilson was checking his phone.

'Any news?' she asked.

'Sorry, ma'am, we have to go now!'

CHAPTER 60

Tara, running only on adrenaline, followed her colleague out of the door, the coffee abandoned on the table and her coat lying on the chair.

'What's up?'

They were rushing down the stairs, unwilling to wait for the lift. Tara ached all over; she could hardly keep up.

'They've got a lead on Ewing. He was trying to board the ferry for Belfast.'

Wilson roared the car on to Wapping and then Strand Street, his siren blazing in the evening traffic. They made their way through the tunnel and hurried to Birkenhead.

Within a few minutes, Wilson pulled up outside the main passenger terminal for the ferry to Belfast. A single marked patrol car was already sitting by the door of the building, two officers standing beside it as if they were already expecting Tara and Wilson.

'Where is he?' Tara asked the policewoman.

She shrugged.

'Don't know, ma'am. We caught a call regarding a suspicious vehicle in the queue for the ferry. The number plate was on our list. The car is registered to a Mr T Ewing.'

'And you haven't seen the driver?'

'No, ma'am.'

At that point, a member of the terminal staff in a high-vis coat approached them.

'He just ran off,' said the man. 'His was the next car to be checked through. He got out of the car and ran. I suppose he saw your patrol car driving in.'

'What direction?' Tara asked. Wilson was already back in the car with the engine running.

'Out the gate,' said the man pointing to the exit.

Tara joined Wilson and they sped from the terminal.

'Which way, ma'am?'

'No idea. He's panicked. Could have gone anywhere.' To their left was the road into Birkenhead town centre, to the right, the bridge leading to Seacombe. 'He can't have gone far. Go left.'

* * *

Thirty minutes later, with several patrol cars on the lookout, there was no sign of Ewing in the roads and streets of Birkenhead. Wilson doubled back towards the ferry terminal and crossed the bridge. Instead of making for Seacombe, he turned left along Dock Road. This was an industrial area with several large factories and other medium-sized units. There were also several open spaces where old buildings had been demolished and nothing had so far replaced them. As darkness fell, and still no sign of the fugitive, Tara by chance spotted a lone figure traversing an area of waste ground. She couldn't be sure that it was Ewing, but she thought it unlikely for anyone to be merely wandering in that area at this time of day.

Wilson searched for a way on to the open ground, but there was no obvious entrance, only mesh fencing, although it was broken in several places.

'Stop the car!' said Tara.

Wilson braked hard and Tara was soon out and running across the rough ground of broken concrete and tarmac towards the figure. Within a few seconds, having noticed Tara's approach, the figure began to run. She knew she couldn't maintain her pace for long. Every joint, every sinew ached, and her fatigue sapped her breath. A few yards further on, she halted and watched as the figure continued to run.

'OK, my friend, where are you going to run to?'

Tara saw that soon the open spaces would come to an end. Ewing, if that's who it was, was running towards a brick wall. She waved at Wilson, signalling for him to drive further along the road. She took several breaths and urged herself forward again.

From twenty yards, she saw him clearly for the first time. Toby Ewing stood at the edge of a quayside. To his right, the brick wall, more than six feet high; to his left, stood Tara and straight ahead the prospect of a jump into dark and cold water. Tara could see that he was stressed. He muttered to himself, he paced back and forth. He seemed oblivious now to the fact that Tara was approaching.

'Give it up, Toby. Come and talk to us.'

He took a step closer to the edge. Tara feared he would jump.

'There's no need for anyone else to die, Toby. You know that. Jez is gone. You don't have to do this anymore.'

'I loved her, you know. I bloody worshipped her.'

'I know. Let's get away from here and we can talk.'

'No. I can't do that, Inspector. You should be dead, too. Why couldn't you leave well alone?'

He gazed down at the water. Tara was convinced he would do it. He was going to jump. Suddenly, he screamed in anguish. He rushed towards her. In a flash, he'd barged straight into her; she tumbled backwards and thumped to the ground. Ewing kept on running. Wilson by now had found a way to get the car through. He caught Ewing in the headlights, as the blue light flashed on the roof. Ewing tried to outrun it. He changed direction, but it was a bad decision. Wilson swerved then hit the brakes as the wing of the car clipped Ewing and he went sprawling into a puddle of water. Wilson climbed out of the car. But the fight had now deserted Ewing. He remained destitute, on all fours in the filthy water, still muttering about how much he loved Jez Riordan.

CHAPTER 61

Tara hobbled wearily into the office. She knew she should be feeling relieved, excited even, at the prospect of wrapping up this gruesome case, but her physical state could not support such a mood. What she craved right now was sleep in a warm bed and someone to tend to her every whim. She knew that was never going to happen. She flopped into her chair, wishing the day was already over. Murray came in shortly after looking for her.

'What have you got for me?' she called, knowing the answer full well.

'They're ready for you, ma'am.'

With her hands on the desk for support, she got to her feet and returned his smile. She could tell that he was examining her: her clothes, the state of her battered face, the state of her battered mind.

'Let's not keep them waiting,' she said. 'Lead on, McDuff.'

'Just to warn you, ma'am.'

'Warn me about what?'

'Ewing's brief.'

'What about him?'

'It's a she. It's his wife.'

'Great. I can hardly wait.'

* * *

Tara and Murray, as they had done 24 hours earlier, entered the interview room with their files and notes ready to extract the truth from another player in this hapless episode. Catherine Ewing sat bolt upright and business-like, a lever-arch file before her on the table. She looked every bit as studious as she had done on their first meeting, wearing a dark trouser suit and a plain white blouse buttoned to her neck. Beside her, Toby Ewing sat blank-faced, without glasses, staring at some point deep in the floor, his eyes red and his face etched with fear, remorse, guilt; Tara couldn't judge nor did she care.

'Mrs Ewing, I didn't realise you were a lawyer,' said Tara, her attempt to establish some rapport before the nastiness began.

'I am a barrister, Inspector. Criminal proceedings are not usually my area but needs must, I'm afraid.'

Tara noticed that the woman did not even glance sideways at her husband.

Murray began with the formalities of cautioning the suspect and explaining that the interview would be recorded. Toby Ewing showed little emotion to anything that was said.

Tara opened a file, checked some information and then asked her first question.

'Let's begin by discussing the poison used to contaminate food in several local supermarkets. Where did you obtain this material, Mr Ewing?'

There was no reply from Ewing. Tara looked at his wife in case she was to reply by proxy for her husband. Nothing came.

'The substance was identified as palytoxin, a marine bio-toxin. Were you aware of the nature of this material? Were you aware of the potency of this substance?'

Tara was happy to continue with her questions. They had sufficient evidence for a conviction, but things would be much simpler if Ewing would admit to his crimes and agree to co-operate.

'Did you know that people could die if they ingested this poison?'

Still, Ewing remained silent. Tara hoped she could hold back her disgust for the man opposite her. She would remain in control of her temper.

'OK. Let's look at some of the details, shall we?'

Murray produced several prints captured from CCTV recordings. He slid them in front of the Ewings.

'Can you confirm if that is you in picture number one, Mr Ewing, taken on 2 October at the Tesco store in Bootle?'

The image showed a man in dark clothing, wearing a baseball cap, standing in the refrigerated food section and holding a package containing a ready meal.

Ewing did little more than glance at the pictures before him. Tara was seething at his attitude but she held her tongue. Murray proceeded with similar questions referring to each picture as he did so. At each presentation, Ewing did not comment. Murray produced a final picture from a folder. It showed the 1972 blue Triumph Stag in a parking space.

'Same day as the first picture, Mr Ewing. This car is parked outside the Tesco store in Bootle. Can you confirm that this vehicle belongs to you?'

Again Ewing hardly took notice of the photo, although his wife studied it then glanced at her husband.

'Just for the record,' said Murray, 'the licence plate confirms that the vehicle is registered in the name of Tobias Ewing.'

'It doesn't mean a lot, Sergeant,' said Catherine Ewing, 'I'm sure there were many cars parked there on that day.'

Tara decided on a different tack. She wanted to rouse the man before her. She wanted to hear his version of the sorry tale that had left six people dead, seven if Richard Andrews were to be included.

'Let's discuss your relationship with Jez Riordan, shall we, Mr Ewing?'

Instantly, the man's face coloured and he couldn't help a nervous glance at his wife. Tara noted the exchange with glee.

'When did you first meet Jez?'

Ewing seemed determined to maintain his silence, probably on instruction from his wife, thought Tara.

'Was she the person who supplied you with the toxin?'

There was no verbal response, but Ewing shifted uncomfortably in his chair. Tara was rising to the challenge. By the end of the interview, she would have this man saying exactly what she needed to hear. He would not get the better of her.

'Was it Jez Riordan's idea to contaminate food, in particular, Harbinson products, with the toxin? What was her motive in doing so? How did she enlist your help?'

'Inspector,' said Catherine Ewing. 'I'm sure you can tell by now that my client is unwilling to answer this line of questioning. If you have nothing further to present by way of evidence, I suggest you allow him to leave.'

Tara ignored the woman. 'When did you begin your affair with Jez Riordan?'

Toby Ewing suddenly looked skywards. It was all that Tara had left to hit the man with.

'Really, Inspector,' said Catherine Ewing looking very displeased. 'Is that all you've got?'

'Was it before she took Richard Andrews as her lover?' Tara persisted.

Ewing now glared into the face of the young detective. Tara felt she was getting closer to rattling him.

'Was it before she had her fling with Edward Harbinson and then set out to blackmail him?'

Suddenly, Ewing looked as though he was floundering.

'Did she ask you to kill Maggie Hull? Why would you agree to do such a thing for her? Why would you poison innocent people? Did you do it all for her? Was she blackmailing you as well as Edward Harbinson? What did she promise you, Mr Ewing? It must have been a hell of a lot. Why did you do so much for her?'

Ewing slammed the palm of his hand onto the table.

'Because I loved her!'

CHAPTER 62

Catherine Ewing, following the morning session in interview room four, and as a consequence of private discussions with her husband, had removed herself from the case. By Tara's reckoning, she had probably removed herself from the marriage. Before leaving the station, she asked to speak privately with Tara.

'I've enlisted an associate of mine to represent Toby,' she said, maintaining her professional front. 'His name is Matthew Greenwell. He is more experienced in criminal cases. I've spoken to him briefly about the facts of the case as I know them. Please bear with him while he gets up to speed.'

'I will, Mrs Ewing.'

'I'm quite sure you noticed that what Toby finally admitted this morning came as a shock to me. He had not been entirely truthful with me, his solicitor and also his wife. I have removed myself from the case, although I spoke to Toby before I did so. One or two curious things have happened recently that I did not understand before this morning.'

'Oh?'

'Some weeks ago Toby's behaviour, his mood, changed dramatically. He told me that he was under pressure at work. He was having to work late on some new projects. I wasn't to worry. But he was very agitated about something. From the time Richard Andrews died, he has been totally unapproachable and very secretive. I had put it down to the recent food scare involving the company and to Richard's death. Of course, I only realised this morning just how withdrawn from me and our marriage he had become.'

'Was there anything specific that he did or said to you that made you suspicious of him?'

'He had asked me for a divorce.'

'Can you remember when exactly?'

She removed her glasses and dabbed at her eyes with a tissue. 'About a week after Richard died, and certainly before this Riordan woman disappeared.'

'I think that may help explain one or two things about his motives in this case.'

'You are certain that he killed all of those people?'

'I'm fairly sure, yes.'

'I've spoken to him for what I hope is the last time, Inspector. Apart from granting him his wish for a divorce, I also gave him some professional advice. If he takes it then your task this afternoon should be less arduous.'

'Thank you, Mrs Ewing. I appreciate your help.'

'Goodbye, Inspector.'

She walked defiantly from the room, passing her husband in the corridor on her way out. She didn't speak. Toby Ewing sloped by awkwardly, looking crestfallen.

Murray introduced Matthew Greenwell to Tara, and together with Ewing, they sat down to resume their enquiries. Greenwell was an affable sort, although probably making just a little too much light of the situation. Tara put it down to nerves, the man was quite young for a solicitor, newly qualified perhaps, and having to handle a case involving a colleague's husband.

Catherine Ewing had been happy to leave her husband's fate in the hands of this young man. Whether or not that was a good thing, Tara was unsure. By the look on Ewing's face, he was past caring. When Tara had recommenced the interview, with the usual patter for the sake of the recording, Greenwell was quick to have his say.

'After some consultation,' he announced, rather too brightly for the occasion, 'my client has decided that he would like to make a full statement regarding this matter.'

Textbook stuff, thought Tara, nevertheless, home in time for tea.

Murray had the handwritten statement typed up on computer by five o'clock. Tara, angry, frustrated, feeling duped, had waited to read it over before going home. As she read, she had to battle to keep her emotions in check. Jez Riordan had become a friend of sorts, but that was before it was discovered exactly what she had been doing.

CHAPTER 63

I am Tobias James Ewing of Fillmore Cottage, Barnston. I am a director at Harbinson Fine Foods, Liverpool.

In March of this year, I began a relationship with Jez Riordan, an employee of the above-named company. In August, she explained to me at her home, that she intended to embark on a campaign to discredit the company CEO, Edward Harbinson. At this time, I did not understand what she meant by discredit, but a week later she showed me several small vials containing a clear liquid. She told me that there was sufficient poison within the vials to kill several dozen people. I asked her where she had obtained the substance, and she said that she had been accumulating it over several years. I asked her what she was intending to do with it. She said that she wanted to bring down Harbinson's company. I was shocked by what she was planning, but she warned me that our continuing relationship was dependent upon my helping her.

On 14 September, I entered the ASDA store at Hunts Cross Shopping Centre and, using a small plastic syringe, inserted several millilitres of the liquid I believed contained poison into a package containing a chicken curry ready meal, I knew to be supplied by Harbinson Fine Foods.

On 24 September...

There followed a list of occasions on which Ewing had entered shops and supermarkets to contaminate

Harbinson food products. The statement then outlined Ewing's actions relating to the murder of Maggie Hull and his most recent association with Jez Riordan.

> *...On the evening of Monday, 21 October, I called at the home of my secretary, Miss Maggie Hull of Bartlett Street, Wavertree. The time was about six-thirty. I had watched her as she arrived home from work. I knocked on her front door and she opened it. I explained that I needed to discuss a delicate work-related matter with her and she invited me inside. As she entered her living room with her back to me, I removed a spanner from under my coat and hit her once on the back of the head. She fell to the floor, but I believed that she was still conscious. I hit her again, this time drawing blood. I kept on hitting her until I was sure that she was no longer moving. After several blows, I believed that she was dead.*
>
> *I placed the spanner into a plastic carrier bag which I had taken with me. It was dark outside, and it was raining. There was no one about in the street, so I left by the front door. I was then supposed to leave the spanner close to the home of Mr Tommy Gracey on Priory Road, Anfield, but I was very upset by what I had done and didn't feel up to driving straight away. Once out of Bartlett Street, I tossed the bag containing the spanner into some bushes and hurried back to my car which was parked several streets away from Maggie's house. From there I drove to another location. I can't remember where. After about thirty minutes, I stopped the car and called Miss Jez Riordan on my mobile telephone. I told her that it was done, that I wanted to come and see her, but she told me to go on home and that we would discuss it the next day.*
>
> *On the morning of Wednesday, 23 October, I spoke to Miss Jez Riordan by telephone from my office. I*

told her that I couldn't take much more of this anguish and that I wanted to give myself up to the police. She told me not to be silly, that we had come too far and it would not be long before everything was finalised. She had already told the police that Maggie had debt problems and had been threatened by Tommy Gracey. It was likely, she said, that he would get the blame for Maggie's murder. She told me that she loved me, and I asked her to marry me. She said yes, on condition that I did not go to the police because I was of no use to her in prison. She told me to get on with my everyday activities as though nothing had happened and that the pain would soon disappear. She told me that Maggie had to die because she knew too much. Maggie was well aware of who Jez really was and was aware also that she had already conducted affairs with Edward Harbinson and Richard Andrews. She told me that Maggie had been very upset by Richard's suicide and Jez was worried that she would go to the police.

Jez promised to meet me that evening, 23 October, after work. We often met in Royden Park near to my home. When I arrived there that evening I could not find Jez. Her car was in the car park but there was no sign of her. I waited for about twenty minutes. I also tried to call her but there was no reply. Then I drove home. I am not responsible for the death of Jez Riordan. I was completely in love with her.
Toby Ewing

Tara tossed the papers across her desk and sat back in her chair. Exhaustion washed over her, her head throbbed, and her eyelids were ready to shut tight. It felt like she'd just been short-changed in a pub and she was too drunk to do or say anything about it. Tweedy would be delighted with the result; she knew that much. Maggie Hull's killer had been found and there was little doubt that Jez Riordan

231

had been murdered, although Ewing had not admitted to it. Since Toby Ewing had freely admitted to the Hull killing, it seemed there was little reason for him to deny the murder of Jez Riordan unless, of course, he was truly innocent.

Tara wasn't convinced by that portion of the story. She had no justifiable reason to disbelieve Ewing's statement, but she was certain to the pit of her stomach that Jez simply hadn't been knocked over by a random hit-and-run driver. The problem was, how the hell was she going to convince Tweedy that the case should not be closed?

CHAPTER 64

Tara slipped the black sequin top over her head and stood before the mirror in her bedroom. Her first night out in months, and she was determined to make the most of it. A new top, skinny black leggings and a pair of shiny heels. It would be so easy to stand in front of the full-length mirror and count the bruises from her most recent conflict or the scars remaining from past turbulent episodes, but tonight she let all her cares drift away. She was more concerned with her new look. Not so much the clothes but the daring hairstyle. She could not recall ever having such short hair. It remained devilishly blond, but it no longer fell below her shoulders. Now it matched her friend Kate's, although not in colour. Purple hair such as Kate's was not a style she felt confident of carrying off around St Anne Street station.

Tonight, she and Kate were stepping out for the first time since she had lost her baby. They would dine at a really good restaurant. They might well drink too much wine. They might find themselves acting like teenagers, dancing at a club. Nothing mattered other than to have a good time in each other's company. If they were approached by a couple of good-looking fellas, then so be it. But they could just as easily do without.

Gathering her coat and bag and closing her door behind her, Tara knew well that her pain had not gone away. She had merely swept it all beneath a mental carpet. Compartmentalise, isn't that how people termed it nowadays? How to survive a major trauma in one's life – box it up, tidy away. Lying on the coffee table in her lounge was a typed letter – her resignation from the Merseyside Police.

They ate dinner and drank two bottles of their favourite wine. Later, they found themselves in a noisy club, booming music, thronging crowds, mostly kids. God, but they were getting old. A couple of shots each and a laugh on the dancefloor. Two guys swooped in; lads, nothing fancy but brimming with confidence. Tara was sure they had school the following day. That made Kate laugh. They drank some more shots and had a few laughs with the lads. They snogged them on the dancefloor, leaving the boys in no doubt what they had stumbled upon. But that was it. All they needed to round off their evening.

By two in the morning, they were comfy on Tara's sofa, drinking tea and eating toast, planning a summer holiday. Life had to go on. Tara must keep all of her hurt under that bloody carpet. She stared at the letter on the table. Could she hold her nerve long enough to hand it to Superintendent Tweedy?

As Kate dozed beside her, *Love Actually* playing on TV, Tara could not prevent her mind from raking over the recent case. Her inability to understand what had motivated Jez to do what she had done remained uppermost in her thinking. To manipulate a man, several men in fact, and then entice one of them to commit murder so that she could settle an old score on her father's behalf. How did she manage to wield such influence with

Toby Ewing? Four people had died, entirely innocent and ignorant of Jez's plight. Two more had died, Richard Andrews and Maggie Hull, because at some point they had become too close to the woman. Then Jez had perished, her terrifying scheme unfulfilled. The company she had set out to destroy, the people she wished to bring down were all alive and well. Tara would never understand the craziness of Jez's actions, but what jarred most with her was the stance of the killer Toby Ewing. Why had he admitted so readily to the killing of innocent people but not to the murder of his lover? Then, at the last moment, before the case was handed over to the CPS, to finally enter a guilty plea for killing Jez. Somehow, Tara could not sit comfortably with the outcome. Something was not right.

CHAPTER 65

Last night's storm had brought down trees, caused power blackouts and some roads were flooded. Nicole did not usually travel this road, but the diversion sign had directed her this way. Traffic ahead was slow, huge puddles of water lay at intervals on either side of the road. The school run was taking ages. She shivered at the very thought of driving by this place. Of course, she should feel relief now that it was all over for her. Richard was gone and she and the kids were on their own, but at least she was getting this second chance. A chance of a new life, and she was determined to make it work.

Traffic slowed again; she stopped by the turning and gazed at the sign. Royden Park. Forever, it would mean so much but she prayed that soon it would no longer strike fear in her heart. She closed her eyes and tried to purge the images from her mind.

Four months had slipped by. Time seemed to accelerate from the day she lost Richard. From the night also when she had last driven through this area. At first, on that night she had driven on by, wondering how her little Simon and Chloe would cope without their father. So deep in thought, she almost did not see the car. It was that woman's car, a silver Peugeot SUV, and Jez Riordan was at the wheel. In a fleeting second, she decided that she had to know what Jez was doing there. Was she meeting someone? Why here? She must confront her. She wanted to look her in the face, ask her why she had taken her Richard. She would tell Jez how she had destroyed the lives of two innocent children, and how she had never been worthy of a good man like Richard Andrews.

It was dark and she should have been home with her children, but this wouldn't take long. Have it out with the bitch and surely she would feel better.

She turned her car on the road and followed the Peugeot into the country park. Slowly, easing along the laneway she saw the red brake lights come on ahead of her. She halted briefly and looked around for signs of any other vehicles. Surely Riordan had come here to meet someone. As far as she could see there were no other cars. Moving on and into the parking area, she saw Jez, already out of her car and pacing around. The woman, looking very well dressed, turned to face the approaching car. She was caught fully in the glare of the headlights. Suddenly, the urge to speak with the bitch left her. It was well past the time for words. Jez Riordan smiled into her light beam, probably thinking that her companion, or her latest lover, had arrived.

Nicole Andrews pressed her foot hard on the accelerator. The engine roared, wheels spinning on the gravel. Her car rushed forward. The bitch didn't stand a chance. Her body thumped on the bonnet and somersaulted as the car raced on by. Checking her mirror, Nicole saw the dark shape of the woman struggling to rise to her knees. Slipping into reverse, the rear lights picked out the stricken body. Again, she floored the accelerator, releasing just enough clutch to spin the wheels on the gravel and then to race backwards. She felt the thud below as the body was hit and dragged underneath. Clear again of the obstacle, she saw Jez in her lights. This time there was no movement. Once more would do it, she thought. She had seized her chance. The car again rolled over the unconscious body. There was no more fun to be had.

More from curiosity than bravery, she ventured from her car and stepped close to the body. There was blood but somehow, in the darkness, it did not hold any trauma for her. She peered into the face of Jez Riordan, the woman who had ruined her life. In the violence of the moment, she had somehow avoided disfiguring the beautiful looks. The body though was lifeless and battered.

Suddenly, nerves engulfed her. Had anyone seen? Was someone coming? She never realised her strength. In a panic, she gripped the coat of the dead woman with both hands and dragged the body over the gravel to a grass verge. She noticed that the verge sloped away into darkness. With one final effort, she grasped the body and pulled downwards until it found its momentum and rolled into the ditch and out of sight.

The tears Nicole cried on her way out of the park were not for herself and certainly not for what she had done to Jez Riordan. They were for Richard.

Her father became her strength. He was brilliant. Unable to sleep, feeding herself with pills and vodka, that same night Nicole finally picked up the phone and called him.

When she related the details of how she had killed the bitch he told her to stay put, to tell no one. Immediately, he came to the house and collected her car. Within a day, it had been sold on and a brand-new Range Rover sat in its place. She was worried still that the police would come for her. What would she say? That detective, DI Grogan, was sharp; she would smell her fear. They would take her away. She would lose the kids. First, the loss of their father and then they lose their mother. What the hell had she done? One moment of blind fury would cost her kids their happy childhood.

Then Toby was arrested. She could hardly believe it. He had poisoned all of those people, and he'd battered poor Maggie to death in her own home. He was charged with the murder of five people but strenuously denied killing Jez Riordan. She was astounded to learn that Toby, like Richard, had been smitten by this woman. Her power over them was so strong it had driven Richard to suicide and Toby to murder innocent people on her behalf. Jez Riordan was a monster, and for what? To avenge an injustice from fifty years ago – an injustice that never actually happened.

Her father had gone to speak with Toby. May as well admit to killing Jez, too, he'd told Ewing. Then the whole sorry mess could be closed for good. Why prolong the agony for everyone? He had caused enough heartache.

And so, in due course, Toby Ewing confessed to running down Jez Riordan. It was easily believed. He did, after all, have a strong motive. She had taken control of his life and had driven him to kill four people and beat Maggie Hull to death.

This morning, her father, Skip McIntyre and Jimmy Ewing completed the sale of Harbinson Fine Foods to a French food manufacturer. Ironically, The Moondreams album, *The Food of Love* re-entered the charts more than fifty years after its release. Recent publicity surrounding the band's story had sparked interest in the musical tour de force.

She hardly noticed the traffic moving on ahead of her. Her foot pressed lightly on the accelerator and the Range Rover moved forwards smoothly.

CHAPTER 66

Saturday, 27 April 1968.

Anne Gibson could scarcely breathe. She longed for fresh cool air, but she didn't want to miss a beat. Jammed next to her was her friend, Beverly, trying her best to sway in time with the music, but that necessitated everyone else swaying as one, such was the lack of space in The Cavern. The room was a hive of noise, laughter and music, thumping bass and pounding drums. The place reeked of sweat and damp, cigarette smoke and the odd aromatic notion of weed – sneaked inside more easily than a bottle of beer. This was a night like no other. Nothing of this quality had been seen or heard in this underground temple to musical art since John, Paul, George and Ringo said their goodbyes nearly five years earlier on Saturday, 3 August 1963.

Her cotton skirt was soaked with condensation. It dripped from the ceiling and ran down the brick walls in rivulets. Her hair was soaked and matted, as was Bev's, and her white blouse had become see-through, not that she cared. No one cared about anything that night except for the sounds coming from the five lads on stage.

Anne was over her brief relationship with Roddy Craig. She knew, just looking at him now, that he was well beyond her reach. He was destined for immortality. His pink ruffle-front shirt was soaked in sweat and open to his waist, his leather trousers looked so tight even on such a slim frame, but nothing could detract from the sensual voice. She could tell that every girl in the room was feeling the same attraction. Her brother Paul was lost somewhere in his musical zone, some parallel world that gave him strange powers over his guitar. Anne was so proud of him at that moment. Eddie, Skip and Jimmy seemed to relish the occasion, more so than Paul and Roddy. Skip, though, looked nervous at times, especially since the electrics had fused because of the dampness on stage. Eddie had already suffered a mild shock from one of the microphones.

All of them looked every inch a rock superstar. Anne had witnessed them recording their songs in the studio at Abbey Road. In time, they would surpass the Stones and maybe even the Fab Four. Everyone was saying so.

The crowds outside in Mathew Street peeled away as the lucky few who had savoured this final show swarmed from The Cavern, their ears filled with the haunting sounds of *The Daring Night,* the last song The Moondreams would ever play live in Liverpool and, as it turned out, would play anywhere.

When bodies had cooled in the night air and clothes had somehow dried, leaving the tell-tale and unsavoury aroma of The Cavern Club, the five Moondreams found their way to The Grapes where band manager Tony Walker had set up a small private area for them to unwind. A few close friends joined the celebration. Anne had brought Beverley along, she hoping to get closer to Roddy, although Anne knew she didn't stand a chance of anything more than a one-night stand. Paul had Eleanor in tow, she already stoned and egging her boyfriend to catch up. Jimmy and Molly were both quickly drunk but with eyes only for each other. Tony and Skip chatted quietly in a corner, both supping pints of bitter like any Liverpool lads on a Saturday night.

That left Eddie Harbinson who was throwing double vodkas down his neck as if he had a point to prove. Anne watched him turn down advances from three delicious young girls, all eager to spend a night with a pop star and quite willing to give up their bodies. But Eddie showed little interest and soon was joined at the bar by Skip who had abandoned Tony, a man likely to be going home with a young lad who'd been hanging around him all evening. Anne wondered what the press would make of it all.

She kissed her brother goodnight, while a desperate Beverley threw her arms around Roddy. He was hardly in any state to notice. He managed to kiss her and peel her off his body at the same time. In an instant, he was in the embrace of another girl as Anne grabbed Beverley's hand and pulled her away. There was no point in prolonging her agony. After waving a final goodnight to Paul, she and Beverley sucked in the cool air as they meandered through the town, high on their laughter and happy for the night they had experienced.

It was well into the early hours when the band toppled into a quieter, near-deserted Mathew Street. Eleanor Riordan steadied herself on the arm of Molly. All other female company had somehow dispersed, leaving the lads to wander the streets just as they had done a year earlier when their lives were less complicated and more private than they now were. But fresh air, alcohol, weed and whatever pills had been downed made a sorry concoction for the members of The Moondreams. All but one of them would forever regret playing The Cavern one last time.

CHAPTER 67

Early hours of Sunday, 28 April 1968.

'We should record that.'

'What?'

'*Ferry Across the Mersey*,' Eddie slurred gleefully, watching his best mate Skip McIntyre standing by the quayside singing for all he was worth. 'It could be like a signature tune for us.'

'Fuck off!' said Paul. 'We don't need any bloody signature tune. Certainly not a song written by some other loser. Isn't that right, mate?'

Roddy managed to look up briefly from the pool of vomit he was at that moment depositing on the bonnet of a Ford Zephyr.

'Ugh?'

'I said we don't need any songs written by losers. We can write our own signature tunes.'

'Just thought it would be good for us since we come from Birkenhead.'

Paul, rocking on his feet and holding a bottle of Black Label in his hand, scoffed at Eddie's suggestion. He had never been a sociable drunk. He tended toward aggressive. Skip was still singing to the heavens, casting his voice over the dark river in a futile attempt to reach the town of his birth. Jimmy was between the clutches of both Molly and Eleanor, all three trying their best to keep each other on their feet. Eddie's heart raced. He had been fearing this moment for weeks, but he knew there were things to be said. It was such bad timing, with all of them being either drunk or stoned. But he could not let the moment pass. He had to tell Paul how he felt.

Paul, however, was first to blow off steam.

'Me and Roddy make the decisions on what we record, not you, Eddie.'

'We're a band, Paul. I thought we all had a say in what we do.'

'Bollocks! The rest of you are nothing without me and Roddy. Isn't that right, mate?' Paul turned to Roddy who was hardly aware of anything never mind contributing to the angry exchange.

'The Moondreams are my band, Paul,' said Eddie. 'I started it with Jimmy and Skip in my dad's factory. It was us who asked you and Roddy to join the band.'

Suddenly, Paul was standing face to face with Eddie, both men breathing heavily and eye-balling one another.

'So fucking what? You three are nowt without me and Roddy. Who writes the songs, eh? You think I can't get another bass player? Two-a-fucking-penny, mate! Same goes for drums and organ.'

He spat his words in Eddie's face. Skip stopped singing and made his way over. Roddy had somehow taken in what was being said. Paul and Eddie weren't finished.

'Not all the songs,' Eddie shouted back in Paul's face.

'What are you talking about?'

'*The Daring Night* is my song, Paul. I wrote it and brought it to you and Roddy.'

'No, you bloody didn't! You brought me a few lines and a riff. I wrote the song, made it what it is.'

'You're fucking lying, Paul. You know it's mine, and you and Roddy took credit for it. I'm not even listed in the credits on the record. You fucking stole it!'

Paul grabbed Eddie by the collar of his shirt and pulled tight. Eddie caught hold of Paul's hair. Suddenly, Jimmy broke away from the girls and rushed towards them. Then Skip joined in. The pair danced around each other and drew closer to the edge of the quay.

'Come on, lads,' said Skip. 'Leave it alone. We can talk about it tomorrow. Don't spoil our last night.'

Eleanor tugged at Paul's sleeve, but the guitarist continued to fume. Molly tried to pull Jimmy away from the fracas. But the scuffle continued.

'I'll fucking kill you!' Paul shouted.

'You're out of the band, Paul!' Eddie yelled back.

Somehow, Roddy had staggered over to join in the row. Jimmy had his arms around Eddie in a bear hug, trapping his arms and trying to pull him away from Paul. Roddy attempted the same by reaching for Paul.

'Come on, Paul, calm down will ya.'

'Stay out of it, Roddy. This bastard needs to know who's boss in this band.'

The girls screamed at the guys to stop. Paul jerked himself away from Eddie and as he broke free, he spun around and pushed Roddy hard in the chest. The singer was unsteady on his feet. He stumbled backwards. He was too close to the edge of the quay. In a fleeting second, he dropped from sight.

The girls screamed in panic.

'Roddy!' Skip yelled, stepping to the edge and peering into the darkness of the river.

Jimmy still had a hold of Eddie. Paul, standing alone in the space he'd made for himself, looked bewildered by what had just happened.

The entire group called out for Roddy. Their shouts were met only by silence.

'Roddy!' Paul cried out. 'Come on, mate. I didn't mean it.' He looked in desperation at the others. 'It was an accident. I didn't mean to… he just let go of me.'

Skip ran off to fetch help. Those who remained by the quayside gazed forlornly into darkness. As the minutes slipped by, it became clear that Roddy was not going to make it out of the river.

Fifteen minutes felt like an age before a car braked to a halt and Tony and Skip got out. There was nothing to be seen but the look of helplessness on the faces of all who stood by the edge of the quay.

'He's gone, Tony,' said Eddie. 'Can't even see his body.'

'What do we do, Tony?' Jimmy asked.

'We'll have to call the police,' he replied.

Paul looked pleadingly at the band's manager, tears and snot covered his face.

'I didn't mean it, Tony, I swear. I just pushed him away from me and he fell.'

'It's all right, Paul,' said Tony. 'I'll take care of it. Nobody needs to know what happened.'

Tony looked at the others for signs of protest. No one said a word in opposition. Eddie and Paul, tempers cooled, could only stare at each other in disbelief. Molly and

Eleanor sobbing in each other's arms were comforted by Jimmy.

'We should get the hell out of here,' said Tony, already weary of gazing into the river.

'I didn't mean it,' Paul continued to say, looking at the others for understanding.

'It was an accident, Paul,' said Eddie. 'Roddy was stoned. Nobody's fault.'

'Remember,' said Tony, 'not a word. He just fell in, OK? I'll take care of everything.'

Paul reached out for Eleanor and she fell into his arms. Tony suggested that Paul and Eleanor travel in the car with him. As the car sped away, the others walked briskly from the quayside.

In the light of the morning, Tony Walker reported to police that Roddy was missing. A few hours later, the body was sighted by the crew on the Mersey ferry. Roddy Craig was dead and so, too, was the life of The Moondreams.

If you enjoyed this book, please let others know by leaving a quick review on Amazon. Also, if you spot anything untoward in the paperback, get in touch. We strive for the best quality and appreciate reader feedback.

editor@thebookfolks.com

ALSO IN THIS SERIES

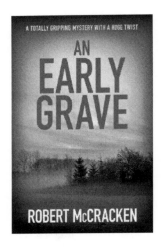

A tough young Detective Inspector tackles a case that
rakes up a past she'd rather forget.

Available on Kindle and in paperback!

Printed in Great Britain
by Amazon